MOMENT OF TRUTH

Carbines scattered long echoes through the timber across the ravine. The sun threw its hard yellow glare against this waiting column, burning wherever it struck. The troopers held double-ranked formation, loose in their seats, but black-jawed and showing the flash of excitement in the rounds of their eyes.

Benteen studied these men carefully, noting how calm the old-timers held themselves. But Trumpeter Patch had never been in a fight before; he kept rolling his eyes around him, watching his companions, as if seeking some sort of comfort from them. Benteen understood what was in the boy's mind. He could remember back to his own first engagements, catching again the rush of blood, the quick squirming fear, and the even greater fear of showing fear. This was what Trumpeter Patch would be going through now, and Harry Jackson who sat with his head down, staring at the knuckles of his hands. This was the silence of the column, but behind that silence were the crowding hopes and fears and the back-reaching memories.

Mixler pulled his horse over to be beside Benteen. Benteen grinned at him and Mixler nodded gently, and turned his glance to the pines on the far ridge.

Suddenly the yonder firing strengthened and dust began to show. Benteen murmured: "They're coming out of the trees . . ."

ERNEST HAYCOX
IS THE KING OF THE WEST!

Over twenty-five million copies of Ernest Haycox's rip-roaring western adventures have been sold worldwide! For the very finest in straight-shooting western excitement, look for the Pinnacle brand!

RIDERS WEST (17-123-1, $2.95)
by Ernest Haycox
Neel St. Cloud's army of professional gunslicks were fixing to turn Dan Bellew's peaceful town into an outlaw strip. With one blazing gun against a hundred, Bellew found himself fighting for his valley's life—and for his own!

MAN IN THE SADDLE (17-124-X, $2.95)
by Ernest Haycox
The combine drove Owen Merritt from his land, branding him a coward and a killer while forcing him into hiding. But they had made one drastic, fatal mistake: they had forgotten to kill him!

SADDLE AND RIDE (17-085-5, $2.95)
by Ernest Haycox
Clay Morgan had hated cattleman Ben Herendeen since boyhood. Now, with all of Morgan's friends either riding with Big Ben and his murderous vigilantes or running from them, Clay was fixing to put an end to the lifelong blood feud—one way or the other!

"MOVES STEADILY, RELENTLESSLY FORWARD WITH GRIM POWER."
—THE NEW YORK TIMES

ERNEST HAYCOX

THE BORDER TRUMPET

PINNACLE BOOKS
WINDSOR PUBLISHING CORP.

PINNACLE BOOKS

are published by

Windsor Publishing Corp.
475 Park Avenue South
New York, NY 10016

First Pinnacle Books Printing: December, 1992

Printed in the United States of America

Chapter One

Two weeks from San Francisco the *Newbern* dropped anchor in the tangle of sandbars and willow banks at the mouth of the Colorado, transferring its freight and its sole passenger, Eleanor Warren, to the steamer *Cocopah,* Captain Jack Mellon commanding. Three days later, under a brass-colored midsummer's sun, they reached Fort Yuma, tarried briefly and went on.

"Ordinarily," Captain Mellon told her, "a military escort would have met you at Yuma. The direct way to Camp Grant is down the Gila, past the Pima villages and over the desert to the San Pedro. But there ain't any military posts along the route and the Indians are very bad, so you'll follow the supply line."

She stood in the useless shade of the *Cocopah's* texas, with a parasol tilted against the beating glare of white earth and metal-yellow sky, and watched the low adobe outline of Fort Yuma fade behind a pulsing, iridescent haze. A little hat made its rakish angle on her auburn head and a dove-gray dress, meant for more modish travel than this, fitted itself tightly at neck and shoulders and waist. She was a slim girl and a straight one and carried the unmistakable army mark—for she had been born in a wagon bed ten miles short of Fort Snelling, Minnesota, army regulations and the laws of nature not concurring, and had spent all her twenty-one years, save the last three, following the guidon. Now with the genteel training of

5

Mrs. De Launcey's Boston School for Young Ladies behind her, she was rejoining the regiment at its most recent frontier. Twenty years ago that frontier was Minnesota and Kansas. Ten years ago it had been the Civil War and Texas; now it was Arizona.

Beneath her brows was the inquiring line of direct gray eyes. She had a long composed mouth and a temper that could at once charm a man or chill him to his bones; this was the competence a girl acquired on the frontier, this was the manner of a girl raised by men and taught by them. She was a little better than average woman in height, with the bony structure of her face making definite, strong and pleasant contours. Two jade eardrops stirred when she turned her head and a cameo brooch, once her mother's, was clipped to her dress at the curve of her breast line. Her skin was smooth and fair and flushed now by the constant heat.

"For a fact," Captain Mellon admitted, "it is average warm. A hundred and nineteen in the wheelhouse. It will be hotter up the canyon but by then you will not mind it."

The canyon walls grew high and narrow as they chugged on. The river was the exact color of chocolate and, since this was late summer, at quite low stage. At night they tied up to any convenient boulder and by day had their troubles bumping over the tricky gravel bars. "One time," said Captain Mellon, "I was hung up fifty-seven days on a bar." Yuma squaws now and then pushed their short, copper-colored shapes out of the shore willows and stared at the boat through the disheveled fall of their hair. Sleeping, in such weather, was impossible. At mealtime the butter was an oily liquid on the plate and neither the beans nor boiled potatoes were palatable. On the eleventh day the *Cocopah* whistled for Ehrenburg and pushed its nose against the gravel.

"Captain," said Eleanor Warren, "it has really been a nice trip."

Captain Mellon was young enough to pull at his mustaches and old enough to feel worried about her. She was

6

a tall, fashionable girl who had made no single complaint on the trip and now was obviously eager to rejoin her regiment. But Mellon thought of the desert beyond, its scarifying heat, its stinging clouds of alkali powder, its discomfort and its danger. She was leaving the last semblance of comfort behind. "There's always something about an army girl," he told her. "Damned if there ain't. Would there be a young lieutenant in that outfit you're so anxious to reach?"

Her smile was long and soft. "Captain," she said, "you have a sharp eye."

"I wish you luck," he said, reversed the *Cocopah* from the gravel bar and steamed upriver. His farewell whistle blast slammed back and forth between the canyon walls.

Ehrenburg was a scatter of miserable dobe huts on a treeless bluff, one general store and the government warehouse which received army supplies from the river boats and shipped them out by freighting teams to the military posts scattered deep in the Territory. A young lieutenant with cheeks broiled lobster-red, and the lieutenant's exceedingly lonesome wife, welcomed Eleanor Warren.

"You are," said the lieutenant's wife, "the only white woman I've set eyes upon for eight weeks. Stay awhile. A more cheerless camp does not exist and I think sometimes I shall lose my mind."

But a detachment of the Sixth was waiting to escort her on. She had hoped to see the men of the Third, her own beloved outfit, so that she might sooner get the common gossip so dear to her; nevertheless she was extraordinarily happy when, next morning, she set out westward in an army ambulance drawn by four service mules, flanked by eight sun-blackened raw-boned Irish troopers and a lieutenant with blue eyes and a tawny yellow mustache like Custer's. She was with her own kind once more and nothing else mattered; there was no feeling in the world like that of an army woman returning to her outfit.

Westward was the pure flare of the desert, broken by silhouetted cacti and the blue blur of Arizona mountains

7

rising suddenly from the plain. The ambulance bounced along the stony soil and fine alkali dust rolled up solid as flour, stinging her eyes and skin. Within her small wall tent at night she listened to the drowsy talk of the troopers around the camp fire, hearing the names of Geronimo and Casadora and Antone, of Crook, of massacred wagon trains and ranch houses in ruins. The edge of San Francisco peak was a constant lodestar in the deep East. On the third day they passed Date Creek, on the fourth they pulled into Fort Whipple, hard by the little mining town of Prescott. This, the headquarters of the military district, was in the cooler hills. Two days later she crossed the hills to Camp Verde, and there was whirled away by still another escort, high up to the timbered Mogollon range, from the rim of which she had her views of the Tonto Basin, wild and dark and rugged. This was slower travel and the elevation brought a breath of sweet wind at evening; but she noticed the escort rode with an aroused vigilance, throwing out flankers by day and guards by night. Five days from Verde the escort crossed Camp Apache's parade ground. Dropping out of the ambulance she confronted Major McClure's wife, the first familiar face of the old Third Cavalry.

"Why," said the major's wife, "you're a grown lady," and cried shamelessly as she embraced Eleanor Warren. "Has it been that long since I packed your trunk at Fort Stanton and watched you go? Three years? I guess I'm just another dried up, leather-skinned old army woman. What a pretty dress. Is that the Eastern style now? How long have you been from Ehrenburg?"

"Twelve days."

"Well, it is three more to your father at Grant. If you think the road so far is bad, wait till you see what lies ahead. The detail from Grant hasn't come yet. Meanwhile we'll have a party tonight and talk about the East. It's been three years since I last saw lace curtains or a hotel room. I hope you can stay a week."

But that night, sometime short of tattoo, a party of

8

horsemen crossed the hard-baked parade with a sudden clatter of hoofs and a man's voice spoke from the porch of the McClure quarters. "Has Miss Warren arrived?"

The officers and ladies of the post were all in this room; suddenly they were smiling at Eleanor Warren as she rose and half turned from the door. There was a quick step in the hall and Major McClure drawled, "She's here, Phil," and then Eleanor Warren swung about, soberly disturbed and afraid of the things that might at this moment be on her face. She said in a small uneven voice, "How are you, Phil?"

He stood before her, this Philip Castleton, his trousers and shirt turned gray from riding and his naturally dark face further colored by the intense Arizona sun. He was a big, black-eyed man, quick and solid, with a driving energy that came out of him even though he stood wholly still. He was straight-backed, physically hard. There was a blaze of feeling in his eyes, and change came to his face. He had presence enough to bow to the group of ladies, but he said "Eleanor," as he stepped toward her. Her soberness went away and regardless of propriety she walked into his arms. This was the man she had loved as a girl of eighteen at Fort Stanton. Now she returned to him as a woman, and all her intervening fears faded and she knew nothing had changed. At this moment she was happier than she could remember ever being.

The trumpets were blowing morning fatigue call, sunlight rushed yellow and hard over the world, and the ambulance and ten troopers of old K were waiting on the parade when she stepped from Major McClure's quarters. They waited at the heads of their horses, these bronzed rough men of her father's outfit. Most of them were old friends—Sergeant Tim Hanna, whose tough Irish lips were broadly asmile, and the Dutch sergeant, Conrad Reichert, and Corporal Oldbuck who had carried her on his saddle when, as a girl, she had visited behind the lines at Bull Run. She went along the rank, shaking hands. "Hanna," she said, "what

9

happened to that Mexican girl at Stanton?"

Hanna brought a gauntlet up across the sweeping tips of his dragoon mustaches. "Ah, now, you remember her still? So do I, but I must be tellin' you about it in private someday. Nawt all the men in old K troop are the gentlemen they look." There was a low run of amusement along the line, and pleased approval. One last private of the detail cantered across the parade and joined the line. Lieutenant Castleton's voice hit him with a severity that surprised Eleanor. "Jackson, report to me as soon as we reach Grant. Eleanor, if you are ready—"

Eleanor Warren paid her respects to the gathered officers and ladies and accepted Castleton's hand into the ambulance. Major McClure's wife called, "Give my love to Harriet Mixler—and tell her to come up here as soon as she can!" Castleton spoke a quick command, the troopers mounted and wheeled as twos, the ambulance rolled over the parade, took something less than a road down a ravine, and soon left Apache behind.

Eastward lay the high rock rampart of the White mountains; in all other directions the domes and spires and ragged edges of hill country lay below the brilliant flash of sunlight. The ambulance rattled along the road, traversed a narrow valley and entered the rough ravines again. A cavalry detail passed them, homeward bound; the officer in command lifted his hat, showing Eleanor a face dull for want of sleep. Her own detail swung loose and straight-backed in saddle leather, each man dressed in blue pants, high boots and gray shirt opened against sunburned skin. Tim Hanna, K's top sergeant, rode at the column's head, his slouched hat turning constantly left and right in search for trouble that might lie in these roundabout piney peaks. Low cactus and sage and catclaw and amber forage grass scattered the slopes. The way was windingly downward into a rougher country than she had ever seen, leading southwest through the smoky heat to Camp Grant on the San Pedro, a hundred and ten miles away.

Phil Castleton rode beside the ambulance wagon, now

10

and then speaking to her, but always breaking off to watch the trail. This was a part of that same alertness she had noticed in previous escorts. Everybody in the command rode heads up; every man swept the rough contours and parapets of the surrounding hills, and some of this tight, uncertain feeling got into her until she too found herself eyeing the catclaw clumps and the scattered rocks.

Phil Castleton said, "The detail we passed was from A Troop, out on night scout. Up this way the Coyotero Apaches are pretty tricky. But we've got it worse at Grant. The Chiricahuas drift up from the Dragoons and part of the Aravaipas are disaffected. We have been chasing a sub-chief by the name of Antone for six months."

"Phil," she said, "thanks for your letters. They were a comfort."

He said, "Sometimes I hoped they'd make you lonely enough to come back. Three years is a long time to wait, Eleanor."

She sat with her hands gripping the seat of the ambulance as it pitched over the rough road, watching him with a solemn sweetness. He was a man who seldom smiled, who was hard with himself because of ambition, and sometimes hard with others because of the wilful energy that drove him. It showed in the uncompromising blackness of his eyes and in the set lines about his mouth. All the way westward on the new Pacific railroad, and on the boat and all across the wastes of Arizona she had been afraid of this meeting, afraid of what the three years' separation might have done to her as well as to him. But now, seeing him, she was no longer afraid and small excitement lifted her heart. Nothing was changed from that day when, as a girl of seventeen she had first seen him ride up to Fort Stanton, fresh from West Point and assigned to her father's troop, K.

"Phil," she murmured, "I wondered if it would be the same," and looked down at her gloved hands.

He said, swift and certain, "I could never change, Eleanor. But you have changed."

11

She was startled by his tone. "How, Phil?"

Sergeant Hanna called back, "Lieutenant." Castleton cantered ahead and for a while both men rode side by side, studying the trace of prior travel on the trail. They fell out of a low ravine into a level, narrow valley and pursued it briskly, through silver-gray clouds of fine-rising dust. Heat closed in strongly and the smell of arid earth and of sweaty horseflesh condensed around her. At noon they halted in the shadow of another narrow canyon for bacon sandwiches and cold water from a spring, and pressed forward into the black tangle of mountains. That night they made camp beside the shallow trickle of the San Carlos deep in the rugged wilderness of hills near Natane's Butte.

Sitting before her little wall tent, Eleanor watched the blackness of an Arizona night close down, thick and solid and mysterious. Against it the yellow point of the campfire burned with a motionless glow and the peaks of the range made faint silhouettes high up, and the sky was a cloudy wash of stars. Somewhere in this darkness part of the troopers lay on guard; in the shadows beyond the fire the rest were rolled in blankets, talking in drowsy, tired tones. Phil Castleton sat near her.

"Phil," she said, "how have I changed?"

He spoke with a dry, reluctant voice. "It is hard for me to explain. I never was very sentimental, was I? But you've grown up. I knew you would and was afraid you'd not be the same. When I came into Major McClure's quarters last night and saw you standing there, it hit me very hard. You were tall and composed. You were a lady, Eleanor. Better than that, you were a woman a man gets to thinking about when he's out alone at night in these hills. For me it has been a difficult wait."

"Phil," she whispered, "here I am, and very glad."

She stood up and watched him rise and remain still before her; and was remotely disappointed that he let the distance remain between them. His voice was short, holding many things back. She heard the strain in him and

12

wondered why he should seem to be fighting this moment, with all that it could mean, away from him. He had always been a man to hold himself in severe check, yet it was odd that he should let it be so now when her own answer had been clear enough.

He said, "Well, it changes a pretty drab world into a pretty pleasant one for me. Though I ought to tell you that Camp Grant is a hellhole for a white woman. Harriet Mixler has been the only one there for six months and I think it has aged her five years. I don't believe you know her. She came out from Baltimore a year ago to marry George Mixler. She never did like the country and now she's about to have a baby and if you weren't coming along to keep her company I think she'd go crazy."

"Nothing could be that bad, Phil. I'm happier in an army post, no matter how drab it is, than anywhere else in the world. It gets in your blood, Phil."

"Well," he said, "Grant is pretty bad." Then he was silent. She thought he was listening to the abrasive sounds running through the blanketing black. A coyote howled high on the ridge and nearer at hand an owl hooted and was still. Sergeant Hanna came into the firelight, listening to that sound; and later retreated from the fire.

"Might be an Apache's signal," Castleton said. "It's one of their favorite ways of calling." Then he added at once, "Nothing to fear. They don't attack at night." But the stillness of the camp was deep and indrawn and she knew every man was awake in his blankets, waiting for the call to repeat. "Eleanor," Castleton said, very abrupt, "I hope we do not have to wait too long."

She knew what he meant. But the abruptness of it surprised her, as other signs of his changeable temper had surprised her. He went on in the same strained and half-awkward voice. "I have never asked you. I thought it was something understood. Let's not make it too long, Eleanor. I'd be a happy man if we could be married within the month."

She was half listening and half controlled by the race of

her own thoughts. Then she said, "Yes, Phil. Yes."

He came forward and brought her shoulders forward with his hands and kissed her and stepped back at once. "I'll apologize for that. I shouldn't have presumed—"

Her question was thoroughly puzzled, and a little forlorn; the sweetness of this moment was all lost. "But why not, Phil?"

"You're alone here. I should have waited until you reached Camp. Good night, Eleanor."

Lying on her cot later, she thought of him with a happiness broken only by faint wonder at the unbending streak he had displayed. He was a man with close-guarded emotions but it was strange that at the one moment when he must have felt the same upwhirl of tumultuous happiness she had experienced, he still could not break through his reserve. She thought about it through the long, still minutes. Nothing broke the camp silence, yet gradually as she lay there the intimations of this land's savageness and wildness and uncertainty began to color her thoughts until it was a relief to remember the troopers crouched out in that blackness, waiting and listening. This was the moment she realised that the security of the last three years was forever gone and that the deep safe sleep of those years was also gone. As long as she remained on this frontier she would be forever listening into the night mysteries. By day she would be watching the trail as the troopers watched, alert and never sure.

In the middle of the following morning Castleton dropped back to the ambulance and pointed to a high, black cone in the near distance. Above the cone little wisps of smoke rose, one following another. "Indians signaling. They know we're on this road. Probably Antone's band."

They continued southward through the hills, the growing heat indicating descent. Now and then they reached a dry creek bed and rattled along it until some ravine closed about them and the sun disappeared and the sound of their progress bounced from wall to wall. This way they traveled, by steady marches and brief halts, leaving a gray wake behind. Once, on the high rim of one such narrow canyon a rock dislodged and fell and she heard it strike and fall and strike again until the sound of it was lost, though it still fell. That afternoon they rounded into a mountain-cramped meadow and came upon a dobe whose doors and oil-papered windows were ripped open. A horse lay warm-dead in the yard and the smell of smoke still clung to the air. Castleton and Hanna went into the dobe, soon reappearing. Castleton's eyes were quite black; he showed his anger this way. "God knows what happened to Bill Lay. This happened less than two hours ago. Hanna, throw flankers on that bluff." Short of dusk he came to the ambulance again, pointing to the tall column of a saguaro cactus higher on the slope. An Indian arrow stuck there, imbedded as far as its feathered end.

They camped on a high roll of ground that evening; and in the blue last dusk of evening horses' feet slashed through the gravel of an adjoining ravine and a man called forward. The troopers suddenly rose to stand by their guns, remaining this way until a file of cavalrymen broke out of the canyon. Castleton walked out to meet the detachment a few yards from the fire. She heard him say in a half-curt voice, "What luck, Benteen?"

He sat in the saddle with a weary looseness, this tall thin-flanked officer Castleton had called Benteen. He had no shoulder bar, which marked him as a second lieutenant; the insignia on the crossed swords of his campaign hat indicated I troop of her regiment. Being a thorough army girl, Eleanor noticed these details first and was afterwards compelled by a rising interest to study the man himself. Riding dust covered his blue uniform and sweat had caked this dust on cheeks deep-tanned by the sun. He had extraordinarily long legs and his hair showed a sandy red when he lifted his hat to release the sweat collected beneath it. His hands, quite large-knuckled, lay on the saddle swell, and a pair of gray, sleepy eyes lifted from Castleton and sent one direct glance toward her. Afterwards he spoke with a voice that was quite even, quite soft: "So far, just the ride. Antone's hand came down this way and scattered."

"They fired Bill Lay's ranch not long ago," said Castleton. Eleanor, listening to Castleton's voice, believed she heard something unfriendly and condemning in it.

"We'll have a look," Benteen answered. He turned in the saddle and considered the half-dozen jaded troopers with him, and Eleanor knew he was calculating their endurance, as a good officer should. He raised his band in signal, broke into a canter and came on with a loose swing of his shoulders, passing within a few yards of her. As he went by he raised his hat, gave her a direct, unsmiling glance, and was soon lost in the dusk.

When Castleton came back she said, "Who was that?" and watched the way his face remained in its set position.

"Tom Benteen, second lieutenant of I troop. He came to the outfit about a year ago." Castleton let the information stand a moment, later adding with some reluctance, "You'll meet him at Grant when he returns from scout."

It was quite clear to Eleanor Warren that he had no liking for Tom Benteen and since she was a wise girl in the ways of army jealousies she put the information back in her head, remaining silent. Darkness fell at once, black and complete beneath the cloudy glitter of the Arizona skies. The fire bombed its yellow brightness against the solid dark. Young trooper Jackson came into the light and stood there with his bead down until Castleton called:

"Get away from that light."

The boy faded. Castleton said in a shorter, smaller voice, "He's mooning about a girl that lives down the San Pedro. Not much of a soldier. I think you must be tired. It has been a long ride, and tomorrow will be just as rough. Good night."

Lying in the tent, Eleanor Warren listened to the long, far wail of coyotes on the ridges until she found herself tense in the blankets, half waiting for the unexpected to strike. There was a picture before her, which was of Lieutenant Benteen swinging like an old trooper in his saddle, as though he were part of the saddle, lifting his hat as he ran by; not smiling, yet with his smoky gray eyes alive to her.

This was all she remembered before sleeping. At gray dawn they were on the road again, turning through one canyon and another on the last descent. They struck the San Pedro and followed its bone-dry bed down a flat, cramped valley asmoke with the tinder heat, and at near dusk came to the junction of waterless Aravaipa Creek where Camp Grant's dobe houses and tents made a kind of square on the baked earth. Lights were shining through the blue fog of evening and men moved from quarters as the detail arrived. Paused by the brush-covered porch — the ramada — of the longest dobe, Phil Castleton saluted and said:

"Sir, Lieutenant Castleton reports back from Fort Apache. Your daughter is here."

Eleanor dropped from the ambulance seat, too eager to wait for assistance, and saw the heavy shape of her father in the thick shadows beneath the ramada. He didn't move and he didn't speak. As she walked toward him she saw the lines running across his plump cheeks, beneath the sweep of his white mustaches. He had removed his hat and she observed that he had turned completely gray in the three years of her absence. All he said was "Well, daughter—" and raised his arms.

She wasn't quite crying when she kissed him, but an emotion, so strong and so full, wouldn't let her speak; it was the feeling that she had once had long ago as a little girl running to him for shelter and comfort when her own resources failed her. This was what was in her now, its memory carrying her the long distance back to childhood. It lasted a moment, then left her completely, and she stepped away to smile at him through tears, sadly knowing her girlhood and her girlhood's sweet, irresponsible happiness was forever gone. She could never again go to him and be sheltered from trouble.

She said in a tone that had to be swift to be steady, "You haven't changed, Dad."

He was a plump elderly man watching her with a soft-smiling gentleness. "You look uncommonly like your mother did at twenty-one. I must say you've turned into a damned pretty woman, Eleanor."

Chapter Two

A woman came slowly forward beneath the black shadows cast by the ramada. Major Warren spoke with a quick courtesy. "Eleanor, this is Harriet, Mr. Mixler's wife. She has been the only white woman at the post."

Harriet Mixler's eyes were wide and round and unhappiness lay tightly across her face. She said in a low voice, "It is nice to have you here, Eleanor."

"If you will show Eleanor her quarters," said Major Warren and, by old habit, he stepped out to inspect the returned detail. The two women turned through the low door of the major's quarters into a room's stale, dense heat. Lamplight showed a rammed-earth floor and the flimsy partitions separating other small rooms. Harriet Mixler led the way into one of these and stood still. Her hand described a weary gesture toward an iron cot, a chair and a wardrobe made of packing-box boards. Two pieces of fresh chintz hung beside a single narrow window. "Your father wished me to make this presentable, Eleanor. It is the best I could contrive."

"You must remember," said Eleanor Warren, "I was born and raised in places like this one. I love it."

"I hate it," said Harriet Mixler. Her accent was softly Southern. She had been a slim and black-haired girl with sharp, responsive features, obviously the daughter of some old-line plantation owner; once lively and very gay and very quick-tempered. All this, Eleanor Warren saw, in profound pity, was gone. "George is out on a scout detail. I think you know him."

"Yes," said Eleanor. "He was at Stanton before I left, and quite an eligible bachelor." She smiled at Harriet. "I think he was one of my first secret attachments."

Harriet Mixler touched Eleanor's traveling dress. Her mouth sagged at the corners. Her expression displayed bitterness. "That is such lovely material. In Norfolk I used to dance all night. We'd ride home by first daylight and eat johnnycake and oyster fries. Didn't you just die when you had to leave the East?"

"No. I counted every day until I could come. You'll like it here. You really will."

"Never," said Harriet Mixler, doggedly resisting the thought. "I hate everything about the army. I shall be an old woman with a leather skin and a ruined complexion in one more year. I sit in that unbearable hovel down the line and hate the sight of myself. I should have left here. Now it is too late. It is fifty-five miles to Tucson, and nothing there but mud huts. It is more than a hundred miles to Fort Apache, which is no better than here. It is like being buried alive." She stared at Eleanor Warren with those great, dark eyes so full of unhappiness. "Do you know what I fear most? Doctor Shiraz is gone three quarters of the time with the troops. When my baby's time comes he will be gone again. I shall die without him. My mother died with me. Even the Indians treat their women better than the Government treats its officers' ladies." Suddenly she put both her arms against Eleanor Warren and dropped her head. Her body trembled and she cried in a choked whisper, "It's a blessed thing to have you here. I'm so afraid—so afraid."

Eleanor Warren placed her arms around this girl. She murmured, "Nothing will happen, Harriet." Men's voices ran through the still, deep night and boots tramped the hard earth. Harriet Mixler pulled back, smoothing her hair. She said in despair, "I'm such a sight," and turned into the main room with Eleanor. Major Warren came in with Captain Harrison of I troop. Harrison was a raw-boned man with a long red nose and a black beard cropped close. His taciturn eyes lighted up, which was rare for him. He said, "Dammit, Eleanor, maybe we'll have some fun around here now."

A voice in the other corner of the room spoke up. "We got beef croquettes, Miss Eleanor."

"Cowen!"

Cowen wore a black broadcloth suit and a white starched shirt. On his vest the huge links of his watch chain gently moved. His hair was carefully greased down against his head, his mustaches were shined and his face showed the nearest approach to pleasure its grave wood-enness permitted. Cowen, the Warrens' cook since '63, took unto himself most of the credit for raising Eleanor through the stage of long legs and bad grammar. Cowen shook her hand with the precise formality which was his idea of good manners in public. "I have things to tell you about this regiment," he said under his breath and left the room. The other officers of the two companies were coming in, Ray Lankerwell, Howell Ford, and Doctor Shiraz, who wore a set of flame-red burnsides. Shiraz said, "You're still an army child, Eleanor," and claimed his kiss. He turned at once to Harriet Mixler, gently pulling her to a chair. "Harriet, I want you to take some wine tonight."

She held to the cloth of his coat sleeve. "Are you sure to be here during the next two or three weeks?"

He had a deep, patient voice. "I'll be here. Right here."

Cowen brought in the supper and the group sat up to the table. Major Warren's face was round and ruddy and cheerful as he raised his wine glass, and for a moment all of them felt the emotion lying behind his silence. He tipped the glass at his daughter and said, "To a lady."

"To a lady," repeated Shiraz.

"And," said Major Warren with a gentler tone, "to Harriet."

They drank on that and suddenly the conversation was strong and pleasant even though dull heat smothered the room. Shiraz rapped on the table and pointed a finger at Eleanor.

"Let's see now how much you remember. The column is in fours, approaching a narrow defile. What do you do?"

"The command is by twos, march. Numbers one and two of first fours continue on. Number three and four oblique to right and follow in. Other sets repeat."

"Who carries the guidon?"

"Ranking corporal, sir. His place is left file of first platoon."

"Very good," said Shiraz, "Tomorrow I shall try you on a horse."

"Doctor," said Eleanor sweetly, "do you remember falling off the big roan, at Stanton?"

The other officers except Castleton let out a tremendous hoot and even Harriet Mixler smiled. Eleanor noticed that Castleton watched her and seemed untouched by the burst of amusement. He sat to the table with his shoulders straight, though the other men were slouched and easy; as though even then he could not quite let go, as though his fiery energy held him in a strict and dark and impatient mood. The campaign had thinned him and blackened him but it had made no change on the sharp, half-handsome detail of his features. He was as he had been at Stanton, a strict and ambitious officer who drove his men hard and himself harder.

"I hope," said Shiraz, "you don't learn the subsequent catastrophes I've had with horses."

"Cowen," said Eleanor, "will tell me all about it tomorrow."

"Ah," groaned Shiraz, "you always knew more about the regiment than anybody else."

22

She said, "Will you ride the hills with me in the morning?"

Major Warren put down his knife and spoke plainly. "This is not Stanton, Eleanor. That's the first thing you must know. Nobody leaves this post at any time except under escort. There are Apaches within ten feet of the sentries this minute. Tomorrow when you look beyond the picket line and see a clump of yucca it is exactly an even chance that there's an Apache's head underneath it. We lost a teamster two days ago. He only went forty yards beyond the stables. We found him with an arrow through his chest. No riding, Eleanor."

Castleton's searching glance brought Eleanor Warren's attention to him. There was a question on his face, plain and demanding. The yellow lamplight showed strong, sudden color on her cheeks. She dropped her eyes, hearing him say in a voice brushed by excitement, "Major Warren, I should like—"

Out in the darkness a sentry's challenge rode the night and a slow sleepy answer came forward. The sentry called, "Corpr'l of the guard, post number one!" Major Warren excused himself and left the room, and on the parade was the arrival scuff of horses. There was a little silence, with the other officers curiously watching Phil Castleton. "What was that?" asked Captain Harrison in his blunt way.

"I think I should wait for Major Warren's return," said Castleton.

Quiet and quick-eyed, Eleanor Warren noticed the way they watched Castleton. With interest, but with reserve, as though something held them off. He had so little of their loose-muscled comfort, he had so strong a will to get on in his profession. It was an impetuous quality, it was his strength. Yet—and this she thought slowly and with a certain reluctant admission—it was a weakness too. Garrison life was a close-knit society; there had to be a good deal of give and take. She thought, "I shall

23

have to warn him of that."

Her father's voice was hearty and cheerful in the yonder dark. Somebody spoke to him in soft-sprawling words; the dismissed troopers moved across the parade. Major Warren returned to the room with the long-legged lieutenant she had seen the previous night in the hills.

"Eleanor," said Warren, "I present Mr. Benteen of I troop. My daughter Eleanor, Mr. Benteen."

Benteen pulled his hat from a head of sandy-red hair. He was taller than any officer in the room. A day's growth of red-glinting whiskers covered his face, chalked with alkali dust and the dry stain of sweat tracks. His eyes showed weariness clear down to the gray depths and his shoulders showed it, lying slack beneath the gray campaign shirt. He had heavy cheekbones, with a small scar making its white cut on the right side, and long lips that came definitely together.

Eleanor Warren put out her hand. "I'm glad you're in the regiment, Mr. Benteen."

Shiraz said, to Benteen, "I give you warning, Tom. She's been in this army a long time and knows the regulations better than most officers."

His hand was extremely wide and heavy at the knuckles. There was a deliberateness about him and she knew, as the silence ran on, that he took his time about all things. This was the way he stood, steadily considering her, as though he meant to have his good look and find out what she was like; and for some odd reason she had the feeling that, behind those gray and indolent eyes, he was placing her against other women he had known and making comparison. In a way it put her on the defensive, it disturbed her. When he smiled, his lips spread back from heavy white teeth. His voice was effortlessly slow.

"You have been mentioned many times. I wish I had been at Stanton. As it is, I'm getting a late start."

It was a polite man's reply and yet the casual

24

inflections of his voice stirred her strong curiosity.

Captain Harrison said, "Did you cut Antone's tracks?"

"He's eighty miles back in the Pinal Range by now. But I know something about his habits which will be useful on the next chase." He moved over to Harriet Mixler, his long body bending a little. Eleanor saw his expression turn gentle. There was a definite affection in his voice. "I passed George's detail yesterday. He'll be back tomorrow."

She noticed the little glow of pleasure this man brought to Harriet Mixler's face. It was a way he had, it was some knowledge he possessed of women. Phil Castleton, she noticed at once, was seemingly disinterested in this scene. His glance touched Benteen and came away; and she realized again that he didn't like Benteen. It was a knowledge that strangely troubled her. Phil Castleton turned to her, the question again in his eyes; he moved beside her.

"Major Warren," he said with a kind of curt nervousness in his talk, "Eleanor and I wish your consent."

Warren had a black Mexican cigar in his mouth. The tip of it flew upward and he reached for it and withdrew it, sincerely astonished. Doctor Shiraz breathed a long "Well, I'm damned," and then this silence grew quite strange. Eleanor Warren took Castleton's arm, embarrassed by the combined scrutiny of these people. She felt the rigidness of Castleton's body, as though it resisted the room, as though he were prepared for trouble. Something here was very odd, something in the silence. Benteen moved around the group, his head riding over all of them. His glance drew her attention and again, as before, she knew he took her somewhere into his deeply-lying thoughts.

Her father said in reflective tone, "It is a nice thing to know. Of course you have my consent." He offered his hand to Castleton and he looked at the younger officer in a way she never forgot—in a way she was never able to describe to herself. Harriet Mixler came over. "Eleanor," she said. "Eleanor."

A sentry challenged across the darkness and a call rang back along the line for the corporal of the guard; boots trotted over the parade. She didn't realize until that moment how highly keyed this post was to the black mystery crowding down from the hills. All the men stirred as though catching the scent of trouble. Howell Ford slipped from the door, but was soon back. "Nachee is here with something."

Warren turned out, followed at once by the other officers. Eleanor Warren started to go along, to be held back by Harriet Mixler's sudden-reaching arm. She was visibly shaking. "Don't go!" she said. "Stay here!"

From the doorway both women watched the forming scene on the parade ground. A man ran up with a lantern, holding it high. By this light Eleanor saw the Apache Indian half surrounded by officers. He was small and wiry, dressed in a shirt, breechclout and moccasins whose leggings were folded down. A headband held back jet hair, and his eyes, struck by the lantern light, had a distinct gleaming. He carried a sack over his back.

Her father called, "Where's Manuel Dura?"

A civilian brushed through the shadows of the parade and came to the group. Her father said, "Find out what he wants, Manuel."

Manuel Dura spoke in a soft, sliding, twisted tone, moving a finger back and forth in front of the Apache. The Apache's face was impassive, unstirred. He answered swiftly.

Manuel Dura said, "He won't talk unless Nantan with the Long legs comes. He knows Mr. Benteen best."

Eleanor hadn't noticed until now that Benteen was at the corner of the house, well away from the parley. He stepped forward.

26

The Indian talked, Manuel Dura interpreting. "Major, he say you want the Indian that keel the teamster. Nachee is good Indian but the other wan was bad. So Nachee bring you the bad wan."

Benteen said something in the Apache tongue. The Apache lifted his chin and grunted "Enju," and threw the bag from his shoulder. Some object dully struck the earth, whereupon Castleton swiftly stepped forward, to hide it from the women. But he had not been quite quick enough. Eleanor wheeled against Harriet Mixler, turned cold and sick, trying to block Harriet's view. Out of the sack had rolled the severed head of an Apache.

"Dammit," grunted Warren, an involuntary break in his voice.

"What was it?" whispered Harriet Mixler.

"I didn't see," answered Eleanor. The Indian slipped into the darkness without another sound. Doctor Shiraz reached down, pushed the head into the sack and took up the sack. He said, coolly, "Very good specimen," and went along the parade toward his quarters. The other officers broke away. Major Warren returned, with a most wry expression on his lips. He looked at Harriet Mixler and at once lied, "Brought me a broken jug. That's the Indian sign for punishment to one of its people." He went on into the room and poured a drink of wine. Castleton stood at the doorway, watching Eleanor a moment. He said, "I'll see you tomorrow," and cut across the parade.

"Walk back to my dobe with me," said Harriet Mixler.

They turned along the officers' row. Tattoo call broke the heated dark, each note cutting a clear long echo over the parade, over the adjoining valley. Sentries were passing the hour call from post to post, that ritual running from number one at the guardhouse all the way out to lonely number ten in the tangle of sage brush at the mouth of Aravaipa Creek. Along the right side of the walk, on the parade, lay the silhouette of officers' iron

27

cots. Lights winked from the windows of the irregular quadrangle, and somebody in the barracks sang out, "Canreen—Canreen."

Harriet Mixler stopped by her door, supporting herself against the frame with an arm. She said, "I wish George would come back. It is such a cruel country. When the baby is born—as soon as it is able to stand traveling— I'm going East. I'll never return to the army."

"How long have you been in the army, Harriet?"

"A year."

"Wait another year, and you'll never like another kind of life."

"Not me," said Harriet Mixler in that same dead, resisting voice. "I won't stay. Good night."

She walked uncertainly into the house. Eleanor strolled on, her shoes striking quick echoes through the increasing quiet. Directly in the east lay the black bulk of the Galiuro Mountains, their summits high and vague against the sky's grayer black. There was no wind and scarcely any lessening in the heat of this smoldering air. Lights died here and there along the quadrangle. The smell of dust and nearby stables, of sage and of newly baked bread, of leather, of canvas—all these old familiar odors of an army post were here, comforting to her, sinking into her consciousness, welcoming her home.

She had turned the corner of officers' row when she heard Captain Harrison's disgusted voice drift through the doorway of the last dobe house. "Three aces—and you catch a flush. Someday, Benteen, you'll break your neck trying to fill those damned things."

Benteen's tone was as it had been earlier in the evening, drowsy and let down: "An agreeable way to die."

She turned and watched them a moment, through the doorway. Harrison and Shiraz and Benteen and Howell Ford and a civilian sat around a small table, half obscured by the heavy drift of tobacco smoke. It was Benteen she found herself watching, with a definite curiosity again rising. He lay back in his chair with a complete looseness, as though no single muscle were alive. His feet sprawled beneath the table and his long arms lay on it, one hand touching a glass of whisky. A black Mexican cigar slanted from a corner of his long mouth. She had a partial view of his face, again noting that though he wasn't smiling, the hint of some smiling knowledge lay below. She guessed that he was not more than twenty-five or twenty-six, which made it odd that he should have a kind of seasoned completeness about him, and the suggestion of so much mature feeling behind the faint skepticism of his solid features.

Captain Harrison said, "What are you going to do with that damned grisly head, Shiraz?"

Doctor Shiraz spoke: "Let the dry air mummify it. I think I shall send it to the Smithsonian. It's a rare piece."

"Only an army doctor would have such a hellish interest," commented Harrison. "I'll take three cards."

Eleanor turned back, walking faster, and saw a dark shape waiting near her father's quarters. Her heart quickened a little when Castleton spoke.

"Eleanor," he said and came to her. There was a swiftness in his words sweet to hear, sweet and yet strange. "Eleanor, God knows I'm glad you're here. I've been lonely." In this darkness his constraint was gone. He took her and kissed her and for a little while she thought of nothing else; after three years of waiting this was the way she had wanted it, this was the way it ought to be.

She stepped back from him, breathless and close to laughter. "Why should you be lonely, Phil?"

He said, "I'm not the poker-playing kind, Eleanor."

She recognized the indirect comment on the game at the end of officers' row. Some of this man's opinions, she admitted, were shaded by an envy or a narrowness

29

which sprang from the intense pride she so much admired. He had never permitted himself the luxury of being idle or foolish in the manner of the average officer. She was an army girl, completely understanding these vigorous and open-handed and extremely simple men who rode through the desert dust; and she knew the solace they found in a cigar, in a drink of whisky, in a game of poker after the routine and the hard work were done. It was, she thought to herself, something she would have to make Phil Castleton see before the unrelieved tension of frontier garrison life turned him sour. She said gently, "It would be good for you, Phil. Why don't you join them?"

In one short phrase, he told her why—though he didn't realize it: "I have not been asked to join them."

She said, "Oh, my dear man!" But she said it under her breath. It was a revelation that shocked her and roused her protectiveness and drew her nearer him. Some act or some phrase or some manner of his had created their quiet dislike, and this was a terribly serious thing in so compact a family as the regiment. Men could be cruel in their judgment of other men; cruel and realistic and sometimes unforgiving. Whatever he had done to turn them against him had to be undone. She had to find the cause and make it clear to him.

"You must put it in their way to ask you," she said.

His short answer showed his freshening resentment. "I have no time to learn post politics, Eleanor."

"You will be handling men all your life. It isn't politics. It is your career." But she was thinking, "I shall have to manage it better than this." He was a square, tense shape in the darkness; he was silent, involved in his own grievances. She put her hand on his shoulder, lightly reassuring him. "Wait until we're married, Mr. Castleton. I've been in the army a long time and I know the fine print at the bottom of the regulations."

He said, "It has been a long wait, Eleanor," and

30

pulled her to him again. This was when all trouble dissolved, leaving her hopeful and excited. Yet it was strange that one part of her mind remained cool and critical. Even as he held her he was not, she felt, thinking of her. He was locked up in himself, involved in his own reasoning. She stepped back, murmuring, "Good night, Phil," and watched him swing down officers' row to his own boxlike dobe. She went directly to her father's quarters and found him waiting.

He had something on his mind. "It occurs to me," he said, quite carefully, "that perhaps I didn't express myself very well when Castleton broke the news. It took the wind out of an old man, daughter. But you know how I feel. It is a damned nice thing to know you'll be in the regiment —"

She said, "How did Mr. Benteen come to us?"

He looked at her a puzzled moment, trying to fathom the question. "Well," he said, "Benteen worked up as a private in the Civil War and took a presidential appointment to West Point. He had quite a war record. They assigned him to the engineer corps but he liked our arm best and got a transfer. The man's a soldier down to the marrow."

"Does he rank Phil?"

"Yes."

She said, "Why do the officers —" and killed the question, knowing she would never get help from her father. He wasn't the man to favor one officer over another, or to express opinions about them. So she turned into her own room, hearing him say, "Up to your neck in post gossip already."

She undressed, threw on a robe and pattered out to her bed on the parade. Lying there with her face turned to the far, cloudy starlight she listened to the fading sounds of the camp. Presently her father moved through the darkness and dropped on his cot with a long, contented sigh. Coolness at last faintly cut the edge of the

31

heat, tremendously relieving. In the distant corner of the parade a trumpeter tentatively breathed sound into his instrument and then blew taps, those sad strong notes carrying far through the shadows. Lights died around the quadrangle and the muffled tramping of the sentries ran around her. Lying there, buoyed up by her return to all these familiar things, Eleanor thought, "I shall have to find out why they dislike him," and then was remembering the manner in which Benteen's steady eyes had watched her and absorbed her into his memory. Thus she fell asleep.

A voice said "Major Warren!" in hard-breathing excitement and she woke, bolt upright. Shadows raced over the parade. Someone called, "The Summerton wagon train—down in the canyon!" A trumpet blasted out its call To Horse and lights broke the shadows and men were shouting all along the barrack and picket line. "I got through," said the exhausted voice. "The rest—I do not know—"

She could not mistake Lieutenant Benteen's long, solid voice. It called, "McSween, rout out the men."

Chapter Three

Her father's long white nightshirt swayed through the curdled shadows. Benteen crossed the parade on the trot. Her father said, "Take the first twenty men you find ready and go out. You know the place?"

Benteen said, "Yes, sir. In the canyon," and wheeled around. His voice ran down the night, strong-toned against the rush of men along the parade. "Sergeant McSween—twenty men, either troop. Oldbuck, fill up some extra canteens."

Major Warren called, "Dr. Shiraz, you will accompany the detail."

Troopers were already forming in the center of the parade, hustled to it by McSween's bronze-throated urging. Phil Castleton came up to Warren. Eleanor heard excitement sing in his words. "May I be permitted to go, Major?"

"Certainly—certainly," said Warren. He walked toward quarters and swore one passionate oath when his bare feet snagged the porch boards. Howell Ford ran by. He said to nobody in particular, "That's Antone again!" Sitting upright on her cot, cold in spite of the night's heat, she saw the troopers forming line. They were mounting off.

"Prepare to mount! Mount!"

She heard them hit their saddles. Dust rose along the parade. "Right by twos, march!" The line moved by her.

Benteen's voice was long and cool. "Gallop!" The detail swept out of the parade, hoofs solidly pounding the parade. Harriet Mixler was calling, "Eleanor — Eleanor," but Eleanor Warren waited another moment, following the detail with her ears as it reached the bed of the San Pedro, rushed over the gravel and struck into the southwest. Presently, when the clatter and rumble was quite gone, she went to Harriet Mixler's cot and bent down. Harriet's body shook. She seized Eleanor's arms. She breathed, "Don't leave. Stay right here — right here."

Benteen led his detail southward up the dry course of the San Pedro, following the rutted freight road to Tucson. As long as the way was open he kept on at a gallop past the lights of Valley ranch and onward through this solid night, against which the tracery of paloverde and high-stalked pitahaya made a ghostly show. They dipped over the gravelly bottom of a wash and dropped to a walk. Dr. Shiraz rode at the column's rear. Castleton drew abreast Benteen.

"Who was it?"

"Two wagons freighting supplies to Summerton's ranch. It was after dark. There were four men. The wagons were burned and the mules killed. I don't know about the men."

"Don't understand how old-timers would ride into ambush," said Castleton, unfavorably. "These people grow too careless. It would be Antone again, of course. I thought you said you tracked him into the Pinals."

"Maybe I was mistaken," said Benteen.

"Maybe," Castleton answered. This was the way Benteen's presence always affected him, rousing a resentment he could not wholly conceal. The tall sandy-haired man's manner, casual to the point of indolence, affronted his own conception of an officer's demeanor. To him Benteen was loose and slipshod, neither a student nor a disciplinarian, possessing none of that hard and

34

lonely detachment, none of that driving sense of duty Phil Castleton had set his life by. Yet this man was considered the best Indian campaigner in the regiment.

The lights of the fort died behind and the little valley swung west, sidling against the edge of the Tortillas. Eight miles onward the party entered a defile between the Santa Catalinas and the Tortillas, and sank into deeper darkness.

Benteen broke from his long riding silence to ask Castleton a question that stirred the latter's surprise. "You like this country, Phil?"

Castleton said, "I take my tour of duty at any post, like or dislike."

"No," said Benteen softly, "that wasn't what I meant."

"It is a little late at night for philosophy."

"The later the night the better the philosophy," said Benteen. "The stronger the cigar, the deeper the drink, the more beautiful the women—the better the thoughts that come. There are no nights like Arizona nights, no sound or smells or colors as sharp as these. It is a land that does everything full tilt, it burns a man black, it dries him as brittle as a bleached bone, it puts him closer to heaven than he's ever likely to get."

"Poetic fancy," said Castleton.

Benteen's chuckle was deep and loose and free. "You're missing something, Phil. You will not find it in Cooke's Cavalry Tactics."

The footing was rocky and rough, against which the shod hoofs of the horses rattled, those sharp reports running ahead. Every sound grew larger—the squeal of leather, the faint jingle and clack of metal. When they stopped for a brief rest, silence pushed down like a weight. The canyon closed in to twice a wagon's width, its walls were smooth faces reaching five hundred feet above. Above them the sky was a glitter of distant stars.

Sergeant McSween murmured, "The Mexican said

'twould be at the first open spot. 'Tis a half a mile ahead, sor."

They went on. Benteen said, over his shoulder, "Close up." This was the heart of night, this dense two o'clock hour that blindfolded a man with the thickness of its shadows. Somewhere water spattered out of a rocky fissure and a sluggish current of air blew faint coolness against the detail; and in the air was the smell of smoke. The walls, as they progressed, fell back a little. Castleton, riding as second man in the single-file column, saw Benteen's shoulders weave and seem to rise. Benteen halted without command, the rest of the file gently bumped together. Ahead of them a fire's red eye showed dully; the smell of burnt wood and of cloth and coffee was very strong. Benteen called forward, "Hello, wagons."

The call rolled over the small clearing and re-echoed against the canyon walls. The smell of powder still clung to the air. When Benteen moved forward again, Castleton pulled out his holster flap and lifted the revolver; he came abreast Benteen. Both of them rode toward the solitary eye of fire. Benteen murmured, "McSween," and dismounted, stumbling at his first forward step. Castleton saw his shadow sink against the earth and he heard Benteen's grumbling curse. "This is one of them—dead as sin."

Troopers moved around the clearing. Going forward, Castleton brought up against some kind of a solid box dumped from the wagon train. Supplies had been scattered around. Heat from the recent fire moved against his face and, closer to the single red eye of light, he touched a still hot metal of a wagon tire.

McSween's voice came from the far side of the clearing. "Nawthing over here, Lieutenant."

Benteen waded the warm ashes of the burnt wagons, exploring the area thoroughly. He returned to the dead

36

man and struck a sulphur match. It was a Mexican, face upward and his arms flung out. The match struck an orange glitter across Benteen's iong jaw and died, and the blackness was greater than before.

McSween said, deeper in the canyon, "The mewels are in a bunch. The damned savages led 'em here and kilt 'em."

Benteen said, "One dead. The other three got away in the dark. They were very lucky. McSween, leave five men here. We'll send an ambulance out in the morning to pick up this fellow."

"Benteen," said Castleton, "it is two hours until daylight. I should like permission to stay here and pick up the tracks of the Indians. It will save a good deal of time."

"This," said Benteen, "happened sometime after dusk. Six hours ago. By now the Indians are forty miles away."

"Do I have your permission?" insisted Castleton.

"No," said Benteen.

Castleton stamped back to his horse, boots grinding deep in the loose gravel. Benteen said, "McSween—" and quit. A voice—a woman's voice came coolly from a corner of the night. "Will you take me to Camp Grant, Lieutenant?"

Benteen muttered an astonished, "In God's good name," and ran rapidly toward the source of that sound. "Where are you?" He lighted another match, throwing its first bright flare out from him against the suddenly rising figure of a girl in a gray dress. She had been lying on the ground, motionless and still through all this, controlled by some sort of caution that had kept her from speaking until the last moment. She had a round, dark face. Her black hair showed the streaking of dust. Her lips were tight together but, in that last sputter of matchlight, he saw no fear visible. He walked on

37

through the dropping blackness and caught her arm.

"That Mexican said nothing of a woman in this wagon."

"No," she said.

"Were you in the wagon?"

"Yes."

"How did you escape the Indians?"

She said, "I crawled out and ran." Her voice had no lift, no excitement in it; it was passive, completely indifferent. He held her arm, returning across the gravel. She didn't seem to need his help, walking as surely as he could walk. He said, "I'll take a horse from one of the men staying behind." McSween said, "Noreen, your horse." Then Noreen came up with his mount and stood by. The girl moved away from Benteen and before he could assist her she was in the saddle, her voice coming calmly to him. "I can manage."

Benteen mounted and turned back through the canyon. The rest of the detail silently followed.

She was beside him. She bent until he felt her arm touch his shoulder; and her voice was a faint stage above a whisper, her words carrying only to him. "There was $3000 in gold in that wagon, Lieutenant. They got it."

"Antone?"

Her arm dropped from his shoulder; she didn't answer.

Beyond sunup Eleanor Warren stood in the doorway of commanding officer's house and watched the detail come across the bed of Aravaipa creek. Men gathered from the four corners of the post and Major Warren, emerging from the house, said, "Godfrey's bells, a woman!" The detail halted. Benteen left his saddle and gave the woman an arm to the ground. She stood a moment in the powerful sunlight, looking around the quadrangle with a calm indifference—and afterwards put her attention on Benteen. She was around twenty-five, Eleanor judged, with a strong body showing through the tight dress material and a smooth, dark skin and deep black hair pulled severely away from a middle part. It was her eyes that attracted Eleanor's attention. They were shadowed and obscure and reserved—as if the hardness of the land lay in them and would let nothing through. But she kept watching Benteen, this robust girl with the dust-stained dress; and Eleanor, sharp in her observations, witnessed the way Benteen looked at her and found her interesting.

Benteen said to Warren, "One man—a Mexican—is dead, sir. The others got away. The wagons were burned and the mules killed. I found this lady. I left a detail there."

Warren spoke to Howell Ford. "Take an ambulance and six men out there, Mr. Ford."

Benteen brought the girl to the ramada. He said to her, "I do not know your name."

She seemed to think about the question a moment; and afterwards shrugged, as though it didn't matter. "Lily Marr."

"This is Miss Warren. This is Major Warren."

Eleanor took the girl's arm and led her into the commanding officer's quarters, Warren and Benteen following. There was a difference between the two women—the difference of poise, of this Lily Marr's close-mouthed silence against Eleanor Warren's light and pleasant voice.

"You will want to clean up and rest. Probably you're starved. Was it very terrible?"

"No," said Lily Marr. "It wasn't that bad. Nothing's bad, if you don't think about it."

"How can you help thinking about it?" said Eleanor Warren in an astonished voice.

39

The girl considered Eleanor, her eyes watchful, her expression still reserved. "You can help anything."

Benteen said, "The Mexican who brought in the alarm last night didn't mention a woman being in the wagon."

Lily Marr lifted her shoulders and let them fall. "He didn't know I was on it. Nobody knew, except Summerton. I crawled into the wagon at Tucson and hid underneath the tarpaulin. Summerton thought it safer. When the attack came it was pretty dark. The men walked out into the night, keeping up their fire. That gave me a chance to run. It didn't last long."

Major Warren said, "How did you happen to be along?"

The girl, as before, considered the question over a considerable interval. Her answer was dry and brief. "I was going to Summerton's ranch to be cook and housekeeper."

Eleanor Warren said, "Don't answer any more questions, Lily. These men are too curious. I shall get Cowen to make up breakfast for you." She went into the kitchen. Major Warren walked out of the room, saying, "Meet me at the office, Mr. Benteen."

Benteen put his back against the casing of the dobe's door. His head was dropped and his eyes held this girl's face with a considering attention. She stood in the middle of the room, meeting his glance. Her lips faintly parted and some of her gravity gently went away; suddenly she came over to him and looked up with a warm expression in her eyes. "Lieutenant," she murmured, "could I stay here awhile?"

"Yes," he said. "Was it Antone, last night?"

She let him wait for his answer, until Eleanor's returning steps sounded beyond the kitchen door. Then she came quite near him, her voice dropped: "It wasn't Antone. It wasn't Indians. Indians don't care anything for gold."

Coming into the room, Eleanor Warren saw them this close together, with the girl's head tipped up and an expression on her face easy to define. Benteen drawled, "Thanks," and left the room, ducking his head to avoid the top of the doorway.

He found Major Warren and the other officers gathered at post headquarters. Manuel Dura and Al Hazel, two of the post guides, were in the room. Al Hazel squatted on the floor, drawing a quick map across the rammed earth with the point of a stick. He was a middle-aged man with a heavy clipped beard and a pair of eyes, never fully opened, that went restlessly from point to point. He wore a faded black serge suit, a loose vest and a narrow-brimmed black hat; and he had a reputation as the best scout in Arizona.

"You go up the creek to here. Pools of water standin' in the rocks and some grass for horses. You go north by a little west, between the Pinals and the White Mountains, cross the Salt here and make a dead point on the Sierra Anchas. That's Antone's favorite country."

Benteen settled on his heels and watched the map grow. Phil Castleton said, "Antone was in the Pinals night before last. How could he get from there to Summerton's wagons so fast? My belief is that if we follow his tracks away from those wagons we'll discover him back in the Galliuros now."

The grip let that remark go unanswered for the moment. Al Hazel lifted his head and gave Castleton a blank, polite survey. "It may be," he said softly. "And it may not be. An Injun's tracks don't mean nothin'. Where he was don't mean nothin' and where he will be don't mean nothin'. Only one thing means anythin' regardin' Apaches—which is where he is when you see him."

"Those tracks lead somewhere," insisted Castleton.

Al Hazel said, "I never got to the end of a breeze by

41

followin' it, and I never caught an Apache by chasin' his tracks back from the spot he made his raid."

"Well, then," suggested Castleton, in somewhat of a temper, "how do you find them?"

Hazel rose from his haunches. He reached for his knife and plug tobacco and sheared off a comfortable chew. The snap of the knife blade, when he closed it, was sharp in the silence. "Maybe I talk too much," he suggested with a smoothness that fooled nobody. "Guess I better just listen." But his dislike for Castleton's question was apparent.

Captain Harrison said, "It might have been some of the Chiricahuas up from the South, not Antone."

"Possibly," agreed Major Warren. "But the fact remains that Antone's the source of most of these raids and the cause of most Apache disaffection in this district. I conceive it my duty to bring him in, or kill him off. When that is done I think the job of pacifying the rest of the tribes hereabouts will be a good deal easier. Nachee can command most of his people and could command more if it were not for Antone's renegade bunch."

Castleton said, "Permit me to say, sir, I do not trust these so-called peaceful Indians around the post. Nachee is an Apache and all Apaches are born to deception."

Benteen drawled from his squatted position on the floor. "Don't agree."

Castleton's voice jumped at Benteen. "Then how is it that whenever we take a detail out on the heels of Antone the news of it seems to spread before us? We never find Antone. His camps are always deserted when we come up. It is my belief that Nachee watches our details leave the post and immediately sends runners out to warn Antone."

"What would you do then?" asked Major Warren.

"A harsher remedy," said Castleton. "I should bundle

42

up Nachee and his people and put them in a stockade, or move them completely away from this post. I should treat any Indian who shows himself around this post as a hostile. Bullet for bullet, trick for trick."

Major Warren touched the white ends of his mustache carefully. "In the last three years seventy-five people, more or less, have been killed by Apaches in this section of Arizona. Most of the cattle stock has been butchered, practically all of the ranches have been attacked and burned. There is no safe road in this quarter of the Territory. A man setting out alone from Tucson has no prospect at all of arriving here alive. Two weeks ago a herder was killed within sound of the Tucson church bells. The mines are deserted. For all purposes it is worse than during Mexican occupation."

"Just two ranches left in the whole length of the San Pedro," said Harrison.

"So far," continued Warren, "I have sent you gentlemen out on scout primarily to learn the country and break in the men to the kind of campaigning necessary. I propose now to set to work. We shall throw details after Antone steadily, keeping him on the move, breaking up his rancherias, pushing him out of his choice camp spots. I want him pushed so hard that he'll have no time to stop to bake mescal, no time to rest up. I expect we shall take our losses but I also expect we shall learn the game as the Apache plays it. We cannot hope to move as lightly or as fast as he does; but we can hope to maneuver him eventually into a bad position, and then close in. I hope somehow, during this time, to capture some of his people and gain information that will betray him. One other thing. When we set traps we must also expect to have traps set for us. That is the constant danger. We are dealing with the craftiest fighters in the world. These are the things I want you all to remember. So far this has been a schooling period.

The men are toughened up, our horses are in good shape. Now we shall go to work."

Castleton stepped from the corner of the room. He said in his quick, suppressed voice, "Major, I should like permission to take a detail out on the trail from the Summerton wagons."

"Your turn will come," said Warren. "Mr. Benteen, take out a detail of twenty men with rations for three days. Hazel goes with you. You are to cut Antone's trail and follow."

Benteen said, "If the major will let me, I'd like to let that trail go and try another. I learned something of Antone's habits on the last chase."

Major Warren studied Benteen through a considerable silence and afterwards put his glance on Al Hazel. He was a round, ruddy and easy-going man, this Warren, and deceivingly smart in his judgment of other men. Now, considering Hazel and Benteen, he formed his conclusions largely from Hazel's attitude toward Benteen. The civilian scout gave Benteen a full and grave attention. It was an interest that the guide, with his slight intolerance toward young officers, had not bothered to show Castleton.

Benteen added, "I don't believe the trail of last night's raiding party will lead toward Antone."

Al Hazel's eyes, never fully open, showed a narrower light. "In that, Lieutenant, I'd guess you was right."

Castleton spoke at once. "Maybe you have additional information, Benteen."

"Ain't always that," put in Al Hazel shrewdly. "Some men get so's they smell the right and the wrong of Indian sign."

"You have my permission," decided Warren. "What is your plan?"

"Up Aravaipa Creek and over to the Gila, circling the Mescals. If Antone has gone into those hills we should

44

cut his sign. I should also like to start tonight, well after dark."

"Agreed," said Major Warren, and left the room.

Benteen walked out with Al Hazel. Al Hazel pushed his hat well forward to shield his eyes from the bitter flash of the sun; his jaws worked gently on the cud of chewing tobacco and his close-shuttered eyes watched the smoky distance of the San Pedro. "Lieutenant, whut was that woman's name you picked up?"

"Lily Marr."

"Just so," murmured Al Hazel, and sauntered off, hands deep in the front pockets of his serge pants.

Chapter Four

Sunlight burned against the earth, catching up the thin and bitter flashes of mica particles in the soil, and heat dropped over the post, layer on layer until it was a substance that sluggishly stirred when the weight of a body was put against it. The flag hung lifeless against its pole; the sprinkling cart traversed the parade, damping the dust and leaving its steamy smell behind. A few Indians came from the camp outside the post and crouched in the false shade of the commissary building. Al Hazel's wife crossed the parade for the Major's washing, her olive Mexican cheeks smothered in a dead white flour paste. Lily Marr slept in an exhausted sleep in Eleanor Warren's bed. Drill call brought two skeleton troops, I and K, to the parade where Captain Harrison, his cheeks turned a lobster-red by the sun, drilled them briefly.

At noon Lieutenant George Mixler brought his detail down Aravaipa Creek and reported. He was a heavy young man whose naturally cheerful face was overcast by worry; after he had welcomed Eleanor he went straight toward his own dobe quarters. From her position under the ramada of the commanding officer's house, Eleanor heard him speak to Harriet, and heard Harriet's voice rise unreasonably and dissolve into crying.

The day droned on, the terrific summer's heat pressing down on a parade bare of life. Eleanor soaked her hands and face in tepid water and, unquenchably curious in spite of the weather, followed the walk around the quadrangle, past headquarters, post bakery, guardhouse and sutler's store and down along the line of men's barracks. Back of the commissary she saw troopers beneath the open shed of the blacksmith shop. Tom Benteen, stripped to his waist, had the hind foot of a horse between his legs, fitting a shoe. When she came nearer she heard him explaining to the troopers; and she paused to hear him explain. "Set it up tight, make your clinch clean. We'll take a few extra shoes along. I want no crippled horses on the trip."

Sweat streamed down his skin, it rolled out of his sandy hair, down across the flat of his cheeks. Troopers led their horses from the stables and back again, Benteen standing by. "This one will blow his tendons ten miles out. Pull a fresh mount from the corral, Levi. That's about all. Check your cinches and buckles. If you've got any bad saddle blankets, go to the quartermaster. Fill your canteens after supper. You'll get rations then. Twenty rounds extra for carbines and ten for revolvers."

When he came around she saw the pull of heat on his face. He took his shirt from the ground and put it on; he came forward, removing his hat; and there was, again, the nearness of a smile behind his eyes, and the same strong curiosity.

She said, "Come along. We've got some Sonora lemons."

The skin below the open roll of his shirt collar was quite dark; his hands were long and broad against heavy wrists. His trouser belt was cinched against a typical cavalryman's small flanks and the yellow stripe on the trousers made him seem longer-legged than was actually so. She wanted him to talk, curious as to the way he might break the strangeness between them, but he had a kind of indifference that covered him. All he said just then was a matter-of-fact, "It is a damned kind thought," and that oath was as natural and inoffensive as anything could be. Once, in turning across the parade her foot turned on a slick-sided piece of gravel; his arm pulled her up at once and then, looking up to him she saw how alive was the interest of his powder-gray eyes.

He followed her into the dobe's kitchen, and went back to the porch basin to wash up while she ground the lemons and pulverized the coarse sugar lumps. He brought in the ollas hanging to the porch rafters and poured the tepid water into the glasses. He sat on the edge of table, lifting his glass to her. "To you," he said, and drank with the lusty, audible relish of a thirsty man.

"It would be good to have some ice," she said.

"The trick of getting along in this weather," he told her, "is to let nothing bother you. Watch the Indians, or the Mexicans. They bend but they never break. Sleep when it is time to sleep and work when it is time to work. They're admirable people and they know something most Americans don't, which is how to get fun out of living."

He was thoroughly relaxed, his muscles loose, his legs sprawled. There was no strain in him, no haste or worry. She said, "That's the way you are, but you didn't learn it from the Mexicans. You were born that way."

"Eleanor," he said, "you're a smart girl."

"No," she said, "I was raised among men."

She refilled his glass and sat in a corner chair, more and more interested in him. The room held a deep shade and no sound stirred the post. Even in the half-light her auburn hair held a shine. Her long lips were gently set, showing gravity, showing will. Her shoulders were square and definite against the chair's back; they were strong. In the lengthening silence she was aware of his continuing, careful attention. In many ways he was an odd man, sharper with his eyes than other men, more attentive to details than other men. There was deception to him—the deception of a swift mind lying behind seeming indifference. She had lived in the army long enough to know that in all men there was a liberal streak of vanity and false pride, making them easy targets for flattery; these things were in Benteen, because he was a man, yet she was rather sure that it would be harder to reach him through flattery, because of the irony in his eyes, irony that controlled his judgments of himself as well as of other people. It was a definite impression she had.

She spoke on impulse. "Tom, would you do me a favor? Next time you play poker, please ask Phil to join you."

It was always dangerous to interfere with the likes and dislikes of men, yet she had a feeling that between herself and Benteen was a quick understanding. In some ways they were the same kind of people, both able to stand apart and watch the world run by. She felt this about him. He had lowered his head. His long forefinger gently rubbed the rim of the glass. He said, "Of course," but the lack of interest in his voice told her more than he intended.

She said, "What is it?"

He raised his head "What?"

"No," she said. "Nothing. It would have been a foolish question."

He shook his head. "Useless, maybe. But not foolish. Some questions have no good answers. That's one of them." He stood up and came on until she saw the flaky grayness of his eyes and the entire gravity in them. Inside him, deep away, some change occurred, swift and violent enough for her to feel that wash of its force. She realized that he was trying to tell her something in his

49

own reticent way. "You can change the color of your dress, or the way you do your hair. You cannot change the kind of a woman you are and you can't change a man into something you want him to be. Don't try, Eleanor."

She murmured, "How do you know that?"

"I tried it once."

"You sound very old," she observed; and her woman's curiosity grew greater and greater.

He could smile. It was a long, sound smile that showed the white surfaces of his teeth. "I got into the first battle of Bull Run at fifteen and went clear through to Appomattox, Two things bring a man along pretty fast, if he's the kind to learn at all—war and women."

She was a practical girl who had seen too many soldiers not to know them. So she said, "When was the first woman, Tom?"

"The first and last," he corrected. "At twenty-one. She was an unreconstructed rebel in New Orleans. If you ever go into the deep South, Eleanor, never let the magnolias and the summer twilight fool you."

She had an instant guess. "That's why you transferred, isn't it? To get away from her. Is she married now?"

"I don't know."

"I think," said Eleanor, carefully watching him, "she regretted that as much as you still do. It would be like a woman."

He said, "Do I show any regret?"

Phil Castleton's voice crossed from the front doorway. "Eleanor." He came on to the kitchen. The sight of Benteen brought him up and he stood with his shoulders pulled straight—a betraying expression on his face; and at once the room was too small for these two big men. Of Castleton's resenting dislike there was no question at all, but though Eleanor watched Benteen with a genuine concern, she could make out no visible reaction.

She broke the difficult silence by pouring Castleton a glass of lemonade. "Warm, but wet, Phil."

He took the glass and said, "Thanks," but didn't immediately drink. His manner was pretty clear; he wanted Benteen out of the kitchen.

Benteen said, "Where's that girl?"

"Sleeping," Eleanor answered. "Did you want to see her?"

"Maybe," put in Castleton, "she could add something to what she told you last night."

"What would that be?" inquired Benteen, soft and idle.

Castleton said briefly, "She did her whispering to you, not to me. My observation is you have good luck with stray characters and broken-down Indians."

Benteen swung around, facing Castleton; and this hot room held storm and trouble. Benteen said, "The term stray character scarcely applies to the lady, Mr. Castleton."

Castleton colored. His brief laugh concealed nothing of the swift anger in him. "I do not know her. Pending better knowledge I withdraw the remark."

Benteen looked at Eleanor. "Thanks for the drink," he said and left the room.

Castleton said, "If this is your day for open house, Eleanor, shouldn't you invite more than one man?"

She spoke gently. "That's a foolish remark, Phil."

"A man in love is apt to be a fool," he said and lifted his glass. He was smiling again. "To you." But his eyes, above the rim of the glass, were round and hot with real anger.

Sergeant McSween called, "The detail will leave at tattoo and ye'd better be takin' some rest meanwhile. The lieutenant Benteen is a man that likes to march."

51

Sunlight glowed through the drawn burlap curtains of the barrack room. In this hot semi-dark the men of the K and I troops took their siestas on the close-placed cots. Harry Jackson lay shirtless against the straw ticking and felt sweat accumulate beneath him. On the wall at the foot of the bed hung his saber, blouse and forage cap. A bright sliver of light struck in at the corner of the window curtain. Just above the window, in a crevice of the dobe wall, a tarantula hung in a motionless fur-black ball, half as large as Harry Jackson's fist.

Voices rolled idly and fatiguedly through the half-gloom. From the corner of his eye, Harry Jackson saw van Rhyn seated like a tailor on his bed, bending over a book. Van Rhyn was an older man, close to forty, with a long, shrunken face and a bony frame that no amount of food could fill. Like the rest of the crowd he was stripped to the waist. A small gold locket and chain swung against his flat chest. Van Rhyn was a peculiar man who always kept his fingernails clean and his boots shined and sometimes he used words that none of the rest of the troopers quite understood. It all made a mystery to young Harry Jackson who was twenty-one.

The bunks of I troop ended with van Rhyn; beyond was K troop's half of the barracks. Down there the men of K were arguing about religion, and pleased with the knowledge it was not their turn to go out on detail tonight. Big Mitch Canreen walked to the window, pushing the burlap aside to squint through the barrel of his carbine. "Anyway, boys," he said, "we'll be hopin' you sleep well on the rocks. When you reach the Injuns bring me back a load of baked mescal."

Sergeant McSween never let a man's insult go unanswered. " 'Tis the least to say we'll see Injuns. In I troop we pick no daisies by the wayside. Did I hear any of ye talkin' about the bloody savages ye've shot?"

Corporal Oldbuck answered that one. "Well, Benteen's

got the luck for that—which I will admit. Castleton ain't."

"Castleton," said another man. "I—"

But McSween stopped the comment before it came. "I'll hear no comparison as to officers."

Mitch Canreen spoke from the far end of I's line, "We'll take care of your duties, boys," and laughed a long, flat laugh.

Young Harry Jackson lay quite still, his legs pushed beyond the foot of his bed. His lips closed and he turned the palms of his hands over, pushing them against the bed. His heart quickened its beating; his throat dryly clacked when he swallowed.

McSween shot back his question: "Whut would ye mean by that?"

"Nothin' for you, Sarge," called Canreen. "But maybe another one of your lads will know." He was laughing again. Head half turned, Harry Jackson watched Canreen stroll forward. Canreen was a heavy, wicked Irishman; even in the half-light Harry Jackson saw the blackness of the man's eyebrows and the solid roll of his lips. Canreen was a bruiser and had had his brutal fights; it showed on the scars of his face.

"If it meant anything to me," said McSween tartly, "I'd clip your ears."

"Sure, Sarge, but you wouldn't know anything about love, hey?"

The drowsy talk fell away and Harry Jackson, flat on his bed tick, knew why. Even in this stifling heat a coolness rolled down his arms and the pit of his stomach tightened on emptiness and he felt an old, sick fear. McSween rolled around in his bunk and his words came out softly for Harry Jackson alone. "Ye'd better try to lick him now, son, or he'll make the rest of your hitch a hell of a wan. There's no livin' with the ape if he believes he's got ye scared."

Canreen came on toward the I troop side. He stopped by the window and turned, the ball-shaped tarantula hovering one foot above his black head. His mouth kept changing, it kept loosening and tightening; he had small eyes deep in his head. Both hands were behind him. He said, "Canreen will take care of it. The old soldier will show I troop rookies, hey?" He was at the foot of Harry Jackson's bed. He turned half away and brought his arms to the front, swinging a broomstick across the bottom of Jackson's boots. The sound flattened against the dead air and hot pain shot up Jackson's legs and made him roll from the bed. Canreen's laughter went wildly along the room, but when Harry Jackson came down the length of the bed and faced him, he saw the glitter of evil in Canreen's eyes. Young Harry Jackson stood with his blistered feet apart, his arms idle and as loose as water. There was no strength in him at all.

Canreen said, "She'll never miss you, Harry. I'll spend a night there myself—"

He was still afraid, this young Harry Jackson; deadly afraid of the beating he was certain to take. But Canreen had spoken a thing that turned Harry Jackson inside out, and the fear was less terrible because of it. Jackson pulled up his head, knowing he could never whip that heavy brute of a man, and then saw his saber hanging by the window. He flung out his arm, seized the saber's hilt and pulled it free of its scabbard and made one wild, outward slash that grazed the surface of Canreen's chest, leaving a faint red track there.

Canreen yelled at the top of his voice. "Hey—!" and dodged backward. Men sprang up from the cots. McSween called, "None of that, boy! None of that!" Harry Jackson didn't hear it. The fear and the jealousy in him was a flame that burned at his lungs. Canreen paced backward, momentarily out of range of the swinging saber; he let go with his hard cursing, and turned and seized van Rhyn's saber from the wall. Suddenly all the men in this barracks were crying in full throat. "All right, boy—all right—lick the hell out of him! Knock him down!"

McSween shouted, "Stop that—ye want somebody to hang for murder!"

Canreen stopped and waited, his shoulders drawn together and his round, cropped head lowered. Young Harry Jackson, turned still and half-blind, saw the red gleam in Canreen's eyes and the meaty roll of Canreen's lips. Van Rhyn's whisper came to him.

"Finish what you start, Harry."

It was this soft phrase which drove young Harry Jackson forward so precipitately that Canreen was caught off guard. The point of Jackson's saber caught and drove down Canreen's weapon. Canreen jumped back and brought his saber forward; when it struck the hilt of Jackson's saber a solid spasm rushed up Jackson's arm, as though it had been broken. All Harry Jackson saw was the shape of Canreen's round head and the dim blur of Canreen's bare chest; everything else was gray and formless and the cry of voices was only a confused tone. He rushed on, striking at Canreen in lunging, crosswise, full-armed slashes. Canreen yelled, "Hey!" and gave ground, and the sound of steel on steel went clanging through the barracks. Young Harry Jackson saw the point of Canreen's blade streak past his eyes and felt wetness suddenly along his lips. He heard his own breathing come deep and croupy from his lungs; he kept pushing on, wanting to kill Canreen, trying to kill Canreen. He saw Canreen's saber go crosswise and, sweeping in, he hit Canreen with the flat of his blade on the side of the face. Canreen dropped, knees and hips and shoulders collapsing at once; he lay on the floor and rolled from side to side, raising his boots to shield his stomach. Young Harry Jackson beat Canreen across the knees, hearing Canreen cry, and afterwards he was caught from behind and dragged back and flung completely around, across one of the beds. McSween seized the saber. McSween was saying in a calm voice, "It is enough, lad."

Somebody yelled, "Attention!"

Silence came to the room. McSween reached down to the cot and dragged Harry Jackson to his feet as Lieutenant Benteen swung into the barracks. "McSween," he said, "what's this?"

McSween's voice was even and polite—the voice of the old soldier turned smart by years of service. "A bit of an accident, sor. Canreen tripped on his saber, and it batted him across the head, strange-like. An odd accident, sor. I nivver saw the like of it before."

Young Harry Jackson backed against the rear wall of the barrack room so that he might have its support for his quivering legs. The heat was about to suffocate him. He could not drag in enough air and the sound of his gasping effort told Benteen the whole story. Benteen saw the boy's red-purple face and spoke quickly. "Lie down. Van Rhyn, get a bucket of water. Hurry it up—the boy's about to have a heat stroke. Did he trip on his saber too, McSween?"

"He was runnin' in the sun, sor. I've warned him many a time against it."

Canreen pulled himself from the floor. He put both arms against the wall and dropped his head against them. Blood dripped steadily from his nose. McSween pushed Harry Jackson to the bed and van Rhyn came back with a bucket of water. Nothing was said. Benteen watched Canreen a moment, and turned his attention to Jackson. Jackson's heart moved the skin of his chest; its straining labor was loud enough for Benteen to hear. McSween murmured, "Would the lieutenant be wantin' somethin'?"

He met Benteen's eyes, his own leather countenance gravely wise; these two men understood each other and played the game according to the rules. Benteen said, "You had better put Canreen's saber somewhere out of reach, McSween," and left the barracks.

Sergeant Hanna came from the shadows at the end of the room. "Canreen, get the hell back to your bunk. If it had been Castleton ye'd be walkin' post for a month."

Young Harry Jackson lay flat on his bed, feeling the warm wetness of the water van Rhyn slowly poured over him. Van Rhyn's face was a blur in a mealy grayness that surrounded everything. He kept reaching deeper for wind, feeling starved and choked for want of it, feeling the rack of his heart. His knees shook and all his muscles were trembling. McSween's face vaguely appeared. Van Rhyn's face dropped near and he saw the older man's reserved, odd eyes pretty clearly.

"Good boy. Never run from anything, or you'll be running all your life. Better be dead than that. I'm telling you, son. I know."

But Harry Jackson, in the strange dimness of his mind, was thinking, "I've got to watch out for Canreen. He'll try to kill me."

The ambulance detail returned near three o'clock with the dead Mexican. At five Major Warren stood over the grave in the post cemetery and spoke the brief funeral service beginning, "Man that is born of woman," under the day's last burning sunlight. There was no further ceremony. The officers and small funeral detail turned back to the parade, Lily Marr and Eleanor Warren accompanying them. Mess call sounded in the first blue shadows of evening; then suddenly and completely, full dark fell across the mountains, across the narrow valley of the San Pedro, and once again the outline of the

Santa Catalinas was a black ragged-edged mass against the glittering shine of the high stars. A new moon, tipped over on one of its horns, made a lightless arc of the low horizon. Heat pulsed along the earth, thick-scented with dust and sage.

McSween called through the thin lamplight of the barracks, "We pull out at tattoo." Standing in the dense shadows by the corral walls, Harry Jackson heard the echo of the sergeant's voice, and the clatter of the eight o'clock guard relief coming up to number five post near the edge of Aravaipa Creek. The relief stopped. Number five's Irish brogue cut the stillness: "Halt—who's there?"

"Corporal of the guard."

"Advance, cawprul of the guard, with the countersign."

This was the moment, while the guard stood at the far end of his beat, that Harry Jackson circled the corral, slipped into the dry creek bed and crossed it, thus putting himself beyond the lines. For a moment he lay belly-flat on the rough sand-and-gravel soil, one hand touching the butt of his revolver as he stared into the muddy dark surrounding him. The lights of the post sparkled behind. The small fire of Nachee's peaceful Indian camp made a round glow half a mile away. To the right of that fire, and another half mile onward, the light of Valley Ranch broke the black. These lights meant nothing, for it was a habit of Antone's band to creep singly down from the hills and lie in ambush at the very edge of the post with lance and arrow. Knowing this, Harry Jackson nevertheless took the risk, pushed to it by his desire. Rising, he went forward at a quiet walk until the sound of his boots could not carry back to the guard; thereafter he broke into a trot, every muscle of his body strained and stiff from the afternoon's fight. Fifteen minutes later, well-winded, he drew up at the first of the little scatter of dobe houses forming the

Valley Ranch, and knocked on a latched door.

There was a delay and, to Harry Jackson's attentive ears, the scrape of more than one set of feet; then the door opened and he passed quickly in and faced Rose Smith.

The smell of tobacco smoke in the room revived the torment of his jealous fears. He didn't look at her for a moment. He stood with his shoulder point swung away, staring at the opposite wall—a tall, slender boy whose face was still clear, still unmarked by the roughness of life. He had deep blue eyes and the gawkiness and the sober intensity of youth wrote its mark on him completely. He said, "If you ain't alone I'll get on back—"

She said at once, "Just my uncle. He left a minute ago."

"Oh," he said, flat and relieved. "Well—"

She was a dark, compact girl, full at hip and breast, with red lips that stirred at sight of him. She was older than Harry Jackson, though this he never knew. Older in years and older in her eyes. Looking at him, her face showed a softening, a puzzled change, as though she didn't quite understand him. She touched his arm, letting her hand lie there. "Maybe you'll sit down."

"No," he said, "I got to get back. I leave with the scout detail after tattoo. Just came to see how you were."

"Why, all right, Harry."

"I just wanted to know," he said slowly.

She said, "I'll think of you, Harry."

"Lord," he said, "that's what I do all the time. It is hell to pull out and think of you here. I wish you were in Tucson, or in the post. And it is tough to think my outfit might leave Arizona any time. I think of that a lot of times. I've got a year to go on my enlistment. Where'll you be next year, Rose?"

"Why," she said, "here, I expect. I don't know."

59

He said, "You shouldn't be near an army post, or near soldiers."

"You're a soldier, Harry."

"You know what I mean—the kind I mean."

"Yes—I know."

He said, "Well, I've got to get back," and pulled himself straight before her. She let her hand drop from his arm and remained before him with her lips soft and with a small, formless smile. She had a pliability, a waiting silence, a smoky-eyed expectancy. But this he didn't see. What he saw was a picture built from the eagerness and the hunger and the dreaming of a boy, all fair and all pure. He held his hat, his feelings strong and severe in his eyes. He said, quite formally, "I will see you soon," and opened the door and pulled it shut.

The girl put her arm against the door, listening to the fading run of his boots. Afterwards, when silence had quite come, the rear door opened and Mitch Canreen stepped in. "Who was it, Rose?"

Her shoulders rose and fell for answer. Canreen laughed, his scarred lips pulling apart, and settled down in a chair loosely. "Sure," he said, "sure. The kid. He don't know much, Rose. Come here."

But she stood by the door a long while, strangeness still on her face—the strangeness of the thought young Harry Jackson had left behind him. Presently she sighed and her expressive shoulders lifted and fell, as though it were something that had to be put aside, and moved across the room.

Tattoo ran the parade in strong, slow notes, sinking into the velvet-layered mystery of this night. Equipped for field duty, twenty men of I troop stood by their horses on the parade, a long blur in the blackness. Sergeant McSween's voice struck its grumbling command into the silence and other voices snapped back at him, counting off. Standing at the edge of the parade, Eleanor watched Benteen and Howell Ford cross the shadows and appear before the other officers grouped with Major Warren. They always went through this, shaking hands and exchanging best wishes. But Phil Castleton was in the background, aloof and silent. Major Warren said:

"I wish you to remember, Mr, Benteen, that your judgment always must prevail in the field. You are to catch Antone if that is possible, to keep him moving if you cannot catch him. Should you come upon him, be sure to estimate your chances carefully. Make a fight under any decent odds. If you must lose men to break up Antone's power, then do it. But under no circumstances should you waste a life foolishly. That temptation will be constantly before you. Antone will see to that. I have a great regard for the troopers in this command. They're the finest soldiers on earth and they're in your hands. Be sure you give them proper leadership. I wish you good luck."

Benteen's voice was slow and cool. He said, "Yes sir," and moved on until he stood before Eleanor Warren, tall-shaped against the night. She said, "Good luck," and took his hand. Afterwards he wheeled away with Howell Ford.

Sergeant McSween's solemn voice cross the parade. "Detail formed, sor."

"Prepare to mount. Mount!"

There was the smash of twenty bodies hitting leather, the grunt of horses and the clank of carbines and canteens and belted trenching tools.

"Right by twos, harch!"

The line moved, gray and indistinct; saddle leather made a little song against the ruffled beat of the walking horses. Eleanor went along the edge of the parade,

61

as far as the end of officers' row, following that column as it passed the guardhouse and the breaking corral and blended with the shadows lying over the San Pedro. Standing there, she listened to the slow fade of sound. Right of her, through the open door of the adjacent sutler's store she saw Cowen's stiff shape against the light. Half a dozen troopers sat before him and Cowen's voice was dryly addressing them. "I wish now to read the letter of a man in Switzerland who went down into the horrors of drink and took the pledge. 'Dear sir and esteemed friend—'" This was as it had been in Stanton. Cowen had organized his Soldiers' Temperance Union. At last all sound of Benteen's detail died beyond the San Pedro and only the dogged rumble of Cowen's voice and the lower murmur of dispersing officers remained.

Chapter Five

Benteen led the detail up the dry bed of Aravaipa Creek, soon passing from level country into the shallow mouth of a canyon, and thus onward through the black tangle of ridge and ravine and rising mountain shoulders. Near midnight they struck water and paused for a long rest, all the troopers settling against the stony soil. Lying full length, one arm propped against his head, Benteen listened to the wild chant of a coyote on a nearby ridge. The taciturn murmuring of the men reached him and the shift of the horses on the gravel and the crunch of their teeth on the iron bits. A small wind drifted from the upper country; the smell of damp horsehide and sweated leather was quite strong. High in the blackest heavens he had even seen a falling star make a brief, dissolving scratch against infinity. Howell Ford sat by, saying nothing. Al Hazel settled near Benteen.

"We turn out of this canyon in a mile. This is the main Injun trail. You headin' for the Gila?"

"Al," said Benteen, "I'm hunting small game tonight. Nachee told me this afternoon that some of Antone's people usually come back to a little rancheria on top of a peak this side of Saddle Mountain. We'll have a look."

Al Hazel relieved himself of his tobacco chew with a sharp "pfwutt." He ground his boots in the gravel. "It ain't a bad guess. Fer a young man you ain't been long learnin' Injun ways. Whut kills white men in this country is gettin' reckless. An Injun's got all the time in the world. His belly's his clock and any mescal bush or mesquite clump gives him food. Home's where he lights his fire and he'll travel farther in one day, with nothin' to tote, than this detail could march in a week."

"McSween," said Benteen quietly, and rose to his horse.

The detail turned north from Aravaipa Creek and suddenly was lost in velvet sweeps of land that joined each other at crooked, tricky angles. Al Hazel, who knew this country better than he knew his own mind, disappeared ahead. Now and then the shod hoofs of his horse, striking rock, set up a faint flash. Eastward stood the vague peak of Mount Turnbull. Due north, in the direction they traveled, was the ragged silhouette of stony peaks against a metal sky. At two o'clock Al Hazel dropped back. "Up there," he said. "The crooked hump on the left."

"How far?"

"Hour's ride."

Benteen turned and murmured to the following column. "No talking." They rose from one hogback to another, through the pit-black world. This was the coolest hour of the night, a faint wind fanning Benteen's cheek and bringing down with it the pungency of desert growth. A horse shied violently out of the line, evoking McSween's exasperated grumble. "Sullivan, whut the hell?"

"Snake smell."

The mountain mass in front of them grew higher and blacker as they approached; the land began to buckle up again. Benteen stopped. "Hour and a half until daylight. Howell, take charge. I'm going ahead with Hazel for a look. Sit tight. We'll be back in thirty minutes."

"Would ye be takin' another man or so, Lieutenant?" suggested McSween.

"Too much noise," said Benteen, leaving his horse. Thus on foot he went forward with Hazel, skirting catclaw and nopal clusters and mesquite bushes. They reached the shoulder-high barrier of huge rocks fallen from the crumbling ramparts of the peak, and began to climb over them, monkey fashion, rock to rock, point to point, up a forty-five degree tilt. Al Hazel grunted and paused for breath, and in the interval Benteen listened to the faint clack and rustle and scrape of earth life. Somewhere in these rocks snakes denned up; he could smell them. Al Hazel put his mouth against Benteen's ear.

"Two hundred yards, straight up."

They continued, with Benteen placing each boot on solid support before swinging his weight to it. The stiff tilt continued, the rocks making a kind of rough stairway. Benteen ran his gauntleted hand against a pincushion cactus and hauled his jaws together, suppressing a groan. Higher up he snagged his shoulder into the drooped branch of a catclaw bush. Turned still, he worried the sharp fishhook barbs loose. At this elevation the air was definitely thinner. Hazel touched his shoulder for signal and in thorough silence they climbed the last hard pitch of the ridge. Standing almost straight, his boots on a lower boulder and his elbows hooked over the rim of the hilltop, Benteen stared forward and saw, for this first moment, only a kind of small meadow recessed in the rocks and surrounding mesquite. All this was against the paler light of the sky and though he swept the cleared area very carefully he could not identify the marks of a camp. But Al Hazel touched his shoulder again, and both of them backed down the slope a good hundred feet before stopping. Hazel whispered close to Benteen's ear.

"A camp. Maybe four-five-six. I ain't sure."

Benteen murmured, "Go back and tell Ford to bring up half the detail. Take off belts. Too much noise. Put extra cartridges in pockets. I'll wait here."

Al Hazel faded below, making no sound at all. Benteen climbed back to the rim, hooked his arms over it and searched the area, trying to see what Al Hazel had seen. As far as he could determine this mountain top clearing was narrow and not more than a hundred feet long, with rock cairns breaking it at spots; then, more closely observing, he discovered that one of the rock cairns had a rounded top, which probably was a brush jacal thrown up by the Apaches for sleeping. After that he caught horse smell, and saw a shape stir at the clearing's far end.

The shadows were beginning to pale. Eastward a definite crack of light showed along the rim of the Galiuro Mountains and from this thousand-foot elevation Benteen watched the surrounding mountains gradually break through the night. The San Pedro valley showed its pale streak. Beyond that, through the gap of the Santa Catalinas, the farther desert began to throw off a dim shine. Below him was a sibilant heaving of breath. Al Hazel crawled through the rocks and came beside him and afterwards Ford and McSween reached the rim. The other troopers were halted and silent below, waiting word.

Benteen murmured to McSween, "One at a time—come up and spread."

McSween bent back, his whisper carrying down. Harry Jackson heaved forward, stepping beside Benteen. Van Rhyn, weakened and badly winded, caught Harry Jackson's sleeve. For a moment both of them teetered on precarious balance, until Benteen's arm steadied them. The sheet of light eastward turned into a broad violent band and at once, so sudden was dawn on the desert, all the world lay gray and misty and semi-visible. Turned back to the clearing, Benteen saw the definite shape of the Apache rancheria before him. A brush-covered jacal occupied the middle of the clearing, and half a dozen horses stood on picket at the far end, one hundred yards away; near the jacal a few lumpy shapes along the ground indicated Indians sleeping. Hazel bent against Benteen. "Four-five bucks."

Benteen looked to either side, seeing the troopers crouched against the rocks. He put his hands on the rim for a sudden jump, motioned forward with his head, and sprang up. The deep silence of the breathless hour was broken by the grunt and rush of the troopers going over the rim. Benteen said in a full voice, "No firing unless they start," and fell into a run, carrying the skirmish line with him.

Suddenly the lumpy shapes on the ground were whirling up and a woman rushed out of the jacal, carrying a papoose in her arms. One wiry buck lunged straight at Benteen, his sharp-pointed lance thrust forward, his eyes live as coals against the copper skin. Benteen had drawn his gun. Before he got it lifted he saw the Indian set himself for a throw, and ducked aside as the lance drove by him. That same moment the Indian reached for his knife and swept it half overhead, still rushing in. Benteen's bullet knocked him down. The scout detail raced on, full-throated. Two more women flung themselves out of the jacal and a small boy stood in its doorway, dead still. One of the Apaches, fleeing away, stopped and took a snap shot with his carbine; and suddenly McSween's gun roared. The Indian dropped. Troopers clawed the brush away from the jacal. Harry Jackson was on the dead run, trying to catch the woman with the papoose. Four other Indian men, the two women, and this small boy stood silent and sullen in the ring of troopers. This was all of the fight.

Al Hazel said, curtly approving, "Not a bad job, Lieutenant."

The clearing, all visible now in the first sunless period of morning, was a little below the rocky rim, marked with a few mesquite bushes and two or three stunted pines. Benteen walked down to the north side, meeting Harry Jackson, who said, "That woman just sank into those rocks with the baby."

"Never mind. You couldn't catch her now."

A rough trail wound down this north side of the hill, breaking into canyon country. Beyond this canyon the hills rolled on in black broken crests toward higher summits. Benteen walked back to the jacal. "Jackson, go tell Corporal Levi to bring the rest of the detail around the north side. There's a trail for horses."

The Indians crouched on the ground, impassive as stone except for one woman who spread out her arms and began to speak swiftly to Al Hazel. Al Hazel pushed his hat forward on his head; he listened, his jaws gently working on the tobacco cud. When she had finished Hazel interpreted for Benteen.

"She says don't kill her because that was her baby the other woman ran off with."

Benteen said, "Ask her how many warriors Antone's got now?"

Al Hazel asked it and waited out the woman's slow answer. "She says maybe enough to fill this clearing with their horses."

"Tell her we are not fools."

Al Hazel repeated it in Apache, and later said, "She says it is true. Some Chiricahuas have come up to join Antone, and some of the Tontos are with him."

"Where is Antone now?"

When Hazel repeated the question the woman looked at Benteen through the loose straggle of her hair and was silent. Benteen said, "Tell her we are taking her to Camp Grant and will keep her there, but that if she leads us to Antone she is free to go back to her baby and her people."

There was a long parley, Al Hazel talking, and listening, and answering. The other Indians never stirred. Finally Al Hazel grunted, "Enju," and turned to Benteen. "She says Antone's over in the Mescals. May be a lie but Antone's been ridin' pretty fast lately and he'll have to stop to rest up pretty soon. He always did like the Mescals for a hideout."

"We'll find out. Put a guard on these people. We'll lay over there until nine o'clock."

The rest of the detail came up the north side with the horses. Somebody started a small fire, upon which the men cooked their bacon and coffee. Benteen took the saddle from his horse, carried it to the shelter of a pine tree and stretched full length, using the saddle for a pillow. Flat on his back, he rolled a cigarette and smoked it through, watching the brightening blue of the sky through half closed eyes. Al Hazel came up and crouched on his heels, imperturbably chewing his tobacco.

"The squaw which got away," Benteen observed, "may cause us trouble. She'll walk forty miles with that papoose before sundown. Maybe reach Antone."

"Maybe," said Al Hazel. "You never can tell about an Injun. But you done well, Lieutenant. Cavalry never sneaked up on an Injun in this country before. It will shake Antone some."

Reveille, stables, mess call, fatigue, and drill call. This

was the ancient routine. Standing at the doorway of the commanding officer's quarters, Eleanor watched the parade ground shadows creep back from the increasing blast of sunlight. Ray Lankerwell came up with a small, copper-faced boy from Nachee's camp. He put a catchup bottle on the parade ground, thirty feet away. He said to Eleanor, "Watch this," and motioned to the boy who calmly bent his bow and sent an arrow dead into the open mouth of the bottle. "Well," grinned Lankerwell, "that gives you some notion." He went away, leading the Apache lad.

Out on the parade Phil Castleton ran K troop through dismounted drill, his voice hard and precise and biting in the dead-hot air. Dust rose around the wheeling column; the occasional bright patches on metal equipment flashed against the pouring sunlight. Sweat began to stain the backs of the men's shirts, and black as they were she saw the growing heat flush on their faces. Phil Castleton stood motionless in the parade's middle, heavy and wide-shouldered. "Canreen—pick up that gun. Hep, hep, hep! On right into line—harch! Pull up your shoulders, Flynn! Watch the pivot—come up, come up!"

Three years, Eleanor thought, made a difference in the things she saw. At seventeen she had taken this man at surface value, not quite knowing what qualities in him appealed to her so. She began to see those qualities now, the strength and the weakness of them. He was terribly ambitious, he was a man who could not excuse weakness. She saw how relentlessly exact he was at drill, how he kept repeating certain close-order commands over and over again until it was done as he wanted it done. He had no patience for imperfection; not even on the frontier, not even in this destroying sunlight and suffocating heat.

Her father came from post headquarters and paused

70

at the door of the house, watching the drill. He pulled at the ends of his mustache and she thought he meant to speak to Castleton; but afterwards he walked into the living room. She turned with him, watching him sink into a chair and sighingly relax.

"Daughter," he said, "it's a damned hot land," and wiped his half-bald bead free of sweat. His skin was full pink.

"Dad," she said, "tell me—"

The girl from the ambushed Summerton wagon train, Lily Marr, came in. The heat seemed not to touch her. Against the doorway's bright yellow light she was strong-shouldered and motionless, with her quite dark hair drawn severely back from a central part. Her eyes had a quick and direct watchfulness common to most people living on the frontier; her face had the frontier's rather set and inexpressive calm. Her skin was smooth, though tanned from the sun, and her features were quite regular, save for a generous mouth. She was better looking than her knock-about life seemed to indicate. Her speech, Eleanor had already noticed, was carefully chosen. All of this put together puzzled Eleanor considerably. Behind this girl's gravity and very definite pride was some kind of mystery.

The major said, "Miss Marr, I should like to know what I can do for you."

The girl looked at him, weighing his words. Then she said, "Nothing."

Warren said, "You want me to send you on to the Summerton ranch with an escort?"

She had a quick answer, a very quick answer: "No—not now. Isn't any use."

Warren didn't understand. "How's that?"

But she lifted her shoulders and let them fall. The gesture had a Mexican fatality to it, and Eleanor got the

71

clear impression then that this girl had had a good many illusions and girlhood dreams knocked out of her. She said, "If I am not too much in the way, Major, I'd like to stay here for a little while."

"Why bless your heart," announced Major Warren, "you can stay here as long as the flag flies."

"Perhaps you might let me work for my keep. I can cook."

Warren said at once, "You're a guest, Miss Marr."

The girl turned her glance to the floor. "Thank you," she said in a softer voice, and went to her room.

Phil Castleton's driving voice crossed the parade. "McGuire, dress against the right file. Flynn, pull up your gun! Column left, harch! One, two, three, four! Sergeant, your pace is too slow."

Major Warren pulled out his watch and scowled at it. He rose and walked to the door, looking on at the drill. Eleanor noticed the sudden shadowing expression on his face and knew, because she was a thorough army girl, exactly what he thought about. Castleton was marching the feet off these men; there had been no rest for half an hour—and the outside temperature was beyond a hundred. Castleton hadn't moved from his exact stand in the middle of the parade. Dust made a steady fog around the countermarching troop; the faces of the men were drawn and brick-red, and a little heat-swollen.

Major Warren tugged at the ends of his mustaches. He was, Eleanor understood, thoroughly displeased, but caught in the delicate problem of protecting his men without criticizing an officer in front of them. Presently he called out:

"Mr. Castleton, that will be enough drill for the morning."

Castleton said, "Very well, sir," and turned the troop over to Sergeant Hanna. He came across the parade and stopped under the brush ramada, before Warren and Eleanor. When he removed his hat a trapped sweat streamed down the violent sun-flush on his cheeks.

Warren said, "Come in, Mr. Castleton," and stepped aside. Castleton walked into the room's half-shade. He held his stiff posture before the major, shoulders thrown back. His eyes, Eleanor observed, were a strict noncommittal black. There was, she reflected, something in him that even the blast of the sun couldn't reach or wilt.

Her father, always careful with his words, spoke nevertheless with a suppressed impatience. "Mr. Castleton, you should remember to give your men long rests. You'll run the vitality out of them."

"They're very slack in drill, sir, and the discipline is far too relaxed. I wanted to pull them up so they'd remember."

"You must not expect perfect close-order drill from men campaigning in the field, Mr. Castleton. Barracks and field duty are two different things. There is always a letdown in military niceties when you troop out on daily scout. You do not create discipline, even among Irishmen as tough as those ones are, by undue severity."

"Yes, sir," said Castleton. But Eleanor knew how much dissent lay behind those obedient words. She knew and was afraid. Her father's more suave talk followed in.

"As soon as Mr. Benteen returns, it will be your turn on scout. Those are the men you will be taking. You want them fresh, not worn out. That's all, sir."

Eleanor said at once, "I'll make up some lemonade."

Castleton turned to her, rubbed pride visible at the corners of his lips. "I'd better change clothes and inspect barracks." He made his short bow and went out. She listened to the heavy tramp of his feet on the board walk, and turned to catch her father's speculative glance.

"You're a smart girl, Eleanor. You know the army better than most young lieutenants. Castleton is an excellent officer. A little hard, perhaps. Maybe you can unbend him a little. He needs it."

"Is that the trouble, Dad?"

He sprawled in the chair, taking what comfort there was to be had. He didn't answer until he had lighted a cigar; its blue fog somewhat screened his eyes. "Most young officers are afraid to be human, figuring it is a confession of weakness. They're not quite sure of their straps, or their leadership. Usually it wears off. After three years it should have worn off with Castleton but it has not. I should hate to see him develop into a martinet. He is too promising for that."

"He's very ambitious, Dad."

"So was I," said Warren, quite gentle with his words. "So was I. But the Civil War glutted the army with officers and promotion now is a very small gleam in the remote future. I should be much more impatient with young Castleton if I did not know he was eating out his heart over promotion. The lists ahead of him are clogged with gray-haired first lieutenants and captains. And superannuated majors like me. He thinks now the only way is to make a very impressive record so that somehow he can make his way over the plodders. I wish him luck, but he must not get himself too hated by men and officers in the attempt. He should develop a little philosophy. Like me. Like—"

She immediately supplied the name. "Like Mr. Benteen."

But the Major was too fair a man to be trapped into a comparison of junior officers. He waved his cigar and said blandly, "You're too damned clever, young woman. Go fix me a lemonade."

But after she had gone into the kitchen his voice came back to her, slow and wistful. "Your mother was the same. We had an awful lot of fun. If she had lived I bet I'd been a brigadier now. It wouldn't mean anything to me at this late date, but it would have been mighty nice to see her face when she pinned that star on my shoulder. That's the kind of a woman she was, Eleanor. Everything was a game, and the game was fun, clear to the end."

Chapter Six

Afternoon's heat settled over the post. It was a suction that drew the last residual moisture from earth and boards and living things. The mountains grew dim behind a blue-yellow haze; all along the valley of the San Pedro was a sulky glitter of rocks and sand and mica particles. Even the Indian and Mexican hangers-on retreated to the thin, oppressive shadows of the post. Nothing moved.

Harriet Mixler lay on the bed in their two-room dobe quarters, face upward and her arms lying full length, fists doubled. George Mixler sat by the bed, stirring the air around her head with a fan. He was a solid young man with a pink round young face crossed by a tawny dragoon's mustache; on his face now was a faint, worried smile. "Pshaw, Harriet," he murmured, "nothing bad will happen." Sweat rolled from his cheeks, down past his open collar. He swiped it away and kept on fanning.

Her eyes were wide-round and breathing was difficult for her. "George," she said, "I should have gone to Fort Whipple three months ago. I'm going to die."

"No," he said, "no, you won't. Why, it is a natural thing, Harriet. Major McClure's wife had three of 'em—all on the frontier. Once she had no doctor. It was behind the lines, during the siege of Vicksburg."

Afterwards he could have bitten his tongue in two. She was an expressive girl, quick to feel and quick to change. Fear rushed across her face, stronger than it had been before. "George, Doctor Shiraz will be away when the time comes. You wait and see. He's always gone! You'd think they might remember me. But they don't care about a woman in the army—they don't care!"

"He'll be here," promised Mixler. "Right here."

"You always stick up for the army," she said passionately. "You never see it my way! I hate the army. I wish I never had seen a uniform!"

"I know," he answered quietly. "It is devilish hard on a woman. But it will be all right."

She almost screamed at him. "How can you be so sure, so indifferent? It's me, it isn't you!"

He said, "I'll get some fresh water."

"No, it's all flat and tasteless." She stared at the thatched ceiling, with the shadow of all that she felt making its dark stain in her eyes. "I feel so terrible. Just like an animal in a trap. It is too late for everything."

He was a man, simple and direct and awkward; and in trying to cheer her he said the wrong thing again. "If it's a girl, we'll call her Harriet. If it is a boy, we'll have him in the saddle before he can walk."

She gave him a swift, hating look. It chilled him to see it, and to hear the dead conviction in her voice. "Listen, George. If I live, and if the baby lives, I'm going away as soon as I can. I'll never stay in another army post, I'll never follow you around in another army wagon like a washwoman, I'll never stand at the door of another miserable dobe shack and pretend it

77

is home, waiting for you to come out of those terrible hills."

"I know," he murmured. "I wouldn't talk so much, Harriet. Just lie still."

"No," she told him, more and more quiet. "You think you're just humoring a foolish woman. I'm telling you the truth, George. I wanted you to resign. You could have had a nice position in Baltimore. My father offered it. We could have lived so pleasantly. You wouldn't do that, and I thought you were being gallant, wanting to follow your regiment. You have had your way. Now I shall have mine. I'm not cut out to be an army wife. I have been miserable every day. I'm going to leave you, George, just as soon as I can travel."

"All right, Harriet."

She looked at him, the terrible intensity still in her eyes. "I mean it, George." And then, looking at her, Mixler saw that she did. He kept on fanning, not speaking. Eleanor Warren came into the room and saw the drawn expression on his face, the set and half-wild look in Harriet's eyes. She took the fan immediately from Mixler. "You run on."

"Thanks," said Mixler and got up. He turned through the room, took a long pull from the warm water jar, and stood with his big legs wide apart. He tried to roll a cigarette, but his hands were shaking badly, so he threw the tobacco and paper away and left the dobe.

At five o'clock, in the densest heat of the day, a rider crossed the San Pedro and appeared before the commanding officer's house and slid from an exhausted horse. George Mixler happened to be coming on from the sutler's store at the moment. The traveler managed to gasp out, "Been a shooting at Summerton's ranch—they want the doctor," and then fell to the ground, his lips and face turned purple.

Mixler dragged him into Warren's house, rousing the Major from a troubled siesta. A trooper ran down the walk and presently Shiraz came up, took his professional look at the man and said, "Damn near sunstroke."

Major Warren said, "You'll have to go up to Summerton's ranch, Shiraz. Seems to be a shooting. Mr. Mixler, get an escort and go along. You'll be back by midnight." Twenty minutes later Shiraz and Mixler, with six troopers, crossed the San Pedro and headed toward the gap in the Tortillas.

At six, Eleanor brought Harriet Mixler to the commanding officer's quarters for supper. Afterwards, in the sundown hour, they stood beneath the brush ramada to watch the mounted troopers stand retreat and guard mount, the buglers of I and K sounding the music. It was suddenly dark, with yellow lights sparkling all around the quadrangle; the sprinkling cart came past, leaving behind the steamy pungence of water on hot dust. Phil Castleton walked up from the hard outer shadows, made his bow to the women and expressed his sentiments on the weather. But his talk was no screen to hide his desires and immediately Harriet Mixler turned away.

"I'll come along in a little while," Eleanor said to her.

The silent Lily Marr spoke up. "Let me walk with you, Mrs. Mixler."

For a moment all the others looked at this grave, secretive woman. Harriet Mixler's face turned from the shadows until the beam of the Warren house-light caught it and showed its strange, set pallor. "You needn't bother," she murmured. Lily Marr said softly,

79

"We all get a little lonesome at times," and took Harriet Mixler's arm, and moved on into the night.

Phil Castleton stared after them, holding his remark until they were barely beyond hearing distance. "I don't like that Marr girl," he said.

Eleanor Warren, listening to the flat ring of his voice, realized that all his opinions were like that. Quick and arbitrary, one way or another. She didn't immediately speak, but took his arm and fell into step with him. They passed the corner of officers' row, turning along the north side of the quadrangle. The moon lay at a low angle in the sky, deep yellow from the dust in the air. When they reached the south side of the quadrangle Castleton drew her into the parade to avoid the broad talk of the troopers in the barrack. She said, "Why, Phil?"

"A stray woman in a tough country. She hasn't explained herself, has she? Just a woman out of nowhere."

"Most of us come out of nowhere, Phil."

"I don't mean that. And what impels you to be philosophical?"

"Why," she said, "I guess I've always been. I see people laughing or crying—and I wonder why. I never pass a man but what I wonder at his story, at all the fortune, good or bad, he's been through. Why should you draw me away from that barrack wall, Phil? I know the kind of things men like that might talk about. I know them by heart. I was raised with troopers."

He stopped and turned to her. She saw displeasure on his face clearly. "That's not becoming, Eleanor. If I ever heard one of them speak like that within earshot of you I'd put a pack on his back and march him under the sun until he dropped."

80

"You'd have most of them dropping then," she said, gently amused. "You shouldn't expect so much purity from a trooper, Phil. It isn't that they mean to be rough. They'd cut their arms off for a woman. It's just that they never knew any other way to talk. You shouldn't mind. These men really raised me. I think they spared me nothing in the way of practical knowledge — I'm glad they didn't."

He said, faintly indulgent, "I imagine they left you in the dark in some things. I should hope so."

She said, "They are very real, Phil. How well do you know them? Their stories? Do you know about Harry Jackson — and the woman at Valley Ranch?"

"Good Lord," he exclaimed, "who told you about her?"

She was laughing at him, softly, freely. "I told you I was raised by this regiment. Cowen keeps nothing from me."

"It is damned unpleasant. It isn't right."

"Why not, Phil? It is pretty tragic, isn't it — young Harry Jackson falling in love with a very common woman. And not knowing she's bad?"

"Are you sure he doesn't know?"

"Hanna says he doesn't."

They had walked on. Now he stopped again. "Do all these men talk to you like that, Eleanor? They never talk to me."

She took his arm and they walked on, steps striking together. The eight o'clock hour call ran the posts; the sentry relief stamped by. They passed the post bakery, went back down officers' row, and began the second round of the quadrangle. "Phil," she murmured, "you must be more patient and a little more human with them. Some of them are illiterate, some quarrelsome, some their own worst enemies. But they're the best men on earth—and they'll stick to an officer until he dies if they're loyal to him. But you must be loyal to them."

He said, quite short and dry, "I begin to see. A sermon, Eleanor?"

He had that faint intolerance—that resistance which came from his pride and his own tremendous energies. She knew she had said all she could for one night and so, knowing it, she laughed again and stopped by the barrack's corner. "No—no sermon, Phil. Isn't this a lovely night?"

He put his arms behind her shoulders and she could see how stirred he was; it was a roughness on his face. "By God, Eleanor," he murmured and pulled her in.

Afterwards, when she stepped back, she was laughing again. "You see, Phil? I'm not a graduate of a female seminary. I'm an army officer's daughter. I'm a woman. Isn't that enough?"

He was grudgingly troubled. "I wish you wouldn't use quite that tone. It isn't—"

"Phil," she said, "living is something that should be real. We should take it as best we can, as deep and wide and full as we can. We shouldn't ever be small or ever be afraid. Does that sound like anything to you?"

"I guess," he said, hesitant and dry, "I miss the point."

She sighed. "Most people do. I wish I could find the words—"

That was as far as she got; for the sound of a scream, wild and in the highest possible reach of a woman's voice, struck across the parade. A scream, a cry—and a guttering breath of agony. And silence.

Lily Marr walked along officers' row with Harriet and turned into the Mixler quarters. She stood by, waiting while Harriet lighted a lamp—so still and grave that Harriet turned to her with a certain puzzlement "It is nice of you to be pleasant to me. I think I shall go to bed. You needn't bother to stay. It is so terribly hot in here."

They were about the same age; in no other respect was there a similarity. For Harriet Mixler was a frightened girl who could not forget the shelter and the light and the softness of the home from which she had come; she had never known hardship, she had never known uncertainty until now. All this left her still childlike and dreaming, and frightened by the world she found herself in. Watching with her still eyes, Lily Marr saw this clearly. She took Harriet's arm again, leading her back to the bedroom, and her voice was slow and very calm.

"The heat isn't bad. Nothing's as bad as a woman's mind makes out. I'll sit awhile."

Harriet put herself on the bed, lying full length. The light was against her eyes. Lily Marr moved the lamp to the far corner of the room. She drew her chair near the bed and propped her chin against the palm of her hand. Her face, in its habitual repose, had an expression that stirred Harriet Mixler's curiosity until she found herself trying to find a proper name for it. It was something like sternness, like a gravity that came when someone had seen too much, like the shadow of hidden sadness. This was as near as Harriet could explain it. But whatever the cause, it was pleasant to see the deep, gentle glow in this girl's eyes; to hear the steadiness of her voice. It brought an inexpressible calm into the room.

Harriet said, "Have you been long in this country?"

"Four years."

Harriet murmured in her little girl's wondering

voice, "It is so odd to think of people. Four years ago I was in Norfolk, having so much fun. It was very gay. And you were on the desert, in this wild territory. It is very odd. Might I ask about your people?"

"They were killed by Indians."

"How sad," murmured Harriet Mixler. "Don't you hate Arizona?"

Lily Marr seemed to study the question, as if it aroused an unfamiliar thought. "Why," she said, "I don't believe I do. When you can't choose your way it doesn't seem much point to hate anything."

"I reckon I don't understand that."

"My people started from New Orleans to California. They were killed at Apache Pass. I have made my way on the frontier ever since. Nobody hates living. We are all glad to live. I am. But I guess I can understand being lonely. Don't be afraid—don't ever be afraid."

She put her hand on Harriet Mixler's arm and left it there a moment, her lips turning sweet. The darkness and doubt in Harriet Mixler's face was very real. She stirred uncertainly on the bed. Lily Marr's calm voice was a comfort, it was something real and solid. "Nothing is as bad as you think. Pain makes you cry, but when it is gone you forget it. Hunger hurts, but you can live a long while without food. That's what you have to learn. Don't ever be afraid. You can stand anything. Afterwards it is good to be just alive. I'm telling you something I know."

Harriet Mixler rose slowly from the bed. "I declare," she said, "I think you're a help. I believe I'll undress and try to sleep."

Lily Marr left the chair, moving toward the door. She turned to watch the drawn, thin lines of Harriet Mixler's face; and saw the haunted uncertainty there. She said in her deliberate way, "You have very pretty hair. In the morning I will comb it out for you. Good night."

After she had gone Harriet Mixler stood quite still, her hands supported against the dobe wall. She felt the heaviness of her child, the pressure on her legs. It was hard to breathe this suffocating air and suddenly the silence was so deep that she heard the slugging rhythm of her heart. She moved through the house and out into the rear yard, going along the vague border of a low board fence, holding to the top of the fence. It was minutely cooler here and the stars were whitely glistening in the sky. She passed back to Captain Harrison's house, seeing him rocking in a chair; beyond that was Doctor Shiraz' dobe. For a moment she paused, wondering how soon he would return, and the low, deep fright came to her again and then she looked at the black overhead sky and began to shake, and to hate this country and this post and the people in it, and went down into a dark loneliness that had no light. She walked faster, as though moving away from something—something that kept following her, though she didn't know what it was.

Her hand was on the top rail of the fence and, sliding forward, it touched a rounded, rough surface that gave before her fingers and fell with a soft "tunk" to the ground. She reached down and touched it again and then her fingers moved across the nose and the mouth of the dismembered Apache head Doctor Shiraz had put out on the fence to dry. She flung herself upright, sickness flooding through her, turned cold, turned crazed; and at that moment she screamed at the top of her voice until her breath ran out and would not come back, and fell senseless to the ground.

Captain Harrison came out of his back door, cursing. The sentry rushed around from the parade, bawl-ing, "Cawprl of the Guard, Post number Five!" There was a swift yell all across the post and feet smashed along the loose-boarded walk and Ray Lankerwell ran up from post headquarters, swinging a lantern at each jump. He found Harrison crouched over Harriet Mixler. The lantern light touched the grisly shape of the Apache's head. Lankerwell kicked it away, hearing Harrison's terrible, passionate cursing. "By God, I'll kill that damned doctor! Bear a hand, Mr. Lankerwell! Easy—she's damned near dead!"

The guard relief charged up. Major Warren rushed through the Mixler dobe and settled down by Harrison, his breath bubbling in his lungs. Eleanor hurried out of the night. Harrison caught Harriet under the arms, lifting her; and then he and Lankerwell took her back into the dobe and laid her on the bed. Major Warren had the lantern now, holding it over Harriet. The room grew crowded and all the breathing of these people was quite labored. Eleanor dropped beside the bed, her hands on Harriet's breasts. Harriet lay with her eyes half opened, the pupils rolled out of sight. Her fists were clenched over her chest and she was caught in sudden, shaking spasms.

Eleanor said, "When will Doctor Shiraz be back?"

"Not till midnight."

She lifted her head, staring at her father. "She can't wait that long."

Harrison ground out, "Is there nobody in this post who knows anything about babies—"

Lily Marr came past the men, gently pushing them. She stood a moment, looking down at Harriet Mixler; and suddenly turned. Her shoulders were square in the lamplight, her voice was cool and unstirred. It was a competence, a feeling of sureness they all felt. It was in the way she looked at them, in the way she spoke.

"I know."

Eleanor looked at the men. "You had better leave. Lily and I will do this."

Chapter Seven

Around nine o'clock that morning Benteen started down the rocky hillside with the detail. At eleven, in a piece of flat country below, Al Hazel got out of his saddle and began walking a zigzag course ahead of the troopers. Presently he pointed to a faintly scuffed mark on the flinty soil and to the broken stems of a bunchgrass clump beyond it. "There's your squaw's trail," he said. "And you can figure Antone's at the end of it." He got back on the horse, his hat tilted forward on his head and his eyes following this dim clue.

The land heaved away in a kind of irregular monotony, roll on roll, with always the higher peaks standing black-cut under the strengthening sun. They crossed areas of strewn slab rock and threaded thickets of catclaw. A deer heaved out of a mesquite grove and vanished in an adjacent arroyo, the powdery dust rising behind him in dotted clouds. Howell Ford rode beside Benteen; Hanna followed behind. There was no talk in the double line of troopers. They rode with an energy-saving looseness, hats pulled low across their sun-blackened cheeks, shading the sweep of black mustaches, the blue surface of Irish eyes and long, raw-boned Irish jaws. Their shoulder points were gaunt-square against the grayness of their shirts; the exposed triangles of throat flesh were bronze-black against the sun. Saddle leather squeaked in rhythm and the gentle chock-chock of hoof falls ran forward through the day's drowze.

Benteen watched the land closely, studying the faint darkness at the base of mesquite and catclaw clumps, the rim of the scattered rocks, the sheltering pitahaya columns, the low-lying hummocks of mescal and Spanish bayonet. Behind these covert spots the solitary Apache brave loved to lie and watch and wait with a patience that had no end. There was no security in this land; none by day and none by night. It was a country of extremes, of long silence and sudden wild crying, of bone searching dryness followed by the sudden rush of cloud-burst torrents down some narrow canyon; of drowsy peace and the swift blast of gunfire. This was the Territory, raw and primitive. It scoured softness out of a man, it put an expression in his eyes that never left; and it put a strange recollection in his head so that he never forgot the country, and even in its hardest moments, made him want to stay on.

Benteen thought of these things as he rode taciturnly under the sunlight blast; of these things and of Eleanor Warren. His interest in her had been, from the first, direct and lively, as near to an instant attraction as he had ever felt in any woman. His picture of her now was quite distinct—tall and shapely in a way that struck through any man, good or bad. Her long, composed lips held back some kind of smiling knowledge; her eyes mirrored some kind of wisdom. He remembered the way she held her head, still and straight when she looked at him, with light sliding across the copper surface of her hair. In a woman silence meant many things; he was not sure what it meant in her, but it pulled at him like mystery, it played on his own solitary thinking and lifted a slow run of excitement, as though he was on the edge of discovery.

They nooned under the insufficient shade of a paloverde grove; and went on. At two o'clock, turning out

89

of a shallow canyon, they came before the footslopes of a long sweeping rise. A mile onward and upward stood the rim of another mountain. Benteen pulled in, at once considering the tactical situation. Al Hazel trotted back from a short exploration. "More tracks come together," he said, and pointed toward the summit. "They all go yonder, to the summit."

"If Antone's up there," said Benteen, "he's been watching us travel all day. And if he's there it means he thinks he can whip us. Or maybe he's waiting to see how far we'll come."

"Never know about an Injun," murmured Hazel, his glance sweeping back and forth across the far rim. After a long pause he added, "But he's still there, all right."

Over to the right a break showed in the mountain. Benteen asked about it. "That's a canyon," said Hazel. "It cuts through the mountains. Pretty deep."

"Any other way of getting off that mountain?"

"You wouldn't catch Antone gettin' in a spot where there wasn't no back door. He's got a trail into the canyon, on the other side of the peak."

Ford said, "I think I see somebody moving on that rim."

Benteen shaded his eyes and took a long look. Rocks lay scattered on the slope, as far as the rim. Up there stood a scatter of pines; and presently he made out the stir of more than one figure. He thought about this a little while. "Antone wants us to know he's there."

"That's right," said Al Hazel, dryly. "If an Injun don't want to be seen you wouldn't see him."

"Pretty certain of himself," considered Benteen. "Hanna, how's our water?"

"Half canteens, sor."

The slope lay gray-brown under the solid beat of the sun; at this three o'clock hour the heat boiled up gela tin waves from the rocks and turned the atmosphere smoke blue. The metal strip on Benteen's gunbutt was hot enough to burn the skin on the back of his hand. "It will be a damned warm climb. He may be as strong as the squaw says, which is pretty strong for this detachment. But those rocks will make a strong shelter, if we need them." He went to the saddle, quite carefully reviewing Major Warren's instructions. He weighed those instructions against the situation before him, making a careful balance. The responsibility was entirely his own; this column belonged to him at the moment, to be expended if he thought the results justified it, to be saved if not. This was the hard choice an officer in the field had to make. He looked back at the men, and at the horses; and silence settled down.

"We will close in," he said.

Still double file, the detail took to the slope and started the long climb, carbines canted forward. A defined trail ran irregularly through the rock scatter. High up, to the extreme left of the summit, an Indian on a horse moved into sight and cut a distinct circle on the slope, waving his lance, and moved out of sight again. Another four hundred yards onward Benteen said, "Skirmishers," and watched his column break into a single line abreast him. "Ford, take the right. Hazel, please go over to the left. If we run into more trouble than we can properly account for we'll fort up in these rocks."

He kept sharp watch on the rim above, and saw the furtive blur of Apaches in motion. At this elevation the lower country rolled away, broken and rough. The roundabout rocks emitted a furnace blast of soaked-in heat. A six-foot diamondback rattlesnake sluggishly stirred in the trail, struck and wound, and struck again. Benteen's horse churned up the soil, grunting away from it. Sweat plastered Benteen's shirt skintight against his back. At this moment he saw no more Indians, and gave the command to fight on foot.

The line of skirmishers dismounted, passing reins over to the horse-holders. One extra man remained with the prisoners. The rest spread out and began the last climb on foot, bending in and around the rocks. Watching the stony parapet, Benteen saw a head come into sight and drop back. It was, as near as he could judge, two hundred yards to the top. Van Rhyn marched beside him, hard hit by the heat and the labor of this climb; his face was drawn and pale and his breath jerked through him like a saw. Benteen said at once, "Drop back and replace one of the horse-holders."

But van Rhyn showed him a pair of odd, hurt eyes. "Let me come on, Lieutenant."

Benteen called, "Watch the line, men. Don't get ahead of it."

Al Hazel yelled, "Hyar they come!"

A dozen Apaches, small and wiry and stripped down to moccasins and breechclout, leaped over the rim in one general line, struck the loose talus dirt and slid feet first toward the nearest rocks. Benteen saw their rifles jump forward in their arms. At the same moment other guns began to bang sharply from the top of the rim. Benteen called:

"Fire!"

The troopers had dropped into the rocks. A volley smashed out, hard on the heels of Benteen's command; dirt spouted up where the bullets struck, all around the racing Apaches. One of them fell head foremost, rolling in a ball. A second dropped on his haunches, and slid, without life, feet first into the rocks. Hanna's bronzed voice rode this racket, hard and unemotional. "Come along now—come along now! Waste no shots!" Benteen braced himself against a rock, holding his revolver or those shifting targets. He saw his bullets hit; from the corners of his eyes saw the line of troopers move forward. The firing from the ramparts kept on, but the Indians who had jumped down to the rocks were all out of sight, dead or still. A slug smashed the surface of the rock beside which he stood. He moved forward, calling, "Keep down—keep down. Jackson, pull your head down." A pair of Apaches suddenly sprang up from the near rocks, fired in unison and raced sidewise to escape the converging lead of the troopers. Ford had pulled the right of the line forward to enfilade those rocks. Benteen kept his eyes on the ramparts above, seeing the carbine snouts dip and fire and pull back. He called, "Lift your aim! On the rim!"

Harry Jackson kept moving out of the rocks, he kept standing straight above them to get his shots. Benteen walked into the clear area, crossed to Harry Jackson and pushed him down. A ricocheting bullet whined like a great bee past them. Dirt and rock-flakes flew along the rim, the effect of the troopers' higher-reaching fire; and up there the barrels of the Indians' guns began to fade away.

Ford, completing his flank movement, flushed the last Apache from the lower rocks and then Benteen, watching the rampart carefully, felt the turn of the fight. He walked out of the rocks, pushing his boots against the sliding talus, wigwagging at the men around him. The line surged up the steep slope, throwing occasional pot shots to cover its approach. Harry Jackson raced forward, catching the shoulders of the staggering van Rhyn; he boosted van Rhyn along, using his arms and the point of his knees to keep the older man from entire collapse. Dust boiled around Benteen and caked into the streaming sweat along his face. He dug this muddy grime out of his eyes and licked it off his lips, and seized the rim with his finger tips.

Sergeant Hanna came up to him, heaving heavy wind out of his chest. They slashed the rolling gravel behind them, flung themselves over the rim and dropped bellyflat from exhaustion. The troop came on, one by one, grunting hard with this last huge effort. Private Jackson, still below the rim, yelled, "Wait for me—wait for me! I got van Rhyn here!"

Antone's band ran and rode across the table-top summit, kicking the cloudy dust behind. An arrow skittered the earth near Benteen and a few straggling shots came back, striking nothing. Troopers pulled themselves to a kneeling position, firing through the dust. Benteen got up, trotting forward with the detail after him. Part way over the flat he saw Antone's band sink out of sight into the adjoining canyon.

"Morphy," he called, "run back and signal the horses up!"

He trotted over the clearing, through the foggy dust. The boots of the troopers struck hard and their knees bent and never quite straightened in stride; this was how spent they were. They went slogging, shambling along, the line swaying unevenly, men falling slowly back from the running. A thin grove of pines stood at this far edge of the mountain summit. Ducking in and out of the useless shade, Benteen arrived at the break-off and saw Antone's band rush single file down a narrow mountain trail into the canyon; a bend carried the Indians entirely from sight.

Howell Ford spoke between the windy reach of his breathing. "They ain't far ahead, Tom!"

The troopers came up one by one. Men dropped flat to the ground, sucking in air; men stood upright with their legs braced apart. Harry Jackson came on with his shoulders supporting van Rhyn. The climb had taken all vitality out of the troopers, and the hard-burning heat took all nourishment out of the air; when they breathed it no relief came. There was nothing their lungs could bite into. The horse-holders galloped over the clearing, bringing up the led mounts.

Howell Ford said, "Look here, Tom."

The single file of Antone's retreating warriors showed briefly on a reverse bend of the trail and disappeared soon again. Presently the party showed at the bottom of the narrow gorge, crossed it and faded in a rock alleyway. The bed of the canyon was eight hundred feet directly below this break-off of the mountains, marked by a small quick-running creek that glistened in the lower shadows; the tail of Antone's party crossed the creek, a half mile up the canyon. A pair of Apaches dropped back, squatting by the water. Beyond this spot the land ran into a heavy tangle of hills.

Ford watched the two Indians. "They take their damned good time about it." He looked at Benteen. "Do we follow?"

Benteen considered the narrow trail and the surrounding walls of rock. It was bad country for pursuit. "I think that's what Antone would like to have us do," he judged.

Al Hazel pushed his derby back from his forehead. "Reckon that's correct."

"They didn't all go into that hole," decided Benteen. "Some of them are still in the rocks at the edge of the trail."

"If I know Antone," put in Hazel, "that's whut he's done."

"We're as close to that savage as we have ever got," pointed out Ford. "Seems a shame to let him slip loose."

Benteen squatted on his heels, studying the land beyond with a close interest. The decision was up to him again, and needed to be quickly made—if he intended to pursue. There was no other way of approaching Antone unless he took the troop back down the mountain and circled it, striking the canyon from the lower end. This meant half a day's extra time. The temptation was pretty strong to push on, but he remembered that Antone had chosen this spot, had made a piece of a fight, and had retreated. Antone was a good general, and very probably waiting in the yonder rocks for a foolish young cavalry officer to lead his men into a beautiful trap. Benteen looked around at the troopers, seeing the dead-beat look in their eyes. Midsummer campaigning was tough.

"No," he said. "We'll make camp here and rest until midnight before turning back to Grant."

Hanna's voice began to catch hold of the troopers. They stacked arms and put the horses on picket in the half shade of the pines. Pickets dropped back to the various edges of this mountain summit; the rest of the detail sprawled on the earth. Benteen moved back to van Rhyn who lay full length on the pine needles. Van Rhyn's lips were pressed together and his breathing came raggedly.

Benteen said, "I'm going to have you transferred to Whipple. This low country is too much for you."

Van Rhyn shook his head. "It makes very little difference, does it?"

Sunlight poured out of the low west, the color of fire. Ford still held his position at the rim, watching the canyon. He called to Benteen in a thoroughly exasperated voice, "Those damned savages are still in sight."

"Certainly," said Benteen. "It is a part of the trick."

Al Hazel's shrewd, half closed eyes swung to Benteen; and then to Ford. He said to Ford, "I reckon that's the oldest trick in the book. They figger a white man will jump at bait. Most white men will."

"I'll stack one trooper against five Apaches any day," grumbled Ford.

"Not in this country," contradicted Al Hazel. "Apaches are the toughest fighters in the world."

Benteen sat on the ground with a piece of paper spread before him. He drew a careful map of the country, marking his trail and the exact position of this hilltop. Below it he wrote his brief dispatch to Major Warren:

Sir: We met Antone's band at this spot, had a slight brush with them and drove them back into the canyon. They are retreating in a general easterly direction, about thirty strong. When Lieutenant Castleton sets out he should avoid the canyon and strike into the hills by higher ground. I am returning. Obediently, T. C. Benteen.

Hanna came up. "They been bakin' mescal in some pits at the other corner of this clearin'."

Suddenly the sun dropped below the rim. The sky still held its last brightness but a quick powder blue spread like water across the land; and silence seemed to drop like a blanket over them, so violent had been the sun. Benteen folded his dispatch, handing it to Sergeant Hanna. "Send Jackson and two other privates back to Grant with this as soon as dark comes."

Ford settled beside him, grumbling. "I hate to see those rascals get away."

Benteen stretched out full length, watching the fading color in the sky. "No hurry. We can't fight an Apache in his own style. Our job is to keep 'em moving, wearing down their horses and grub. If they can't bake mescal—which takes three days—they'll have a tougher time eating. My dispatch will reach Grant before daylight. Castleton will be on the trail with his fresh detail in the morning, while we go back to rest up the horses. We just play leapfrog with Antone."

"Not very spectacular campaigning."

"No," said Benteen. "Not very. Twenty cavalrymen dead at the bottom of that canyon would be, though."

Dusk settled in swift desert suddenness and a campfire began to burn against the shadows. Benteen cooked his coffee and fried his bacon and ate it with an active man's unsatisfied hunger. He stretched out on the ground, rolled a cigarette and watched the night stars break through the enamel black of the sky. His men lay blanketed nearby, drowsy in speech; the sentries scuffed the hard earth along the rim. Turned partly on his side, Benteen watched the silhouette of van Rhyn's sharp profile against the fire. Van Rhyn's voice was the voice of an educated man; and he was speaking to Harry Jackson.

"All young men are proud of strength, Harry. And all ignorant men, young or old, are proud of it. The thing you must learn is that faith is the stronger thing."

"What?" said Harry Jackson.

"It is something that will come to you later," said van Rhyn.

Lying back, all muscles loose, Benteen listened to the run of talk, to the little sounds coming out of the broad night, to the shifting of horses' feet on the hard earth. Ease came to him and these surrounding sounds and smells comforted him—being familiar and old, and a part of his life clear back to his first enlistment. There was a simplicity to the smell of sweat and to the gentle grumbling of Hanna's voice; there was an ancient reality to the feel of dust and pine needles against his skin; there was something in the far sky that caught up a man and cradled him with its timeless promise. A man, be thought, was meant to be a part of dust and struggle, to feel hardness and to get his pleasure from the little intervals between. This was his kind of life. Lying like that, with the cigarette burning against his fingers, he remembered the tilt of Eleanor Warren's head as she had watched him from the porch of the commanding officer's house. It was her silence, and all the secret things behind that silence, which caught at his interest, and fanned the faint flame of excitement again. She was a full woman; in her eyes was a knowledge of what life was—what it ought to be. He felt it in her; it was a quality that came across the space between them and touched him.

He fell asleep with the effortlessness of a natural man, and was wakened at midnight. The troop fell in line and turned down the long slope, bound southwest toward Grant. All the stars were brilliant in the sky.

George Mixler had rigged up a hand-operated fan from the ceiling of the room, directly above Harriet's bed. He sat in a corner, patiently pulling it back and forth, stirring the stale night's heat over his wife. She lay motionless on the bed, her black hair loose around the drawn paleness of her cheeks, and would not look at him. This was the thing that gouged through him like the sharp point of a knife; she had not looked at him and had not spoken to him since his return from the detail to Summerton's ranch. The baby was in an improvised cracker-box cradle beside the bed. Shiraz bent over it with his stethoscope, the edge of his whiskers against that wizened-red little face. It was a boy, frail and homely even to George Mixler's partisan eyes. Eleanor Warren and Lily Marr stood in the background, waiting Shiraz' inspection.

Shiraz put down his instrument, rolled it together and shoved it in his pocket He parted his whiskers neatly. "Nothing wrong at all."

Harriet spoke in a washed-out voice, "He cries so much."

"So would you," said Shiraz, "if you were in his place. It is a natural cry." He took out the stethoscope and put it against her chest; his eyes kept watching her face, very kind, very sharp. She looked back at him steadily and he was a wise enough man to see the resentment she bore him, and to understand its reason.

She murmured, "You weren't here."

He put the stethoscope away again. "No," he admitted, "I broke my promise, didn't I?"

George Mixler spoke up. "Harriet, you shouldn't talk like that. He was called out."

She didn't answer Mixler, she didn't look at him. Her lips were straight and tight for a moment. When she spoke, it was to Shiraz. "I know. Orders come first. So you went to Summerton's ranch and set a drunken man's broken arm."

Shiraz stood up, faintly smiling. "None of your fears came true, Harriet. You're all right and your boy's all right. Mark my word, you'll both be old soldiers." He remained cheerful in face of her settled and resenting manner. Afterwards he looked around at the woman, and over to George Mixler, and seemed to listen to the silence in the room, estimating its meaning. He nodded at Eleanor who went toward George Mixler, replacing him at the fan. Mixler rose and immediately left the dobe.

Shiraz followed him. Both men stood in the blackness of the parade. Mixler kept fumbling his hands around his pockets. He blurted out, "She hates me for being away, Shiraz. By God, that's hard to take."

"What else could you expect? That's the time when a woman wants her husband to be somewhere nearby—most women. And it is a time when you should expect no reasonableness at all from her, which is the way nature made it. But she'll get over it—she'll understand."

"No," answered George Mixler. "No, she won't." And suddenly Shiraz was shocked to hear this big young man crying. Shiraz stepped up and hit him on the shoulder. "And you're not the first man that's done that, either, George. I reckon every man and woman in the world think that their baby is the first time such a thing ever happened. It's always the same. You come along with me for a good stiff drink."

Castleton moved through the shadows, his feet briskly striking the loose boards. Mixler pulled himself together, seeing the faint blur of Castleton's curious face. Castleton said, "Anything wrong?"

It was the brusque way he spoke the words that turned George Mixler and stiffened him, and made him rap his answer friendlessly back. "No," he said, and walked on with Shiraz.

Castleton stopped at the doorway, looking through. He put his shoulder against the dobe's edge and listened to the steady, in-and-out crying of the baby, watching Eleanor pull at the fan until her glance lifted and saw him. He made a gesture with his hand.

Harriet turned faintly on the bed. "Never mind, Eleanor. The air seems just as hot when you move it. I wish I were up in the hills, at Fort Apache. I don't think the baby can stand this."

Lily Marr moved around the room, silent and capable. She ran a wet towel across Harriet's face and changed the pillow; her hands smoothed back Harriet Mixler's loose hair. She looked down at the girl, a kind of gentle sternness along her lips, a calm and unhurried faith in her voice. "He will live. Nothing's as bad as you think."

Harriet murmured, "You're both mighty kind. I wish it were a girl. I'd name it Lily Eleanor. What good's a boy to me? One thing I swear—he'll never be a soldier, and drag his wife into some godforsaken place and

101

leave her alone when she needs him."

"Harriet," said Eleanor, but quit on that, knowing nothing could be said now to this tired, bitter girl. Lily Marr stepped back from the bed and saw Castleton beyond the door. She stared at Castleton and when she turned again her face was unstirred and without expression, showing nothing at all; in a way it was like a withheld judgment. She moved over to Eleanor and took the rope guiding the fan, relieving Eleanor.

Eleanor joined Castleton, but for a moment she paused to watch Lily Marr, trying to find in her mind words to define the impression that girl left in the room. Lily Marr's hand, gently pulling the rope, was square-knuckled and strong. She stood straight-shouldered and faintly full at the breasts, watching Harriet with inexpressibly calm lips. She was smileless, as though she had forgotten how to smile, as though some knowledge, iron-hard and gray and fatalistic, had changed her beyond laughter. She had said nothing of herself to Eleanor; she was a mystery. Yet in her was an indomitable reliance, a still, strong acceptance of all that she had seen and all that she had been through. She was, Eleanor thought, a woman who had bent to the necessity of living, who carried the scars of that bending; but who would never break. She was stronger than anything that had happened to her.

Eleanor walked along the parade, thinking of this while she held Phil Castleton's arm. She was tired from a day and a night of constant attendance in Harriet's room, and she was lonely with odd thoughts that she wanted to express and yet knew Phil would not understand. He said, dryly:

"Your Lily Marr is a versatile woman. Where did she get that knowledge?"

"Where did I get mine?" answered Eleanor.

"I love you for your courage," he said and stopping

102

he took her swiftly inside his arms and kissed her.

She laughed and pulled away, feeling the release of that moment. Some of the trouble went out of her and the smell of this night was keener and more pleasant. "You do have your moments of insight, Phil," she murmured. "I really needed that."

He said, quickly, "I love you for your courage, Eleanor, but I hope you never have to do a thing like that again. For a refined woman—"

She heard the strong distaste in his tone, his sense of injured propriety. She said, "You are telling me it wasn't ladylike, Phil."

His voice stiffened. "There are certain rather dismal parts of life that are better left alone."

"It would never make me afraid to have my own children, if that is what you mean."

"No, I didn't mean that at all. Great Scott, Eleanor, what a thing to say. But I hated like hell to think of you in there—that—"

"Phil," she said, "you mustn't be narrow. Don't ever be. I'm glad I was there. As for Lily, she's a wonderful girl, whatever her past may have been."

The distinct dryness came back to him again. She noticed how he reverted to that tone when he wasn't pleased. It troubled her, and it roused her temper a little. He was saying, "I think your tastes are too generous, Eleanor."

"I'm an army girl, Phil."

They had reached the south side of the quadrangle. He stopped to face her. "You have said that before. Maybe I don't understand. What is it you mean?"

"I have never been afraid of anything that is real, Phil. I don't ever want to close my eyes or ears. I don't want to be blind, I don't want to hide. Living is too much fun. It is only when we start running away from it that we grow old and very proper, and very dull."

She paused, trying to find a better way of saying what she felt so deeply; and failed. How was it possible to express the keenness of living as she felt it—the vividness and the sharpness of each day's impressions, the singing, tumultuous force of her imagination? How could she express her own hungers and desires? She looked at him in growing anxiety, knowing that his own conception of her was of flowers and lace and softness—something she could never be.

He said in the same brief voice, "If it weren't for your being here post life would be damnably dull. I shall be glad when my turn comes to go out on scout."

This, she realized, was his only answer. He hadn't understood, and he wouldn't change. He would wait for her to change. She walked on with him, keeping time with his pacing, silently making her adjustments, out of necessity. A woman in love, she reflected, had this hard way to make—to conform and to bend. She was coolheaded enough to realize how ridiculous his opinion of her would have seemed, if she were not in love. But she was bound to him and couldn't help herself; and so her life was no longer her own.

He was saying, "I think the present policy regarding Indians is foolish. How can you tame a savage? They are all alike. Nachee is no better than Antone. They are all tricky, all cruel. But I think we are unduly afraid of them and move too slow. Give me thirty men and I'll track Antone clean into Mexico."

"Phil," she murmured, "you must not be so impatient."

He stopped again. He was stirred as he had not been before. His talk came out, quick and half-harsh, burning with his own eagerness. "This army is a morgue for a man's ambitions! We get into a rut, we drift, we sit around waiting for a fellow ahead of us to die. We quit trying, for fear of making life uncomfortable

104

for the rest of the officers. Not me! I'm damned if I sink into the routine like that. I will not be a gray-haired captain thirty years from now."

She said softly, "How far do you wish to go, Phil?"

He didn't answer her at once and then she knew that he was a little embarrassed by his own ambition—that he hated to show her how deeply he felt, for fear that she would see weakness in him. This was what had drawn her so swiftly and inevitably to him at seventeen—this hard man's pride and this almost arrogant ambition. At twenty-one she still felt the power of that rash pride; but the years had tempered her judgment and now, gently silent, she knew she had to help him over the roughness of his own will.

He said finally, in a more moderate tone, "To the top, Eleanor. Why not? There's only one end to this road and why should a man be content to make just a halfhearted fight of it?"

"Then," she said, "I'll help you get there. I know this army inside out. And an officer's wife can make or break him."

He was laughing as he turned; and when he kissed her again, rough from his feelings, she was satisfied to have it so. Only, in the far corner of her mind she felt that he had carelessly put her offer aside, as though her help was something he didn't need. He had this kind of pride. When he got a little older, she reflected hopefully, he would grow more tolerant. And then he would see. Distant in the corner of her mind a faint flash of critical judgment tried to warn her that he would never be different than he was now; but a sudden swing of loyalty to him put the thought aside. She walked quietly around the quadrangle with him, said good night, and returned to Harriet Mixler's place. George Mixler was at the doorway.

He said in a half whisper, "She doesn't want me in

there. You sleep in the other cot with her tonight, Eleanor."

"Of course," she said, and touched his arm reassuringly. An officer's wife could make or break a man; and Harriet was slowly breaking George Mixler. Watching him walk back toward the sutler's store, she saw the down-slope of his shoulders and felt regret. She turned in and relieved Lily Marr, bathed Harriet's white face—in which the memory of her past hours remained like a permanent mask—and undressed for the night. She was up two or three times during the succeeding hours to watch the baby; afterwards its steady crying wore off and she fell asleep.

Around three in the morning the return of Benteen's messengers woke her. Lying in the darkness, feeling a faint coolness in the air, she listened to men cross and recross the yard until she realized that a new detail was going out. She rose and slipped on her robe and stood in the doorway, watching lanterns flash through the black. Troopers were forming on the parade, and Castleton kept calling at Sergeant Hanna, and her father's voice crossed the darkness, drawing Castleton over. She heard him give his instructions:

"You will take twenty-five troopers out for three days. Your mission is to keep Antone moving, to wear his horses down and make it impossible for him to rest or roast mescal. Mr. Mixler accompanies you and Manuel Dura goes as guide. You will respect Dura's judgment as to the best trails and as to the number of Indians that may be in front of you. I am giving you a rough map sent in by Mr. Benteen. It shows where he left Antone. You will take up that trail, acting on the advice Mr. Benteen enclosed with the map."

"Yes, sir."

Sergeant Hanna's voice harked the shadows. The troopers were counting off, mechanically, sleepy-voiced.

106

Her father spoke again to Castleton, quite soberly and putting insistence in each word.

"Remember, these men are in your hands. Do not permit any enthusiasm or snap judgment on your part to lead you into premature fighting. Do not gamble, do not guess. Don't push your command beyond its endurance. Above all, watch out for a trap. Antone will attempt to suck you into one. You must refuse to follow him through any piece of country, no matter how inviting it may look, unless you are dead sure your flanks are covered and your rear protected. That is all. Good luck."

Castleton walked back across the parade, speaking to Hanna. George Mixler came to the door of the dobe. He said in a low, uncertain voice, "Is she asleep?"

"Yes," said Eleanor.

"Well," murmured George Mixler, his tone discouraged and flat, "I won't wake her. Give her my love. Tell her I said good-by. Tell her everything will be all right." He waited a moment, as if hoping to hear his wife call out to him, then turned away. The command mounted, crossed the parade as a shadowy column of twos, passed through the gap between the bakery and the barracks and struck the loose gravel of Aravaipa Creek. Eleanor listened to that tramping rattle die out in the distance, troubled by Phil's failure to come to her. Long after the last echo had gone she turned back into the dobe. Harriet's voice rose, dead-bitter, from the blackness.

"He knew I wasn't asleep. He just didn't care enough to kiss me."

Eleanor said gently, "Would you have kissed him, Harriet?"

"No."

Chapter Eight

From the doorway of Harriet Mixler's house, Eleanor watched Benteen's troopers cross the parade in the golden glare of middle-morning and swing their jaded horses into line. Weariness bowed the shoulders of the men and cramped their legs. Sergeant McSween's voice, dismissing the detail, was a parched croak.

Benteen went immediately to commanding officer's quarters and remained with her father a quarter-hour. When he came out he walked straight toward her, a slow smile breaking across lips roughened by the sun. Fine alkali powder whitened the red stubble of his three-day growth of whiskers. His cheeks seemed gaunt to her, his eyes more deeply recessed. The trip had dried him out; it had enervated him. Even in smiling he showed her a drowsy fatigue. But she was thinking that it was good to see him. His presence was like reassurance, and then they were as before, a little gay with each other, seeming to understand each other.

She said, "We have news. Harriet's baby came."

"We passed Phil's detail around sunup," he said. "George told me about it." He looked at her with a distinct approval in his eyes. "You're all right, Eleanor."

She returned his smile. "Was there a doubt about that, in your mind?"

He shook his head. "No. Never was a doubt. Can I see Harriet?"

She led him into the house. Harriet lay with her eyes closed, her cheeks set in the same half-bitter firmness.

The baby was sleeping. Benteen bent his tall shape over it, the grin coming sharp and white across his face again. He murmured, "Looks like Harriet," and his voice opened Harriet's eyes. Benteen came against the bed and put his big hand lightly on Harriet's shoulder. He said, "Good girl." There was a raw red scar on the back of his hand. It drew Eleanor's momentary attention but afterwards she was watching the way this man had with a woman. Harriet, so bitter and so full of hatred for everything that was army, reached out and seized his hand and then she smiled—and for that moment she was pretty and pleased and a little like the Southern coquette she had once been. "I declare I'm a sight to look at, Tom. Go 'way until I can fix up."

He kept smiling at her. He reached over and wound a lock of her quite black hair around his finger. "George Thomas Mixler wouldn't be a bad name for the boy."

"Maybe," said Harriet, "it will be Thomas Mixler."

He said, "Now wouldn't that be somethin' to make old George mad?"

Her smile faded and her mouth turned unhappy and desperate. "Tom," she said, her hand pulling him down. He kissed her on the forehead and straightened, and Eleanor, watching this through a swift blur, noticed how gentle he was with her, how kind. He said, "All Southern gals are flirts, Harriet. You let me alone."

He left the dobe, ducking his head at the doorway. From her place Eleanor watched him cross the parade. At this moment Lily Marr stepped from the bakery shop, whereupon he lifted his hat to her. Lily Marr came to the shaded walk along officer's row and stopped. Her glance followed Benteen; her eyes were round and grave and soft.

This was the middle of another hot day. At three in the afternoon, with the full blaze upon the land again, Benteen came to commanding officer's quarters and found Eleanor sewing on a dress. One faint bead of moisture showed on the tip of her nose and the exaggerated heat laid its rose stain on her cheeks. He stopped in the doorway, loosely resting against it, so relaxed that he seemed almost bony. He had slept and shaved, and suddenly she saw the distinct expression of approval in his eyes. She had never practiced the art of ladylike modesty, as taught by Mrs. De Launcey's Boston School for Young Ladies, her army training at once rebelling at the dropped eyelash, the breathless murmur or the hand pressed across an agitated breast. Nevertheless she looked down at her sewing, not quite sure of herself.

He said, "I'm going over to Nachee's camp. Can you stand the sunshine?"

She rose at once, got her parasol and went across the parade with him. "Sometimes," she said, "my own company isn't very interesting. I'm glad you came along."

"Eleanor," he said, "Harriet and George are in considerable trouble."

"I know."

They circled the barracks, cut through the corrals and crossed the dry bed of Aravaipa Creek. Nachee's camp, with its brush-covered jacals, lay a half mile down the San Pedro, within hailing distance of the post; yet she noticed that Benteen wore his revolver and that his glance kept rummaging the roundabout clumps of cacti and catclaw. There was no security in this land, not even in the full blast of a midday sun.

She said, "She's rather high-strung, Tom. And accustomed to much more than an army post could ever give her."

"It's breaking George," he said.

"Do you blame her so much?"

He gave her a slow, smiling glance. "Why, no. It's hell out here on a woman — and she's taking the change from civilian life harder than most. I'm just a little bit afraid she won't stick it out."

"Where did you learn about women, Tom?"

Afterwards she regretted asking the question, for she saw the change it made in him. It took him back into his past life, it pulled the smile from his face. She added at once, "I know. The Southern girl. She would be dark and perhaps very quick, very intense, perhaps like Harriet."

"That's a close guess. How do you figure it?"

She looked at him, judging and calm. "You are partial to that kind. You are very fond of Harriet."

They walked on through the blaze of light, hearing the racket of the Indian dogs in Nachee's camp. A few men sat on the shady side of the jacals; a few women crouched in the bright-traced shelter of a paloverde tree, grinding mesquite beans. Benteen said, "All men carry the picture of a woman in their heads—the kind of a woman they want. But it is usually a picture built up of many women, not one."

"That's not very fair for the woman a man finally gets. How can she live up to all that he wants?"

He was smiling a little. "When he finally gets his woman he sees all the things in her that he wants to see."

"Then you are saying that love is blind."

He shook his head. "No, I should say that it is a very strong light. Makes a man see things he otherwise wouldn't. There is some sweetness and some honesty and a hell of a lot of self-sacrifice in the worst woman that ever lived. Those are the things a man finds in a woman, when he's in love."

"Until she hurts him," said Eleanor, watching his face for a break.

He shrugged his shoulders. "That's part of the bargain, the quarreling and the bitterness. The sand with the sugar. I'd rather have it that way than a lifetime of dullness. People want too much."

"Why, Tom," she broke out, "you are saying the things I have always said."

111

He looked at her, not quite smiling. "I know."

"How could you know it? I've never talked to you—not about that."

They approached the first line of tents. Children came from the jacals and stood around, silently watchful. Benteen stopped and turned to her. There was always on his face a kind of speculative reserve. He had a way of holding his long lips together, smileless and yet on the edge of a smile, and a way of looking at things or people, absorbing them but seeming not to pass judgment, as though some things mattered and many things didn't. She was near enough to see the flakiness of his gray eyes; they could be hard as stone or they could be, as now, the most considerate pair of eyes she had noticed in a man.

"You wouldn't have to talk of those things, Eleanor. Look in your mirror tonight. Now let's pay Nachee a visit."

He turned her into the first jacal, into a hot, rancid-smelling gloom. Blankets and robes made beds around the edge of the shelter, occupied by squatted and sprawled figures. One man rose to a sitting position and said "Nantan," and motioned to the floor. A squaw came from the rear shadows and threw a gray army blanket on the floor, whereupon Eleanor sat down in obedience to the slight pressure of Benteen's hand. Benteen dropped to his haunches, not immediately speaking, and in this interval Eleanor took her first deliberate look at Nachee, chief of the peaceful portion of the Indians on the San Pedro.

She judged he was as old as her father, but he had a round and entirely smooth face, full-lipped and quite kind. A narrow band of red calico crossed a broad forehead to hold in coarse jet-black hair; and though he wore only a shirt—whose dangling tails made him look a little ludicrous,—a breechclout and moccasins with turned-up toes, she was distinctly impressed with the

112

dignity he carried. His eyes were cloudy brown.

She knew enough of Indian etiquette to preserve the silence and to remain grave before all the inquiring eyes around her; but it did surprise her when Al Hazel slipped into the tent a few minutes later and took his place somewhat between Benteen and Nachee.

"Tell Nachee his last advice was very good," instructed Benteen. "Tell him I thank him for it."

Listening to Al Hazel Eleanor, made out little coherence. Apache was a quick, loose language and Al Hazel spoke it as if he held a chunk of mush in his mouth. Now and then he used his hands, or drew swift descriptive lines with his finger points. Finished, he listened carefully to Nachee's answer.

"He says you must be careful of Antone. Antone is very sly. His father was a fox, his mother a wolf."

"Tell him we have heard there are many men in Antone's camp, some of them Tontos and some of them Chiricahuas. Is this true, and how is it so?"

Waiting through Hazel's question and Nachee's reply, Eleanor saw the intent, owl-wide eyes of a small girl peeking in through the cracks of the jacal. Nachee's hand cut downward graphically to describe something. Al Hazel turned back to Benteen.

"It is true. The Chiricahuas have come up from the border because Antone has persuaded them he has the medicine to kill soldiers. The Chiricahuas are very bad. You will have to kill Antone before you can bring in these others and make them peaceable."

"Ask him how far Antone will travel east, if the troops follow?"

Hazel asked it and got his answer. "Nachee says Antone will never travel very far east. He will keep circling back, toward the south, keeping his eyes on the soldiers all the time. But if you don't let him stop to rest he'll grow tired and then his warriors will leave him. That is when he will make a fight, so

113

that his warriors won't think him a coward."

After that Nachee spoke again, nodding toward Eleanor. Al Hazel pushed back his hat and grinned behind his hand. "Nachee says this wife is very good but a man of your standing ought to have more than one. He says one wife wears out too fast."

Eleanor, who considered herself a calm girl, opened her mouth and shot a startled glance at Benteen. He had maintained, through all this talk, an unstirred countenance. It did not change now but when he spoke again it was directly to Nachee. Eleanor felt the heat of this tent; it was worse than it had been before, it began to burn on her cheeks. Nachee was a grave and philosophical and tattered figure on his blankets, but she thought she saw the glint of humor in the obscure depth of his eyes.

"Enju," said Benteen and terminated the interview by rising and giving his arm to Eleanor. They left the village and Al Hazel behind, crossing the rock and cactus-scattered flat.

"Why do you sometimes use an interpreter and sometimes do not?

"I don't know enough of it to carry on an extended parley."

She looked at him. "What did you tell him?"

"I said you had another man."

She looked up and saw the complete indifference on his face—and she realized he had put it there deliberately to hide something; and then, because she knew that this was so, she spoke out.

"It was a complete answer, Tom. I have another man, and am quite satisfied—though Nachee wouldn't know what that meant, would he?"

Dust rose along the upper sand bed of the San Pedro, signal of a horse coming by the base of the Catalinas. Benteen and Eleanor walked on, saying nothing more, and soon reached the commanding officer's quarters.

She turned to him at the door. "Come in and I'll fix some lemonade."

He followed her into the room. Major Warren lay on the corner couch with a month-old *Harper's Weekly* covering his face. The paper fluttered gently to his profound snoring. Both of them went quietly back to the kitchen. Benteen sat up on the table, his long legs swinging down, so turned that he commanded a view of the parade. The solitary horseman came off the San Pedro and reined up in the shade of the troopers' quarters, dismounting there. Benteen watched the man loosen the saddle cinch and settle on his heels against the barrack wall. He pulled off his hat, rubbing away the fresh sweat on his head and, afterwards, casting a long glance around the parade—in a manner that was full of lively caution—he settled to the business of building a cigarette. From this distance Benteen couldn't see his features clearly.

Eleanor handed him his glass and poised her own. "Salud, Tom."

But he waited, not lifting the glass, holding her eyes for a moment. His lips were thoughtfully pinched together. Behind his smooth expression something ran its way, something boiled and was pressed back. She saw the little details of his face then, the heavy, black-red line of his eyebrows, the faint break at the bridge of his nose, the scar on his temple which was from a "Minie" ball—so Cowen had told her—at Bull Run.

He said, "To the other man, Eleanor."

She had a quick answer for that. "I wish you knew him better."

"Why?"

"If you knew him you'd like him. You don't now."

He said, "You're a damned loyal woman."

She considered her words carefully. "Maybe it is as you said. Maybe it is because, being in love, I see things you don't see."

"Salud," he said, and tipped the glass.

Major Warren strangled on his snoring and woke, dashing the paper aside with an irritable arm. He rose and came into the room, scanning them, with hot, bloodshot eyes. He rasped, "Hot enough to melt the hinges of hell's bronze doors," and went out to douse his head in the water bucket. He came back, accepting a fresh glass of lemonade from his daughter; he swallowed it greedily, some of the drink spilling down his cheeks.

"Mr. Benteen," he said, "the paymaster is at Fort Lowell. You will take an escort of six men in the morning and go get him. I'd send Lankerwell, but he's to go out on the next scout with Captain Harrison." He freshened his glass and stirred the lemonade with the tip of his forefinger. "Who's that over by the barrack?"

"Some cowpuncher off the San Pedro," said Benteen and turned out. Eleanor followed him as far as the doorway, and Major Warren, turning his fat body reluctantly about, watched those two with a sharp, smart attention. Benteen continued on across the parade. Eleanor stood at the doorway, and Warren, who was no fool, noticed that even if she was in love with Castleton, this tall officer of I troop had the power to attract her eyes. Nuzzling his whiskers into the lemonade glass, he thought about this and called his daughter back to him.

"You have never seen Tucson. Maybe you'd like to go along with Benteen. It will be a five-day trip. Rough, but better than sitting around here. Maybe you'll get a chance to attend a dance at Lowell, or maybe Benteen will take you to a Mexican *baile*. Wish I was young enough to do that again. By God, it is hot! Think you want to go?"

"Yes," she said. "Of course I do."

"Be a break in the monotony for you," he answered and looked at his glass. For she was smiling at him; she was a damned smart girl and she was reading his mind, and laughing at him.

116

Benteen crossed the parade to supervise afternoon stables. Coming on toward the barrack he noticed the stranger's bright and careful eyes lift to him. He was, Benteen decided, just one more stray rider, one more vagrant shadow from the hills or the desert. The territory had a good many of these men, most of them with unexplained pasts and mysterious occupations. This one had a dry, half-handsome face, smooth-shaven and fairly light of complexion in spite of the sunshine. He had pushed his hat far back on his head, to show a clump of yellow hair.

He was very watchful. Benteen, stopping by him, noticed that his whole figure, motionless as it still was, seemed to tighten. His eyes were a pale, calculating blue.

"From Summerton's?" asked Benteen.

The stranger stared at Benteen and his very brief "No" had a grudging arrogance in it.

"If you're hungry," stated Benteen, "go over to the mess shack and tell the cook I authorized a meal."

"Thanks," said the stranger. "But if I was hungry, I'd eat my own grub."

Benteen let the obvious dislike slide by, nodded, and went on to the stables. The man's unfriendliness toward the army was the reflection of a common attitude on the frontier. These civilians in the territory wanted protection, but many of them disliked the kind of law that went with it. They were a tough, headstrong lot; and some of them feared the uniform — any kind of uniform. Benteen dismissed the man from his mind for the next hour but later, when he left the stables and cut around the breaking pens in the last late flash of the day's sun, he saw a scene that stopped him in his tracks.

The stranger had gone over to officers' row and stood now by Harriet Mixler's dobe, facing Lily Marr who had her back to the dobe's wall. He held his hat in one hand and he was speaking, using his free hand persuasively. Benteen observed that the girl made no kind of an an-

117

swer. She remained still, shoulders pressed against the wall, as if afraid or as if angry. Presently the stranger reached into his pocket and produced something, offering it to Lily Marr. When she made no move to accept, the stranger jerked her hand toward him, slipped the gift into it and waited. Lily Marr flung the gift downward to the dirt.

This was when Benteen moved across the parade, his long legs traveling fast. The stranger wheeled around at once. Benteen observed the wire-tight expression on the man's cheeks, and the white-hot temper in his eyes. "Captain," he said in a way that was a thorough warning, "we're doin' well without your help."

Benteen spoke to Lily Marr: "You know this man? You want him around?"

There wasn't any fear on her face that he could make out. Her reserve held; it was definite and cool. She said, "I know him but I don't want him. Tell him to pick up his money."

Five gold pieces lay in the white dust. For a moment Benteen considered them, remembering the robbery of the Summerton wagon train. He had no proof of this man's connection, but as he turned to the stranger he saw the look in the other's eyes—the quite bright and quite deadly attentiveness. Benteen said, "Pick up your money and go along."

"Captain," said the stranger, "I never took an order from a man in my born life. Or from a woman either. Or from anything that breathed."

The stranger had a gun and would use it. Benteen was sure enough of the man's character to know that. But the insolence and the wild pride was a little thick for him and so, since he was close to the stranger, he whipped his long arm out, seized the man's arm, hauled him in with a hard yank, and seized the holstered gun. He was angry, suddenly and deeply; and felt no scruples at all. He threw the man's gun back into the dust,

118

grabbed him by the shoulders with both hands and shook him until he heard his teeth clack together; and threw him flat to the dust.

"Pick up your money and go along," he said again.

The stranger was face down and half knocked out; he lay motionless for a moment, his fingers dug into the loose silver dust. McSween and a pair of soldiers ran over from the barrack and the guard on this post swung forward with his gun brought down. Ray Lankerwell stepped from post headquarters, buckling on his belt as officer of the day.

From her place in the doorway of commanding officer's quarters, Eleanor Warren had seen it all—the brief exchange of talk and Benteen's swift punishment. She didn't come forward with the others but watched Benteen with a fresh, startled interest, now knowing something she had felt but never had seen, which was his capacity for anger. This then was part of the man; this was a part of all those turbulent things hinted at by the grayness of his eyes and the long calm of his lips.

Meanwhile Benteen reached down and retrieved the stranger's revolver and turned to Lily Marr, observing her stillness and her expressionless gravity. He realized she knew more about this man than she was telling. There was a story here, in her and in the stranger and in the gold pieces scattered on the ground. He put his attention back to the stranger who had risen to his knees. He said, "Do as you're told, friend," and watched the stranger reach into the dust and recover the gold pieces. Afterwards the man got to his feet, brushing himself aimlessly. It wasn't until all this was done that he lifted his face to Benteen. His cheeks were dead white and his eyes had turned the color of slate.

Benteen turned to McSween. "See that this man waters his horse and leaves the post." He pulled up the stranger's gun, kicked the loads from it, and handed it back.

119

The stranger didn't look at Lily Marr again, or at the surrounding men. His glance clung to Benteen with a memorizing hatred, telling Benteen as clearly as speech what he felt and what he someday intended to do. He said, "All right, Captain," and walked away with McSween behind him. "All right, Captain. All right."

The group broke away, leaving Benteen with Lily Marr. Benteen said, "You know this man pretty well, Lily?"

"He knew I was in that wagon train. That's why he held it up. But I got away in the dark. He will kill you, Mr. Benteen."

He said "What?" and made a half turn after the stranger. Lily Marr's voice stopped him at once.

"No. I wouldn't speak against him, Mr. Benteen. I'd never tell what I know."

"He's a killer, Lily."

"Oh that," she said and shrugged it away, as if it meant nothing. "That's because people have tried to kill him. His name is Jack Bean and everybody knows he's an outlaw. But nobody knows as much about him as I do."

"What'd he come here for?"

"For me, Mr. Benteen. And he'll come again."

He studied the impenetrable reserve of her face and knew he could ask no more. She was a dark woman, a woman with a gray and odd wisdom, with a strange realism completely governing her. He said, "All right, Lily," and walked away.

Lily Marr's attention turned toward Jack Bean a moment, as he rode out of the post. Then it veered to Benteen, following his high shape as it cut through the first violet eddies of twilight. She laid her shoulders against the dobe wall, softly sighing. Her eyes were, at this moment, round and wide and expressive.

Chapter Nine

Eight hours' march brought Phil Castleton to the retreating trail of Antone in the broken hills northeast of
Grant. Manuel Dura said, after a considerable scout,
"They go north, maybe to the Pinals, maybe into the
Apache Mountains." Before sundown they pushed over
the Gila and made camp. Manuel Dura went ahead, returning considerably after dark. "In the Pinals, I think.
The trail say so, though I would not believe only that. It
is that Antone like the Pinals and maybe got mescal pits
up there."

"How old are those tracks?"

"Four hours, mebbe."

It was the nearness of Antone's band that caught hold
of Phil Castleton and turned him hard and eager. Lying
in his blankets, he watched the distant crystal wash of
the stars and the thin moon hanging low and smoke-yel-
low in the sky, and was impatient because of the night's
long delay. He felt no weariness, hard as the ride had
been; his ambition keyed him up, it was a quick and
constant stimulant, like food, like whisky. The troopers
were blanketed down for the night, their talk drowsily
carrying on some old, indecent joke. Rising to an elbow
he saw Trooper Sweeney still crouched by the faint firelight, long-lipped face turned into a huge grinning.
Sweeney said, "The rocks are hard. It ain't the same as
quilts and a mattress. Hey, Canreen? No quilts for you

121

tonight. What wud Rose be doin' now, hey Canreen?"

Somebody said, "Talkin' nice with Harry Jackson Sure."

"Hell, the kid ain't got that much green in his eyes.'

"Ye saw him use the sword on Canreen. Young wans are like that, thinkin' things that ain't so. Hey, Canreen why don't Rose tell him?"

Canreen grumbled from his blankets. "I'll be doin' the tellin'."

"Sure," jeered Sweeney. "And then you'll get somethin worse than a beatin' around the head."

"Shut up, Sweeney, if ye don't want that mouth spread a foot wider."

Sergeant Hanna broke in. "No more of that tawk. A for Harry Jackson, let the boy find it out for himself 'Twill be a bad enough time, let alone wan of you Iris apes rubbin' it in."

But Sweeney murmured, "Maybe it ain't him tonight Maybe it is Daugherty. She likes 'em with a smilin way—and with a bit o' money."

Phil Castleton laid his order flat and sharp across the night. "That's enough talk. If you're not tired enough to sleep I'll see you get a longer ride tomorrow."

Silence fell—the stony, obedient silence that only sul len men could contrive. He felt their dislike, he felt th unspoken insolence—and waited for some least murmu from any one of them, so that he might at last lay o his punishment. But there was no break in the stillness their mockery was elusive, beyond his reach. Lying bacl on his blanket and saddle, he knew what they wer thinking of him, as he had known it since his first day with the command. There were a hundred ways a soldie could make a young officer feel the weight of enliste displeasure—in wooden words, in impassive expressions in a kind of obedience that was too exact, neither on gesture more or one less. Between that fire and his ow blanket was a gulf he could never cross.

He had never been able to figure out the reason, and now had ceased to care. But there were times when he wished he had the power of stepping back into the ranks so that he might do as Hanna sometimes did, which was to take a malcontent behind the latrine line and smash respect and the fear of God into him.

This was the way he felt as he lay there watching the stars. He had no fear of them, and little tolerance. He had no way of telling these men of the ambition that fired him, no way to arouse their enthusiasm and their loyalty. In the beginning he had hoped to have this chiefest gift of an officer, to so stir men that they would follow him out of blind zeal, wherever he led. Now he knew he could never do that; and though it left him a little lonely, it had also served to toughen him. These men who would not serve him from liking would serve him because he drove them harder than any officer in the detail. He was not, he told himself again, a man like Benteen; and that thought, coming idly to him, at once set up all the old heart-burning animosity. This was the core of it, this was the natural injustice Phil Castleton never ceased to feel—that this lank, lazy officer who seemed to dream little and to have no ambitions should, by the gesture of a hand, bind the enlisted men fast to him; and having that gift, should ignore it. This was the thing that turned him resenting and so jealous. Long after the camp had fallen asleep Castleton remained awake, made irritable and sleepless by his ambition, made lonely by it, turned a little brutal by it.

Next day they followed Antone's trail along the eastern base of the Pinals, traveling deeper into the broken pocket country, traveling higher into the general hills. At noon Manuel Dura said, "They rest here. Fresh trail. Maybe hour old." Thereafter Castleton pushed his detail on without rest. Horse droppings showed freshly on the trail; the smell of dust still clung to the heated air. At five o'clock that day a canyon opened before them, its

123

hundred-foot walls pinching in a shallow clattering creek and a narrow trail weaving around man-tall boulders. A kind of permanent twilight lay in there. Manuel Dura stopped at once, shrugging his shoulders.

"In there."

"How far ahead of us?"

"Maybe hour, maybe just around bend. I don't know. Very close, I think maybe."

"How many?"

"Maybe twenty go in there. Maybe more by now." Manuel Dura watched Castleton add saw something on the officer's face that troubled him and caused him to point toward the rock walls overhead. Small inset pits studded these walls to either side; the parapets hovered directly above the trail. "Too bad. She's a nice place for trap."

A quarter mile on the canyon the walls bent and carried the trail out of sight. Castleton watched that bend. "What's beyond?"

"Mile, maybe, same thing. She comes out then into little meadow. More hills after that."

Castleton pushed the sweat across his face and stiffened his legs against the stirrups. Nobody spoke. Hanna's eyes, old and black and faithful, watched him. Hanna waited, but he knew Hanna didn't like the canyon; he knew none of them liked it. He washed that consideration out, his impatience growing stronger. Antone was down that canyon, maybe within rifle shot. Antone was growing tired. He balanced the thought against his orders, which were to take no chances against a trap and to return at the end of three days. The second day was up and it was another day back to Grant. Yet he had his few hours of grace and, looking at the rock wall above him, he saw nothing to check his eagerness. He had little respect for Apaches; he had nothing but a desire to close in and end the chase, and thought now he saw the chance of doing it. Antone, he reasoned, would never believe that a cavalry detail would follow through the canyon. Castleton pulled up his reins. "All right. Forward."

Mixler stared at him. Dura's swarthy face came around, openly surprised and dissenting. "She's not good. We better go around, up this hill, come down far side."

Castleton's natural impatience broke out. "Never mind—never mind." The truth was, though he did not quite realize it, he resented the knowledge both Dura and Al Hazel had of Indians, and the manner in which they used that knowledge to caution the post officers. It was his conviction that all civilians on the frontier had built up the Indian scare in order to keep troops on hand, thereby profiting from the selling of feed and supplies, and from the vast freighting business built up from post to post. Mixler was beside him, and Mixler's long silence further irritated him.

"Any suggestions?"

Mixler shrugged his shoulders. "You're in command, I believe."

Castleton lifted his gauntleted hand overhead, motioning the detail to follow, and entered the canyon at a quick walk.

There was still a half hour of sunlight but as soon as the detail got into the canyon a solid twilight settled around the detail. Watching the high boulders in front and the small recesses above him in the canyon walls, Castleton was at once bothered by the thickness of the shadows. The dashing of the creek and the clatter of the horses on the stone under-footing made a strong racket. For a moment he had his doubt, and for a moment it was his inclination to turn back. What checked the impulse was the memory of Dura's skeptical expression, and Mixler's dislike, and the opinion of the troopers. They were watching him now; it was too late to change. He could not permit any of them to see any confusion in his mind. But the feeling of this place was bad. The farther the detail progressed the narrower the canyon seemed and the more smothered Castleton felt. He caught himself eyeing the overhead rim; he found that his leg muscles were pushing against the stirrups. Suddenly, near the bend, Sergeant Hanna clattered through the creek and cut in front of Castleton.

Castleton snapped, "What are you doing?"

Hanna's old-soldier's face, bronzed and hard-boned, swung toward the lieutenant. "K troop has fawrty enlisted men and three officers. 'Tis better arithmetic that wan enlisted man get shot than wan officer."

"Get back," said Castleton, and pushed past Hanna.

Beyond the bend was only the graying vista of water and stone and the blank wall of another bend in the distance. Above them the bright light suddenly left the sky and at once shadows packed down into the gorge layer on layer until nothing was clear but the ragged dance of the water on the rocks. The high rims were blackening silhouettes. Wind scoured faintly through the canyon but sweat collected under Castleton's hat brim and gushed along his nose and eyebrows when he lifted it; his nerves were thin-drawn wires pulling at his fingers, at his shoulders, and at his neck. Somewhere was a sound that was not the sound of water or traveling horses. He said, "Halt," and listened, swung forward in the saddle.

Dura's voice came forward, softly hurried. "Eef Antone is on that rim, he weel be thinking of rolling rocks down now. I would not stop, lieutenant."

Castleton shoved his horse forward. The trail bent again and the walls closed in until this canyon was no wider than the length of a horse. Trail and creek squeezed past black shoulders and then, beyond this point, Castleton saw the fresh clear twilight of a meadow beyond; the canyon walls broke away. He held his horse to a walk, crossed the creek and stopped in the meadow.

"Hanna, we camp here. No fire tonight."

The gates of a pass opened west of the meadow, leading upward into the Pinals. To the east other and shallower canyons fed into the wild, dark hills. Behind lay the now dark maw of the canyon through which they had just passed. Castleton dismounted and turned his horse over to an orderly, watching the troopers stack arms and make cold camp. Manuel Dura crossed and recrossed the meadow, low-bent in the shadows. Presently he returned.

"They stop here and go on. Up there now, maybe." He pointed to the broken-black tangle of the hills eastward.

Castleton looked at Mixler, a tinge of irony in his tone. "I have always thought that Apaches were overrated. Antone is a better fugitive than a fighter."

All Mixler said was, "I should hate to have been caught in that canyon, Phil."

"He wasn't there," pointed out Castleton. "He will never stop to make a fight. We are being held back by a fear of something that doesn't exist."

Settled on his blanket, he listened for the drowsing talk of the troopers and didn't hear it. They lay silent, and in that silence was something sullen and dissatisfied and bone-tired. Sentries moved along the outer shadows, their feet grinding against the creek's gravel. This air was cool, coming off the higher hills; and somewhere an owl hooted once—and was answered from another part of these hills. He saw Manuel Dura rise off the ground, listening. The sentries quit walking and silence poured in, heavy and mysterious until he too felt the strain of it. The owl call didn't come again.

Castleton turned on his side, adjusting his head to the saddle. He was sleepless once more, begrudging the length of the night and hating this delay. Antone was nearby, less than an hour's good march away, which was a knowledge that tantalized him and played on his restlessness until he sat bolt upright and put his big hands together and stared at the felt-black shadows. At this moment he was thoroughly alone, turned hungry and solitary by the intense pressure of his ambition; turned desperate by it until he had the senseless desire to reach out and seize something and break it between his heavy arms. For some men, he thought, life meant a struggle for power and place. This was what it meant to him. He had no patience to drift. He could not stand waiting his place in the slow mill of promotion. The fire in him had to burn; it had to find a way through. And this, he knew in deep sudden bitterness, was why he had no friends among his own rank, and no loyalty from his men. He drove too hard. He wanted success too badly. Other men laughed and made their lives easy. Because he could not stand these things and would not fit into the routine, he was disliked. Once he had seen the commanding general of the army. In the general's eyes was something taciturn and aloof; as though he saw and knew things other men could not. Castleton had not understood that expression then, but now he did. That solitariness, that tightness around the mouth, was the price a man paid for reaching the top—for all the sacrifices and all the hard decisions, and all the lifelong discipline to a driving purpose.

He dropped his head to the saddle again, thinking of Antone's nearness until Antone became the elusive key to his whole career. He knew then that, given the gamble, he would risk himself and his whole command.

He fell into a shallow sleeping and woke around three o'clock. This was the day to turn back, according to his orders, but he had still one hope, and so routed out his command, let them finish a cold breakfast, and put them in the saddle. Manuel Dura said, still not quite awake, "It is better we take another trail back to Grant."

"Not yet. Which way did those tracks run last night?"

"East," said Dura.

128

"We go east."

The troopers traveled in a solid file behind him. At first light they had reached a rising ridge above the meadow and faced a country crosshatched by pine-scattered draws and turning gulches and rocky mounds. Dura had his look at the ground and came back thoroughly awake. "The sign is plenty. They meet here yesterday. See that peak? Maybe there now. Thirty—forty, *quien sabe?*"

A defile with ragged sidewalls marched toward the peak in the northeast; the cobalt shadows of dawn whirled around the land, eddying like water, tricking the eye and giving motion to the country beyond. "That way, Dura," said Castleton.

Dura's horse threw up its head and sidestepped in the trail. Dura studied the ground with a quick attention and saw nothing there to cause the disturbance. He lifted his head, eyes almost shut, staring forward. He said, "Do not take that way, Lieutenant."

"What do you see?"

Dura shrugged his shoulders. "I see nothing and I do not like it. But that trail she is a trap."

"Turn left, toward that barrier of rock."

Manuel Dura spread his arms. "A bad place."

Castleton gestured with his arm and crowded past Dura. The peak was his target, in the east. The barrier of rock, which was a six-foot breastwork heaved up by some ancient slipping of the earth's crust, lay a quarter mile forward; to either side the land rose in broken hummocks. Castleton put the column into a trot, aiming at the lowest section of the rock barrier.

Mixler swung abreast, his light complexion turned pink by the run. "Is that yucca growing along the edge of those rocks?"

The steady run set up a racket of iron hoofs on the solid ground. Saddle gear creaked and Hanna's voice was heavy behind Castleton: "Close up, Flynn!"

"Hah!" rasped Dura and hauled his horse in. His arm whipped straight forward. The clumps of yucca along the rock rim moved and fell away—and became round black heads. A first shot broke the morning, its echo rocketing all up the hillsides. A faint wisp of smoke rose.

Castleton called, "Skirmishers!"

Hanna's voice beat at the troopers as they rushed along a long, broken line abreast Castleton. Mixler flung his horse around and rushed to the right of the line, his ruddy face alive and eager and suddenly pleased. A quick firing broke from the rocks, the smoke showing the Apaches to be scattered along the parapet. Castleton, taking his swift survey, thought there was an empty spot over toward the left of that parapet and promptly rushed for it, signaling his men to follow. It whirled the troopers into an irregular grouping; and this was the way they crossed the front of fire. A horse went down, throwing Trooper Sweeney far forward against the stony soil. He turned and kept on rolling until he reached a dip of earth and fell into it.

On that side toward which Castleton rushed, a series of broken hummocks rose rather sharply. Driving in toward the end of the rock parapet, Castleton came close to the hummocks and at once felt the cross-whip of lead. Antone's warriors showed themselves briefly in the spaces between the hummocks, fired, and fell back. Castleton wheeled, raced at them with his revolver swinging up for a shot. Hanna galloped behind. Mixler, making the complete circle from one side of this area to the other, brought on the last laggard men; they raced between the hummocks. Antone's warriors ducked in and out of sight, firing as they moved. Hanna and O'Grady, close together, rode an Apache down beneath their horses, looking behind to see him flat and dead on the earth. Mixler galloped around the base of a hump, came point-blank before a tall Apache with a carbine already

130

lifted to fire. Mixler threw his horse aside and felt the breathing smoke of the carbine's explosion and, targeting the brave with his revolver, killed him with the shot.

It was a tight and wicked moment, the troopers rushing at the successive hummocks without order or direction, firing at the fugitive shapes around them. The Apaches kept fading and reappearing, from pocket to pocket; they gave ground and were lost, and reappeared again. The Indians stationed at the rock parapet were streaming forward from the rear and the right flank. Manuel Dura saw this first and, slipping off his horse, he ran to the crest of a hump, flattened against it and coolly targeted this new rush of Apaches with his carbine, aiming and firing with unexcitable method.

Mixler, circling a hump, discovered Dura at this business. Immediately Mixler called up the nearest troopers, rushed up to support Dura and dismounted. One man held the horses while the others dug in. Mixler's face was rose red and his blue eyes were bright, almost laughing as he settled down. He said, "No hurry. Be sure you hit something, or don't fire."

Meanwhile, Castleton had gotten deeper in the broken country. Apaches kept retreating before him, vague as shadows. He fired and missed his aim. An Apache dropped out of sight and Castleton, seeing the warrior's intent of circling the hummock, yelled at O'Grady nearby. "Go around that side!"

O'Grady made a rush at the hummock's other edge while Castleton circled his own side. His horse went into a pothole and climbed out at the moment O'Grady galloped dead into the Apache's thrown-up gun. The bullet hit O'Grady in the chest, knocking him out of the saddle. Castleton's bullet killed the Apache. Rushing on, Castleton saw O'Grady's dead face turned toward the first brass-yellow flash of sunlight.

The Apaches were shadows that vanished. There was nothing now to be seen around the potholes. Wheeling

131

back, Castleton saw Apaches trotting away from the fight, in a country too rough for cavalry to follow safely. Over in the clear ground the racket of the carbines kept going; all the troopers were rushing in that direction.

Coming around the last hummocks, Castleton saw the main section of Antone's band break back for the rocks, those brown bodies squirming through the apertures and out of sight; but one Indian raced toward the hollow where Sweeney lay, reached down and stabbed Sweeney to death and ducked away. A dozen bullets ripped the ground around him and caught him and knocked the life out of him. Galloping to the highest hummock Castleton watched Antone's band reach their horses in a far hollow and race back toward the peak.

A few last shots followed them, but in a moment the pines and the rough country hid them entirely. Troopers rose from the ground, walking loose-jointedly along the uneven earth. Hanna came up and stood at the head of Castleton's horse. Sweat hung in bright balls at the ends of his mustaches; his shirt front was gray with dust. His old soldier's eyes turned to Castleton, reserved and waiting—and full of things Castleton could feel.

"What would the lieutenant be wantin' now?"

Castleton watched the slopes of the far peak, seeing his chance of capturing Antone fade entirely. There could be no pursuit in land like that, formed as it was with pine thickets and rock pits against a steep climbing grade. The sun rose, red-hot in the sky, his rations were only for three days, and his horses were jaded from the steady pushing through the rough country. All this he knew with a bitter disappointment. And had he not known it, Sergeant Hanna's black eyes would have told him.

Corporal Oldbuck called, "Sweeney's a dead one."

"So's O'Grady."

These men stood around, the excitement of the encounter fading, leaving them loose and weary. Castleton felt the dull judgment in their heads; he heard it in Manuel Dura's voice when the guide sauntered up.

"Maybe now you theenk Antone can fight, Lieutenant."

"Hanna," said Castleton, "we turn back. Tie Sweeney and O'Grady to their horses."

He rode away from the men, down to where Sweeney lay on his back with two long knife slashes through his bloodstained shirt. Castleton didn't dismount. He sat forward, watching Sweeney's face, curious to catch the shadow of some expression. This was his hard moment, to know that he had led Sweeney and O'Grady to death. This was when he realized how eagerly he had fallen into Antone's trap. He had no particular conscience about the matter, no regret, for this was the risk he took along with the rest of them; this was what soldiering was for. But he knew what Major Warren would say, and what the post would say, and how his men would be judging him. He sat there, thinking of it, turned harder than he had been, enraged and made a little mad by failure. It was the failure that mattered.

Chapter Ten

Eleanor and Tom Benteen, with a detail of eight men, left Grant before sunrise and camped that night in the gloomy jaws of Gold Canyon where, not long before, Apaches had slaughtered the Kennedy-Israel party. The following morning they reached the desert floor west of the Santa Catalinas and struck southwest into a yellow-blue heat haze. All in the surrounding distance was the smoky outline of peaks and buttes rising from the flat plain. Northward, the black summit of the Pinals and the lesser summits of the Mescals and the Tortillas. Westward lay the Picacho, marking the route of the mail stage line.

Along this route were evidences of the Apache scourge in the shape of mounded graves, old and new, scattered at frequent intervals, to mark the sudden end of Mexicans, stage-drivers, ranchers and prospectors suddenly ambushed. A blackened square showed where a ranch house had been; the bleached bones of a horse lay beside the metal fragments of a wagon. Summer's sun was a melting ball in a spotless blue sky and heat waves danced in gelatin layers along the cactus-studded soil. Gradually the low-lying shape of Tucson lifted from the plain and at sundown that day the party crossed the parade of Fort Lowell on the edge of town. The commanding officer's wife, Mrs. Bursom, immediately took Eleanor in charge. "You will join us for dinner, Mr. Benteen," she added.

The troopers moved to the stables, and Tom Benteen reported to the paymaster.

"I shall be ready to leave in the morning," the paymaster said. "Incidentally, there's a Mexican troupe in town tonight, playing 'Eleana and Jorge.'"

Benteen repaired to the post's bachelor hall, cleaned up, and returned to Colonel Bursom's quarters for dinner. Afterwards, in the soft, hot desert twilight, he escorted Eleanor into Tucson.

"This," he told her, "is the Mecca of the Southwest. There is nothing like it from San Antonio to San Diego, except perhaps Prescott up in the Mogollon range. But Prescott is strictly American. This is almost straight old Mexico."

At this half-light and half-dark hour a soft quiet lay over the town. There were no streets to speak of, only casual alleys threading the scatter of single-story dobe houses, along the walls of which strings of drying peppers hung colorfully. The dust was ankle-deep. Near one livery stable a water trough's overflow created a deep mudhole, and in this a hog lay, nothing but his eyes and snout showing. The church of San Antonio stood in the center of a plaza, its steeple and cross standing high over the low dobe dwellings. Around this plaza were shops and saloons and the long, windowless warehouses of the freighting merchant. In front of them canvas-topped wagons were banked, idle after their long runs to Missouri, to California, to Guymas and Hermosillo, deep in Old Mexico. They passed the rankness of the Munoz corral, they skirted the lighted windows of saloons, hearing the restless bubble of talk and the clatter of chips and the call of the roulette croupier. Beyond this, as darkness settled down, they followed the broken remnants of the old wall which once, in the time of the padres, had kept Tucson a safe haven in the heathen wilderness of northern Mexico.

Vesper bells were ringing. People moved through town, toward the quartermaster's corral. Candle lights gleamed out of doorways and the softness of Spanish talk was pleasant to hear. Darkness came down and the mystery of the desert pressed in. Eleanor took Benteen's arm, keeping step with him. "It is," she murmured, "a million miles to anywhere."

He felt the rhythm of her body, he was conscious of the sweet smell of her hair. Long afterward he said, "If I ever left the army, here's where I'd stay. In the Territory."

"Why?"

"Why," he said, surprised at being pinned down, and not quite finding the right words, "I like the desert. I like the hills. I even like the heat."

She said, "Well, that is the kind of a man you are, Tom."

They recrossed the plaza in front of the church. Then he said, "What kind?" and was really puzzled.

She didn't answer him directly. She stopped, coming in front of him, looking up to him with her hand still on his arm. A quarter-moon threw its soft light across her face; he saw its breadth, its strength, and the dark, unknown things lying in her eyes. "Do you think you'd ever leave the army?" she asked.

"Not by choice. Only if a bullet or an arrow ruined me. It is always a possibility a man has to consider."

He said it in a thoroughly impersonal manner, as if it were a contingency that didn't much matter. He had, she recognized, a broad streak of fatalism in him. Many things didn't matter to him; he shrugged them away, he closed his mind to them. It was odd that this should be the way of so vital and so physically strong a man. Once, she guessed, he had been hotheaded and restless—now and then she saw its remaining force, as in the scene with the outlaw, Jack Bean. But he had been through the Civil War as a boy, and had toughened on the frontier; and it had made him older at twenty-five than most men would ever be. This was what made him so brief-talking, so in-dolent. This and one other experience, she added at once

136

to herself. The Southern girl had done the rest of it. The Southern girl had taken all of him and had given back very little. She wondered then how much he still loved that woman; and because she was very curious, she said gently:

"Well, this is Southern, too. You like the South."

"Without magnolias and honeysuckle," he answered. "No more of those."

They crossed the plaza, threading the little alleys near Ochoa and DeLong's freighting warehouses. Mexicans were going ahead of them, toward the quartermaster's corral; all laughing and soft-talking people. Eleanor said, "Are you really that bitter about it?"

"If I were bitter," he said, "it would mean I hadn't forgotten, wouldn't it?"

"You haven't forgotten. I know that much."

"No," he said, "I haven't. But I'm not bitter."

"You think of her a great deal," she said quietly.

"I think of many things. I remember a cavalry charge in '63. I think of the smell of the swamps around Richmond when we were dug in—rotten and full of malaria. Water moccasins slid around your boots and scared hell out of a man. I think of the sound of the Minie balls at Gettysburg, at Little Round Top. I think of the time Mr. Lincoln came down to camp to see McClellan. McClellan kept drilling the army and not doing anything and Mr. Lincoln wanted to know why. Mr. Lincoln was very tall and his stovepipe hat added another foot and he was dressed in old clothes that made him look like a scarecrow. Little Mac was small and very neat. I think of a drink of buttermilk a little girl handed me one day in the summer of '62. This was in the Shenandoah valley. She was ten years old and her father was on the Confederate side with Lee. But she gave me a beautiful curtsy and flirted with her eyes. We gave her a salute when we rode on." He looked down at Eleanor with that slanting expression which was so near smiling and so near irony. "That's what I think of. Just pieces of action and little scenes that don't mean much. Put them all together and that's my life."

"No," she murmured. "You think of her. When you are quite tired. At night. When you are lonely."

He said, "Your eyes see too much, Eleanor," and led her into the quartermaster's corral. Cottonwood saplings had been thrown across the corral for seats. At the end of the corral a row of burning torches indicated footlights. A barrel, a wagon, and a watering trough comprised the stage, on which the actors waited. The admission, the polite young Mexican said, was fifty cents for the citizens, but a dollar for the distinguished Americanos. Benteen paid and escorted Eleanor to the least uncomfortable cottonwood he could find. All the youngsters were down front, making a great racket. Elsewhere sat the men of Tucson, a sprinkling of soldiers and the black-eyed Mexican girls with their ever-present duennas, their cheeks plastered with the customary flour-paste cosmetic. An orchestra — flute and guitar — made a desultory effort to rise above the considerable confusion and presently ceased. A broad Mexican came before the footlights, adjusted his serape and harangued the crowd in Spanish, made a low flourish and retired, whereupon the actors took station, struck their postures with heavy theatrical license, and "Eleana and Jorge" began in the shape of an extremely tearful scene between a rich uncle and his sorrowing niece.

"This uncle," explained Benteen, "is a mercenary old scoundrel who intends to sell his niece Eleana to a rich French officer who is a poltroon of the first rank. Jorge is a poor but very brave Mexican officer who loves Eleana. Of course Eleana loves him. It is very pathetic. But maybe love will win."

Eleanor smiled at his tone. He had turned pleased and gay and skeptical. The cottonwood log made a perilous bench which was the reason Benteen hooked his arm through the crook of her elbow, meanwhile vigorously applauding Eleana's unintelligible but highly dramatic

138

speech. The rich uncle departed and Don Jorge, hiding all this while behind the barrel, sprang up to the tremendous cheers of the audience, made his impassioned declarations of undying love and stalked behind the wagon; at this juncture the French officer, leering and effeminate, rose from the barrel and minced forward.

A storm of hatred rose from the cottonwood benches. *"Muere—Muere—* May he die!" Benteen clapped a hand across his mouth, emitting strong whoops of approval. At the end of the first act Benteen and Eleanor munched edible quinces, listening to the constant clack of the cigarette-smoking duennas. More troopers lined the rear of the corral, the music struggled feebly against the racket and the tar flares made a smoky, saturnine light against the black Arizona night. A frail little Mexican girl with eyes as round as dollars flirted behind her duenna's back at a youth with a dramatic face in the shadows. The second act showed the cowardly French officer's temporary ascendancy and Don Jorge's departure to death or glory. The second intermission brought a payozo, or Mexican clown, to the stage waving a Mexican flag and chanting death to foreign foes. By this time both Benteen and Eleanor were thoroughly hungry. Benteen bought steaming-hot enchiladas and chocolate and both of them ate their late supper while the third act confounded the French cad and the avaricious uncle and brought Don Jorge and beautiful Eleana to the center of the stage in happy embrace. Tucson, man, woman and child, stamped and shrieked its approval.

Benteen guided Eleanor through the crowd. "Everything comes out right and now we go home to sleep in exhausted contentment. Could opera night in New York be any better?"

"I thought Eleana was a little buxom," said Eleanor.

"The Spanish taste," said Benteen. "Anyhow, she has to be buxom to stand three acts behind those footlights. Must be a hundred and ten Fahrenheit up there." Turning

139

from the crowd, they swung the long way home, back through the devious pathways and plazas of Tucson.

In passing from the corral he had not noticed Sergeant McSween in the shadows nearby. But after he had gone McSween swung around and stared into the semi-darkness near the quartermaster's shed. Jack Bean stood there, and had been there during the last half-hour, closely watching Benteen. Presently Bean turned into the night whereupon McSween ploughed his way through the crowd of Mexicans, following Bean at a careful distance.

Benteen and Eleanor, slowly pacing this bland, hot night, came again to the church plaza. A few late worshipers came out and went away; the crowd straggled through the formless streets and a group of horsemen galloped from town. Men filed into the saloon on the far corner of the plaza and the lights there grew brighter. Eleanor settled on the church steps, pulling Benteen beside her. She laced her fingers together, around her knees, watching the high, brilliant stars and the capsized outline of the quarter moon. Silence settled across Tucson, a soft, smothering wave.

Benteen rolled a cigarette and lighted it, the smoke trailing fragrantly into the still air. He sat loosely on the steps, his long legs sprawled before him; he was, she thought, as thoroughly relaxed and at ease as a man could be. His face had softened from its habitual expression of disinterest and for this moment she was sure he had forgotten the past.

"Eleanor," he said, "this is damned pleasant."

Her presence, she thought, did this to him. But immediately the instant pleasure of that knowledge was qualified: her presence, or any woman's presence. For she was an army girl and she knew how hunger built up in a man until the nearness of a woman was the strongest temptation in the world. Even for Tom Benteen. He was a solid man, strong and physically alive; he had his thoughts, he had his desires. The memory of the Southern girl, clear as

140

it might be to him and as near as it might be, wasn't enough. He couldn't live with that pale shadow.

She murmured, "How far are those stars?"

"Too far."

"How near," she whispered, "could we get, if we tried?"

"Why try?"

She shook her head. "I know you better now. You don't mean it. You cover everything up."

He breathed in the cigarette smoke and expelled it. She heard the long sweep of wind in his chest. "Eleanor," he said, "don't be too curious about me."

"Why not?"

"I don't think I want you to know what's inside."

She spoke in the gentlest, most wondering voice. "I won't be able to help that, Tom. I think any woman would be curious about you. Harriet is. Lily Marr is. Should I be different? Remember, we will be in this regiment most of our lives. As long as you are a line officer and Phil is a line officer. Twenty years at least. That means we'll all be thrown together. You two hate each other. I see it very clearly. When I marry Phil I shall take his side, of course. But I know you both rather well, and I'll never be able to hate you at all. It will be hard, for me. Do you see?"

He didn't answer. He sat with his elbows on his knees, his head dropped forward and the smoke of the cigarette spiraling around his face. His lip corners had a tough, sharp set. She watched him with the closeness that could come only of deep, personal interest; his expressions and his mannerisms, the very manner in which his long fingers hung down, registered in her mind. He had a man's reticence and a man's rough humor; he had a man's thorough temper hiding behind his silence, sometimes gay and sometimes hard and hot as fire.

She said, "I should try to do something about that. But you and Phil are the whole world apart and never will be any closer. I'm sorry. It will make our lives difficult. We shall have our troubles."

"I have thought of that," he agreed. "The trouble will not come from me. Been wanting to tell you that the last day or so."

She said, quickly, "I wish you'd marry."

He looked around at her, surprised and on the edge of smiling. "Now why?"

She didn't smile back. Soberness held her face dark and still. She reached out and held her hand toward him until he took it. Her fingers closed around his palm, suddenly strong; holding to him, pressing some of her thoughts into him. The silence went on like this, full of unexpressed and puzzling emotions. Abruptly she drew her hand away.

"I do not believe I can tell you why, Tom. I don't believe I should. I don't think it would be very clear to you—or to me. But it would put an end to one thing. And that, I think, would be good for all of us. Does it mean anything at all?"

"Yes," he said. "Maybe it does."

Somewhere in town a Mexican boy was serenading the window of his own particular love. The melody of his guitar drifted through the thick desert silence, the sound of his voice was quite clear, singing:

> *"No me mires con esos tus ojos,*
> *Mas hermosos que el sol en el cielo,*
> *Que me mires de dicha y consuelo,*
> *Que me mata! Que me mata! Tu mirar!"*

From his position in the shadows of a dobe across the plaza, Sergeant McSween saw Benteen and Eleanor as two close-placed shadows in the vague moonlight. The sight stirred him and the song got into his Irish heart, and he stood there, patient and watchful, and did his own particular wishing, for a moment forgetting why he was here. Then he remembered and turned his attention to a sharp black line under the porch of the Shoo-fly restaurant. This was Jack Bean.

Eleanor said, "I have been thinking of what you said, about leaving the army. Short of death, you never will leave it. It is your kind of life. You would never be happy in any other."

"No," he said, "I never would."

She went on in her clear and sweet and judging voice, "I don't believe the slowness of promotion worries you. I don't believe you think about that much. I don't believe you ever have the heartburnings that other officers have. Yet this will happen to you, Tom. Promotion will come to you. Do you know why? Because you are a natural officer. You live and breathe the army. Your men feel it and the officers feel it. I've watched officers since I got old enough to notice. Some men do the right thing because it is just in their makeup, or in their blood. They were born with it, I guess. Some men have to learn it all. The gift is yours—without even thinking of it." She paused and drew a long quick breath, listening to the fading melody of the distant singer. "Would he be mentioning love, Tom? Let's walk."

They rose and crossed the plaza, close together under the vague shine of moonlight. Fort Lowell's gate lay northward but they paced slightly and slowly southward, on out toward the silver-shining border of the desert. Deep down there behind the black mountain masses lay Mexico; eastward the near peaks of the Santa Ritas cut heavy chunks from the sky; and all around was a loneliness and the smell and hint of sharp danger. The Mexican boy's song had entirely faded. Behind them, though they didn't know it, Jack Bean walked; and behind Bean came old Sergeant McSween, moving like a cat in the dust.

Eleanor said, "What was her name, Tom?"

"Lucy."

"Pretty, and Southern. Is she married now?"

"I never found out," he said.

"You should."

"Why?"

"Because it would close a door. It's open now and you keep watching it, thinking maybe someday she'll come through it."

He stopped, pulling her around. His voice was quite troubled: "You see a lot. Don't rummage through me like this. Why should you be curious? You've got a man."

"You should do something else," she said in the same, even way. "You should either go to her or get her out of your head. For a man like you, Tom, an old lavender and lace memory is bad."

"Maybe," he said. They paced on, saying no more. They rounded the entrance to the fort gate and went through it, quietly circling the parade. The sentry's hour call ran from post to post: "Three o'clock and all's well." Suddenly Benteen was softly laughing in the deep darkness.

"Eleanor, it is a damned short time till reveille!"

"It's been fun."

He stopped again, touching her arm. She came about, seeing the blur of his face, the black cut of his shoulders against the night. She knew he wasn't smiling. She knew what was in his mind. He said, "This is the way it ought to be. A little fun. A lot of riding. Something to cry about. Something to remember when it is all over." The pressure of his hand grew greater, pulling her in. She had lifted her head and her two hands came against his chest, without resisting pressure. This was the way she stood when he kissed her, heavy and long and hungry. If she had never known what was in the heart of this man before she knew now—the wild run of his temper, the force of his will. It came out, it broke through; it was, suddenly, something that passed over to her.

He stepped back, softly speaking. "Regrets?"

"No," she said. "No regrets. It has been a lovely evening, Tom. What did you say—something to remember when it's all over."

They walked straight across the parade, up to the porch of Colonel Bursom's house. Suddenly Mrs. Bursom's

144

voice rose from a corner. She said, faint acid in her tone, "I think it is about time."

Eleanor Warren was laughing. The sound of it ran gaily into the night. "About time. More than that, I think. Past time. Good night, Tom."

He turned down the steps, angling toward the gate of the fort, and she knew then he would be going back to Tucson to a saloon. She knew what he'd do. He'd draw a chair up to a poker game and order a drink, and sit low and loose in the chair, remembering. This was the kind of release a man of his kind had to have. There was too much inside him. Somehow it had to come out. In a kiss, in a drink, in a fight.

Sergeant McSween watched Benteen and Eleanor go into the post, and followed. But he hadn't gotten far along when he heard the sentry challenge again and heard Benteen's answer, outbound. McSween turned himself wearily around and passed the sentry, trailing Benteen back to the saloon near the church plaza. He stood in the black solid shadows, with his shoulder points flattened against a dobe's wall. Inside the dobe a man slept with a heavy snoring, and somewhere in this town a child's high thin cry echoed out. From the saloon came the steady undertone of drowsy voices and scraping feet. A Mexican stepped from the saloon, adjusted his serape more securely over a shoulder and walked across the plaza with a drunken man's extreme care. These were the only lights showing; elsewhere the mealy blackness of a desert night clung to earth and wall and sky, against which the cross of the church spire cut its immemorial shape. McSween, who was one of the faithful, watched the cross and had his own thoughts. Afterwards, looking back to the saloon, he saw Jack Bean.

The outlaw came slowly along the wall of the saloon and stopped before one of the green painted windows. Little glints of bright light showed where the paint had flaked away. Bean put his eye against one of these, look-

145

ing in. He stepped back, traveling as far as the door. Here he paused so long that McSween thought he meant to enter. It was clearly in the outlaw's mind, and the impulse teetered him toward the door until he shoved his hand against it and pulled away. Continuing along the wall, he cut around the saloon's corner, toward its rear. To the observant McSween nothing could have been clearer than Bean's purpose. This big black Irishman left the dobe, came up to the saloon and started for its rear, in the opposite direction Bean had chosen.

Inside the saloon, Benteen walked to the bar and signaled for a drink, which he took straight and quick. Afterwards, carrying bottle and glass with him, he moved to the lunch counter. He spooned a helping of chili out of a hot kettle into a bowl, spread a slice of sweet Sonora onion, as large as a saucer, between two pieces of bread and settled comfortably to a late meal. To a man who had averaged twenty miles of riding a day for the past six months, hunger was something always close and always real. There wasn't any fat on him. He scarcely knew the feeling of a full stomach; the constant activity of his life swiftly burned the food he took, and left him hungry again.

It was for him pure comfort to stand spraddle-legged at the bar, his elbows resting on it while he ate the chili and the onion sandwich, sampled a platter of enchiladas and finished his drink. He lighted a cigar, drawing in the strong smoke with a keen relish, and turned and hooked his arms over the bar to consider the room with a well-fed humor. There were times in a man's life when little things gave him his greatest moments—a drink of pure cold water after a blistering ride, the tremendous softening of a man's body when he dropped flat to the ground after a long run up a hill slashed by rifle fire, the taste of a dry biscuit to a razor-sharp appetite, the biting flavor of a cigar after long abstinence. These were the simplest things in life, but none of them were free. A man had to earn them by sweat and hunger and fatigue. That was why they were good.

It was then past three o'clock, two hours short of the time of starting back to Grant. He considered the poker tables a moment, thoughtfully and with an inveterate poker player's eagerness, and moved toward a vacant seat. In the middle of the room, he stopped, suddenly knowing he had no taste tonight for play. It was this quick and this strong—the recollection of Eleanor Warren's body swaying toward him in the vague moonlight, her rising lips, and the echo of her gently suppressed laughter. He moved out of the saloon and headed for Fort Lowell's gate, and had taken a dozen paces when a voice, even and very hard, hit him in the back.

"Just a minute, Captain."

He knew the man, even as he turned. He remembered that tone. The green-stained light of the saloon window ran a sickly glow across his path and for a long moment he could not see beyond it.

"Here, Captain," Jack Bean said, in that same thorough cold fury. "Here."

Benteen's eyes saw the vague shadow Bean made in the mouth of the ragged alley beyond the saloon. The outlaw stood near a dobe wall, the blackness of the wall dripping on him, covering him with its formless substance. And it was the man's voice, crowded with the memory of his humiliation at Grant, that told Benteen what was soon to happen. He stopped his turning, grinding his heels into the loose dust, watching Bean's motionless shape. He held his arms down by his side, at once outraged for not having a gun on him; and his mind was made up when Bean spoke again.

"You see me now, Captain? I never shoot a man in the back. I always give a man warnin'. You see me now?"

Benteen bent his knees and shoved himself across the green lane of light, low and fast, turning to the right as he plunged forward. Jack Bean's gun threw its round blossom of light and its shattering racket into his face. The breath of the lead touched him. There was a shadowy twenty feet between them, and the projecting edge of the dobe fifteen feet away, a shelter if he reached it. He swung in, toward the dobe, seeing the muzzle light spread again. But his mind changed and, with the dobe wall right before his arms, he suddenly refused the shelter, cut wide of it, and crashed into Jack Bean's swinging arm.

He tasted powder. Jack Bean's gun exploded in his ears, but he caught the man's arm and carried it up and back until he heard the grind of gristle. Jack Bean's finger, jammed in the trigger guard, exploded a last shot at the sky; and then Benteen's long palm wound around the barrel, holding it out of range. He carried the outlaw back against the dobe wall and raised his knee and smashed him in the stomach. Bean's wind belched out, his free fist caught Benteen on the jaw corner, scraping skin; for a moment the two of them heaved and turned and wrestled along the wall in bitter silence.

McSween's voice bawled up the street: "I'm comin', Lieutenant! I'm comin'!"

They reached the corner of the wall, staggered around it into the pure darkness between this dobe and another. Benteen brought up his left hand, sledging the base of Jack Bean's jaw. They whirled on backward, with the outlaw's wiry shape bending and whipping. Benteen was hit on the side of his nose; the outlaw's sharp boot-heel cut down across the arch of his feet and left its fresh, livid pain. Benteen kept smashing his shoulder into Bean, kept throwing him backward and twisting the overhead gun. They came against another dobe wall, Bean's head cracking against the dried mud; Benteen caught the man's small waist and dragged him away from the wall and, with a circling heave, battered him into it again. Bean's gun fell and his knees buckled under him. He capsized into Benteen's arms. Benteen hit him twice in the belly, got him by the neck and dragged him back along the alley.

McSween stood there with his own revolver lifted. "By God, I couldn't fire, Lieutenant! You were in the way!"

Benteen sucked the thin and hot and insufficient air into the bottom of his lungs. Bean, half strangled by Benteen's crooked arm, kept lunging against the ground with his feet, he kept trying to turn and break free, his arms sliding slow punches against Benteen's neck. Benteen got into the green lane of light and threw the outlaw against the saloon wall. McSween targeted the dark muzzle of his revolver dead between Bean's eyes and spoke with a throaty softness. "Be still, sonny, or I'll blow your brains against the saloon."

Jack Bean's eyes were slate-black against the surrounding paleness of his skin. The green light showed this. Blood dripped down the corner of his lip and a round spot, like a burn, began to flush up behind his ear. "Captain," he ground out, "I'll be in this country a long time, and I never forget." Then he let out a hard, furious cry. "You damned fool, why didn't you use your gun instead of runnin' into me?"

"What gun?" said Benteen.

Bean stared at Benteen. "I knowed you didn't have a holster, but was you crazy enough to walk around Tucson without a gun of some kind in your pocket?"

"No gun," said Benteen. "Now you pull out of here."

Bean said disgustedly, "I never brace a man unless he's got a gun. How in hell was I to know? Listen, Captain, you better carry a gun. Next time I call I won't wait."

"Maybe," said McSween, "there will be no next time. Lieutenant, I had better take a walk with this man. A little walk beyond the town."

"Captain," said Jack Bean, a driving anger in his tone, "you made a mistake layin' your hands on me. No man ever did that. I propose to kill you."

"Walk along," said Benteen.

Bean unhurriedly brushed himself and turned into the church plaza. McSween grumbled under his coal-black

149

mustaches and waggled his revolver at the retreating figure. Benteen looked down at himself, and saw the shreds of his gray shirt hanging about his waist. He grinned at McSween and turned back to the post gateway.

McSween waited until both men were buried in the dark. Thereafter be bolstered his revolver, staring up to the dim silhouette of the cross on the church. Presently he walked over the square and up the steps, into the church's open door. "Now it has been a long time," he murmured, removing his hat. "Whut would my mother be a-thinkin' of me, so high yonder?"

Chapter Eleven

A day and a half beyond the limit of his orders, Castleton brought his detail front into line on Grant's parade ground and turned it over to Sergeant Hanna. The two dead men were lashed crosswise on their saddles. For a moment he looked at them, his eyes half closed against the glare of the sun. "Hanna," be said, "put Sweeney and O'Grady in the quartermaster's shed. Send a detail to the cemetery to open up a couple graves."

All the people of the post stood in the shade of the ramadas, looking on. The detail was motionless, waiting dismissal, the sun-inflamed eyes of all these troopers fixed on him. He felt the sullenness behind that impassive glancing; he felt the silence of the roundabout spectators; turning, he saw Major Warren waiting at the doorway of commanding officer's quarters. Castleton left his horse, stiffly crossing the parade. There was no expression on Warren's round, heat-flushed face.

Castleton saluted. "I report back from detail, sir. We had a brush with Antone's party in the Pinals. Privates Sweeney and O'Grady were killed."

Warren said, "When you have washed up I wish to see you and Mr. Mixler."

After dismissal George Mixler walked to his dobe, toward Harriet who at once turned into the house. Lily Marr came from the dobe, gave him a close look, and went on down the walk. Mixler found Harriet in the bedroom. She stood at the rear doorway with her back turned to him, its stiffness and its squareness telling him everything he needed to know. He paused over the crackerbox crib, studying the yellow and wizened face of his son, seeing his small arms turn fretfully in a troubled half-sleep. There was, he thought heavily, something wrong with the child. He said in a hopeful voice:

"Everything been all right, Harriet?"

"No," she said. When he heard the hard, remembering bitterness in her voice, a dullness traveled through Mixler. He went to the kitchen, stripped to his waist and washed and shaved and put on a fresh shirt. It took time, and all the while he waited to hear her step, to hear her voice changed back to the way it had once been. For him there was something unnatural in her manner. He had the actually terrifying fear that childbirth had unsettled her mind; suddenly he had to see her face.

"Harriet," he said, "turn around."

Stony indifference held her still. It left him helpless, it left him in a thoroughly defeated mood. But he spoke again, very gentle. "Is it always going to be like this, Harriet?"

"No," she said. "Not for long. As soon as the baby can travel, I'm going."

"You're sure it's got to be that way?"

She came about, showing the set, white composure on her face. He was a young man and his knowledge of women was limited to this one girl; but he realized that her long dislike of army life and her experience with the baby had at last changed her completely. She was sane enough, but she was free of him. She had put him aside. There was nothing in her eyes now to remind him of the laughing, impulsive girl he had married in Baltimore. The damage was done. He had been away at the one time she had wanted him and nothing he might say about the ways of the army would change her.

"Yes," she said.

There came to George Mixler, whose life had never been complicated by any kind of real trouble, a grinding feeling of injustice. He put his blond head down, setting his teeth tight against the rough and tumble words he wanted to say. He said them all—but to himself; and when he was done he looked up to her, gentle again.

"You know best," was all he said.

Castleton was at the door, calling him. He joined Castleton, going down the walk and stepping into the commanding officer's house. Captain Harrison and Ray Lankerwell waited there with Warren. Warren said, "Where did you leave Antone, Mr. Castleton?"

"We followed his trail from the point near Trumbull Butte, continuing north into Castle Canyon. On the third morning we started west from the canyon. About an hour's march we reached a long rock fault. They were behind it. When we turned to skirt the rocks we ran into another party in a very rough stretch of ground to one side of the rocks. They made a brief stand and gave way, west again toward the top of a hill in the direction of the Apache Mountains."

"How many were in that party?"

"Dura said about forty."

Warren said, "Captain Harrison, take twenty-five men who have not been on the last two details. You will leave after sunset. Lankerwell and Manuel Dura will go along. Rations for five days." Major Warren paused, looking hard at Harrison. I want you to keep Antone moving but do not permit him to pull you into a trap."

Harrison nodded and stood there until Warren said, "That's all." Afterwards Harrison and Lankerwell left the room. Warren's eyes were very blue. He stood before Castleton and Mixler, a round and normally comfort-loving officer who grew more formidable with each moment.

153

"Mr. Castleton, I always give my officers the option of judgment when they are on independent detail. What was your thought in continuing beyond the limit of time I had set?"

"Antone was directly in front of me, sir. Never more than an hour's march after we hit Castle Canyon. I thought it possible to overtake him."

"Did you scout the canyon before entering it? Put flankers on the rim?"

"No sir. I did not believe Antone would try an ambush there. We got through it without a scratch."

Warren turned on Mixler: "What was your judgment when you started into the canyon?"

Mixler flushed a little. He stared at the major. "I had no judgment, sir. Never gave it a thought."

Warren let the answer sink into dead silence. These moments ran on until George Mixler stirred his heavy legs and looked down. Warren pulled at the ends of his mustaches, speaking again to Castleton. "You got through the canyon and continued west until you reached the rocks. Had you scouted the country?"

"No sir. Indian sign was very strong. We knew they were dead ahead."

"You knew they were behind the rocks?"

Castleton remained stiff and straight in the room. His jaws cut hard lines against his cheeks. He met Warren's eyes. "No sir."

"Did you know they were flanking you in the rough country beside the rocks?"

"No, sir."

"Then it was a trap?"

"I should like to say—"

Warren's voice killed Castleton's reply. "Was it?"

"Yes, sir."

"Did Manuel Dura mention it might be a trap?"

"Yes, he did."

154

Major Warren nodded at Mixler. "That will be all, Mr Mixler."

George Mixler left the room at once, glad to be rid of that scene. He turned to the sutler's store. He sat down at a table and had the sutler bring over a bottle and glass, and poured himself two swift drinks of whisky, and sat there staring at the blunt ends of his fingers, loose and moody and defeated.

Back in the commanding officer's house Major Warren asked one more question. "What impelled you to continue then, knowing you were on dangerous ground?"

"I believed we could overtake Antone. It was my judgment the risk was justified."

But he looked at a man who was no longer mild or jolly. When Warren spoke it was with a soft-voiced detachment that made the words so much the worse.

"There are times, Mr. Castleton, when it is necessary to risk a command. Nor do I condemn an honest mistake. It takes a good many years to season an officer in the field. Neither of these conditions applies to you. You are an ambitious officer. In order to further your own particular career you disregarded my explicit warnings, the advice of your guide who knows Indians better than you could ever hope to know them, and rode into a trap, wasting two excellent soldiers. The kindest thing I can say to you, sir, is that you were a fool. My hope is that you will profit by this incident. If you do not there is no place in the army for you."

Warren wheeled away, seized his hat from a chair and stamped out of the house. Slowly turning, Castleton saw him cross the parade and enter the shed where the dead troopers lay.

Castleton braced an arm against the doorsill, shoving the full weight of his body into it. This was the kind of headless fury that moved through him. He put his head down, stretching his lips and pushing them together and

stretching them again; then he looked up and watched
Ray Lankerwell pass by. Ray's eyes touched him, guard-
edly indifferent, but Castleton, turned rash and jealous
and suspecting by all that had happened, thought he saw
contempt in the man's eyes. He stared at Lankerwell's
back, on the dangerous edge of calling Lankerwell back
and making a quarrel of it. What really checked that impulse was the scrape of feet behind him. He turned to see
Cowen come through the kitchen.

He threw his question at Cowen as if he wanted to hit
the man. "Where's Miss Eleanor?"

Cowen showed him a wooden face, but Castleton
thought he saw something behind that impassiveness,
something that was hard to bear. "Lieutenant Benteen
went to Tucson with a detail. She went along, sir."

Castleton's voice stepped up a note. "When will they be
back?"

"Two days, sir," said Cowen, and gave the lieutenant a
straight black stare, falsely respectful, and retreated.

Castleton walked slowly around the room, at that moment willing to give a year of his life for the privilege of
stepping across the barrier that separated him from
Cowen so that he might slam Cowen against the wall and
beat that covert jeering out of Cowen's eyes. He swung
his fists back and forth as he walked, and stopped and
stared at the yellow flare of light on the San Pedro. Tucson lay that way—and Eleanor, and Benteen. He smacked
the edge of the doorway with the flat of his hand and
went down the walk at a heavy tramping pace to his own
single-roomed dobe.

He poured a drink from the olla jar swinging on the
rafter of the ramada, at once beginning to sweat from the
little moisture taken in. This was the quality of afternoon
heat. He sat on the edge of the bed and rolled a cigarette
and afterwards locked his two fists together, staring at the
floor. He thought of Antone until Antone ceased to be a

156

ordinary Indian in the hills, and became, instead, everything that stood in his way. This was how he thought of Antone, hating him increasingly. Then he remembered Eleanor, and Benteen, and when he came to consider Benteen he drew the cigarette slowly from his mouth and held it, forgetful, between his fingers. His lips pushed together, never relaxing. His big shoulders came forward and he sat in this profound dismal study—a man with black cropped hair and a heavy, forward-thrust chin and with eyes narrowed against the little devil-points of light shining out of them.

In this country a dead man needed quick burying. In the last sunlight a file of troopers carried Sweeney and O'Grady, blanket-wrapped, out to the little cemetery. Castleton saw them pass his door. For a moment he sat still, in no degree stirred, feeling no pity toward the two men and no conscience in the matter. But in the end he rose and went to the cemetery and stood in the burning sunlight and listened to Warren's brief service. He looked at the figures in the bottom of the grave. There was, for him, nothing sacred about death and nothing to dread about it. He had no fear of it, no feeling about it one way or other. Nor for that matter did he place any particular value on life, another man's life or his own. So he remained motionless and unstirred, and this was the way Lily Marr, in the background, saw him. She was a clear-sighted and realistic girl—appraising people by her own odd standards; and in Castleton's long, solid face with its taciturn impatience, she saw something on the very edge of brutality. She looked away from him, at the graves.

At dusk Captain Harrison led twenty-five men out of Grant's parade on a five-day scout, Ray Lankerwell and Manuel Dura accompanying him. The straggling Indians from Nachee's peaceful band started back to the camp on the San Pedro. Night fully fell, the increasing moon laying its silver-frost glow across the gravel and alkali earth.

Lamps made a firefly pattern all around the parade and the hour call ran from post to post. At tattoo Castleton took the usual check roll call on the parade and returned to his dobe. He lay on the bed, staring up to the black ceiling; sleepless with all that was on his mind, his impatience turning him more and more desperate.

In the fort this night other people had their thoughts and were prompted to strange speech and odd acts. Lying in his single cot, George Mixler listened to the steady mewling of the baby. There wasn't any light in the room. The thick hot air pressed against everything and the smell of baked earth was very strong. Harriet's white nightgown made a blur on the other bed. He heard her reach out and gently rock the crackerbox cradle.

He said, "Do you want me to pick sonny up and walk around?"

"No."

There was a distance between them pretty hard to bear, as bad as if one of them had died, and it made him remember how close they had been in those few years of married life. He said:

"You remember the boat ride across from Old Point Comfort, Harriet?"

"No."

He pushed the single sheet entirely away from his stripped body and scrubbed the heavy sweat around his chest. Sweat ran out of his scalp. It soaked the pillow and made a wetness that was a comfort against the greater heat. He said, "How soon can sonny travel?"

"Maybe a week."

"I guess you had better go then," he said quietly; and put all his hopes away.

Sergeant Hanna sat in the back of the bakery shop, pushing the table's candle idly around its own drippings. Light turned his feather face faintly red. Herb Levi, second line sergeant of K troop was there, and Corporal

158

Oldbuck, and Cowen. Cowen stood attentively in the background. Hanna used the candle to mark the fight.

"They was behind the rocks. We turned left — and then we saw 'em up behind the humps. So we went at that bunch. O'Grady died behind the third hump. Sweeney was hurt when his hawrrs fell but it was an Injun that ran out from the rocks and stuck a knife in his chest. After we brushed 'em from the humps we beat 'em back when they came up from the rocks. They ran then, the devils — shtraight for the hills. 'Twould have been nawt any of us come back from that, had we followed. And still, I saw the wish in Castleton's eye. For a minute I thought he meant to follow; and in me mind I kissed the cross."

"A fool," said Levi.

"In a way he is," admitted Hanna. "I will never feel very sure of me life as long as I follow behind him. 'Twas a hell of a march on hawrrses and men, but to him we're nawthing to consider."

Cowen said, with a sepulchral solemnity, "Was he afraid?"

"Afraid? By God, no. Had he been in the humor he would have done up that hill after Antone alone. No, no fear. But no reason ayther. And cold, my boy. Dead cold. Have a look at his face and see if ye find a spark o' sympathy there. He is a fine hater, and driven by the wish to be a great man. And he means to do it, if he must kill himself or us." He looked solemnly around. "That is no idle fancy. I do not like the thought of goin' on the next scout detail with him. He will be mad to try his luck again."

"Another thing pushes the boy," said Levi. "That would be Mr. Benteen."

"Ah," breathed Cowen, "you should have seen his face when he found out Miss Eleanor had gone to Tucson with the Lieutenant."

"A bad look," suggested Hanna.

159

"A killing look," said Cowen.

The three of them were old soldiers, with the loyalties of long service ground into them. They remained silent after Cowen's remark, thinking about it and gradually awakening to its meaning. Hanna looked at the other two, a narrow surprise on his blackened checks. "And so the man is — a killer. It had nawt come to me that way before. He has no pity I have ever seen. He has damned little conscience in the way he handles his men, and the Lord put a pride in him that will brook nawthin'. So he is, a killer."

"How is it Miss Eleanor does not see that?" puzzled Levi.

"Ah," grumbled Hanna. "Love. She only sees his strength, not the damned deadly thing behind."

Cowen stiffened. "Hanna, keep your Irish tongue off that girl."

Hanna stared at Cowen. "You fool," he murmured. "I taught her to ride and I taught her to soldier since she was knee-high to a waterin' trough. You should be tellin' me about Eleanor Warren. It is God's pity she cannot see the better man. The Lieutenant Benteen is an officer and a gentleman in the true way. Now it is somethin' to see him ride and somethin' to hear him command. Every man in this regiment knows it. A pity she does not."

"Maybe," said Cowen, very shrewdly, "she sees it better than we think."

"Whut's that mean?" asked Hanna, who loved his gossip.

But Cowen only looked wise and shook his head. "I bear no tales from the commanding officer's house."

Levi drew a round circle on the table with his thumb, and spoke. "One of these days Castleton will be bracin' Benteen. It is in the cards — and not long in comin', I think. A man like Castleton will stand for nothing in his road, and Benteen's in it. It will be a hell of a thing when

160

it comes. I am not sure Benteen can lick him."

"Ah," growled Hanna and rose from his seat. The three of them were darkly pondering it, displeased with what they saw. Hanna shrugged his shoulders. "If they fight and the Major hear of it, they'll be cashiered. So then it will be that dog Castleton who pulls down a better man than he ever could be." It made him angry; he showed it in his somber Irish eyes. But he said, "This is improper talk, outside us three. Say nothing." Taps floated across the parade.

There was an unfinished bottle on the table. Hanna drank his share and passed it to Levi who rubbed the neck clean and, slyly winking at Hanna, offered it to Cowen. Cowen put both his hands flat against the sides of his trousers. "No, of course not," he said irritably. "You know damned well I don't."

Levi saluted him and tipped up the bottle. Cowen sighed, his eyes watching Levi's Adam's apple slide up and down. Cowen's lips puckered. Suddenly he wheeled around, and stamped from the room.

"Temperance," said Hanna, "is a wonderful thing. Save me another drop, Levi. It is a dry damned country."

As soon as the last note of taps had faded, Harry Jackson rose from his cot and slipped out of the barrack. He reached the guard line behind the quartermaster shed, waited until the sentry on that post had walked to the far end of the beat, and quietly crossed it. At the far margin of Aravaipa Creek he flattened on his belly to take a quick survey of the desert. As before the shining of Rose Smith's light, a mile away, was a lure that made him forget the danger of the land, and so he rose and fell into a quick trot. When he reached her door he paused, noting that the inner board shutters had been drawn across the window. Faint light seeped through the cracks and there was a murmur of talk inside. Harry Jackson listened to it, distinguishing no words. And at last knocked.

161

Jealousy and fear grew in him while he waited, bu when she opened the door and he saw the shape of he shoulders and the shining of her hair against the light this went away and left him humble. He stepped inside waiting for her to close the door. Her face came arounc to him, carefully watching him. She didn't smile.

He said, "I couldn't get away last night. On guarc duty."

"Harry," she said, "I don't think you ought to run the desert like this. Antone's Indians are around."

Her words, seeming to carry concern, made him feel good. "I'd come," he said, "if I had to walk ten miles.' There was smoke in the room. He said, "Your uncle been here?"

Her answer came out rather slow and delayed. "Yes.' But on her face was a settled expression; it had a weariness. "Harry, you going back east when your enlistment's up?"

He gave her a puzzled look, "Why?"

"You ought to."

He had his cold run of doubt. "Rose," he said, "this is a bad place for you to be. You ought to have a better home. I never did quite figure out why you got to stay with your uncle. You ought to be in Tucson, or up in Prescott. There ain't anything here for a woman like you—"

She broke in, "It is after taps. You better go back."

"When my hitch is up I'm goin' to Prescott and settle. Maybe you'd like that."

"Me?" she asked and stared at him, her eyes obscure. "Why me?"

Harry Jackson's cheeks were red; his blue eyes were sharp and excited. "We could be married."

"Me?" she murmured. "Me, Harry?"

He said, "Why, it won't be such a long wait, just a year. I've got two hundred dollars, and I can get a job

162

with a freighting outfit any day."

She kept staring at him until he quit talking. The set of her face was odd, her eyes were very round and her lips were pulled together as if she were angry. He heard her murmur, "Thanks, Harry," and then she went to the room's back door and opened it and spoke to somebody in the darkness. She said, "Come in," her tone sounding exhausted. Canreen came out of the night.

Canreen's big-lipped mouth spread apart. He was laughing from the top of his lungs, quick and enormously amused. He said, "Hello, kid. You're kind of late tonight, ain't you?"

"Canreen," said Rose Smith, "he wanted me to marry him."

Canreen quit grinning. His eyelids came together and he stood there, puzzled, not understanding. "Huh?" he said.

Harry Jackson remained in the center of the room. He pulled up his head and his long black hair came down the side of his face, giving it a young, thin appearance. His lips were turned, as though he tasted alum; a kind of cold sickness spread across his features. The girl saw it and Canreen saw it. Canreen at last caught on; his voice ceased to jeer at Jackson. It was a little bit kind. "Kid," he said, "don't you see? Hell, go on back and forget it."

Harry Jackson said nothing in that long, stretching silence. Something went out of his eyes while he looked. The girl saw it die. Then he stared at Canreen and even Canreen, not a quick man, saw murder in the boy's eyes. This was all. Harry Jackson turned out of the dobe, pulling the door behind him.

Canreen grumbled, "I'll be watchin' that kid. He'll try to run a saber through me again." Rose Smith was crying, making no sound about it; she watched the closed door and tears squeezed out of her eyes and traveled along her checks. She dragged her lower lip between her teeth.

163

"Rose," grumbled Canreen, "what the hell?" He reached out his heavy hand and laid it on her shoulder. "Aw, what the hell?"

Young Harry Jackson walked across the desert and slipped by the guard line. He let himself quietly into the barrack, pulled off his boots and lay face up on his bunk, staring at the black ceiling. He doubled his fists together and drew a long breath to break up something lumpy and painful in his chest; but it stayed, and he drew a deeper breath. Van Rhyn, whose bunk adjoined, spoke through the black.

"You all right, son?"

Harry Jackson didn't answer and presently van Rhyn pushed his feet from the bed and scratched a sulphur match, throwing the light toward Harry Jackson. Harry Jackson batted the light out of the older man's hands and turned on his side, breathing deeper and deeper. He didn't know he was crying.

Chapter Twelve

As soon as Eleanor returned from Tucson she heard of Castleton's brush with the Indians. The story came first from her father at the supper table and as usual he confined himself to the strict facts. But she asked:

"Did Antone surprise him?"

Major Warren stroked his mustaches, thus covering the expressive part of his face. She knew he did this deliberately. His answer, as always, avoided direct judgment. "The boy had a little hard luck. They were in rocks and he could not surround them."

The true story would be among the enlisted men and Cowen, who was an inveterate gossip, would know it. After her father had gone for his evening stroll, she turned to the kitchen. "Cowen," she said, "what happened?"

Even with his hands in the dish water, Cowen's massive dignity clung to him. He contained important information and self-consciously showed it. Nevertheless, it did not entirely come out. "Mr. Castleton pursued the Injuns into the Pinals. This was a hot trail and the lieutenant kept on it very strict. He reached Antone in some rocks and made the charge, but was fired upon from the left flank where some of Antone's warriors hid. He rushed 'em and then was surrounded for a bit, but fought 'em away. Sweeney lost his hawrrs and was hurt—and afterwards an Injun run from the rocks and knifed him. The

165

Lieutenant chased a savage around one side of a little hump o' ground and O'Grady went the other side of the hump. That's where O'Grady died. The Lieutenant killed the Injun. Afterwards the bunch ran and t'was too rough a country to safely follow."

"Was it a trap, Cowen?"

Cowen scratched his ear with a soapy thumb. "Now I did not exactly hear that," he countered. "Though I did hear the Lieutenant caught up with Antone very sudden."

"How did they look when they came back?"

"Ah," said Cowen, "like lobsters boiled too long in the pot. And wouldn't anybody after five days of that ridin'?"

"Five days, Cowen?"

"Very near. The Lieutenant had a hot trail and wanted to keep on till he caught the red scoundrel."

She knew most of the story then. Phil had over-stayed his orders two days in order to gamble on his luck, had been surprised, and had lost two men. She stood in the doorway of the dobe, deeply concerned. He was too ambitious and too proud not to feel the sting of failure; and the judgment of the officers would nag at his mind. They wouldn't say anything to him but their manner toward him would reveal it. This was the brutally effective way men had. Knowing Phil Castleton, she imagined his humiliation and began to worry.

She looked around the dark quadrangle and didn't see him. Disappointed and a little piqued by his absence, she went down to see Harriet Mixler. Lily Marr sat in the bedroom, rocking the crackerbox cradle. Harriet smiled out of a face drawn very thin. Neither she nor the baby looked well.

"As soon as he can travel," said Harriet, "we're going up to Fort Apache and get out of this heat. He won't live unless we do. When fall comes I'm taking him East."

166

Eleanor, sympathetic and broadminded by nature, felt only impatient, remembering George Mixler's wire-drawn features. Still, she would not have let opinion escape had it not been for her own confused state of mind.

"Harriet," she said, "what do you expect from marriage or from army life? Every time George goes out on scout he takes his chance of dying. Why should you cry about trouble, why should you put all the blame on him, and make him so miserable he can't eat or sleep? People should stand their miseries. You should stand yours. When you married him you knew he'd be knocking around from one frontier post to another most of his life and that he would never have the freedom of a civilian, or the money, or any of the conveniences. You thought the uniform made him a very gallant figure, and so it does. But don't you know what the uniform means? He made a bargain with the United States. You thought that pretty nice when there was no trouble. Yet trouble is what all his training is for. Now that it comes do you want him to crawl out of it and run back to Virginia and drink mint juleps in the moonlight? I'm disappointed in you."

Harriet flung back her answer. "He can do what he pleases. I can't be an army woman. I'd grow old and wrinkled, and break my heart at it."

"So you'll run away and break his," said Eleanor. "You wanted him to quit the army. You threw the choice at him. Any woman who tries to make a man choose between his wife or his career is a fool. Maybe he'd throw up his career—and you'd have your man. But what would you have? Nothing you'd want. You would have destroyed everything in him that you liked—his self-respect and his loyalty."

"No," said Harriet, "he's made his choice. He wouldn't leave the army."

"I think," said Eleanor gently, "you ought to he proud

of that. But if you want a man you can wrap around your finger you'll be a miserable wife."

"I'm going," repeated Harriet Mixler, in a stone-set voice.

"Yes," murmured Eleanor, "I think you will. But afterwards this is what you'll remember. You'll remember George coming in from a trail, hot and dusty and tired. You'll remember how pleased he was to see you and how you sat around in the shadows, glad to have him back. You'll remember how sweet those few days were—the days between the times he had to go. You'll remember him sitting on his horse at dress parade. I think you'll remember the trumpet calls and the flag at retreat, and the midnight suppers, and how good an orange tasted when you hadn't had fresh fruit for a month. And you'll remember your friends—the closest friends you'll ever have in the world. When you get away from it everything will come back clearer than you imagine and you'll always regret leaving."

She had said all this quite swiftly. It came springing out of her heart, and then when she had finished, she was surprised how deeply she felt, and was quite still—knowing that Harriet had refused to listen. Harriet lay with her eyes turned to the ceiling, the baby had begun to cry again, and Lily Marr's dark eyes watched her—watched Eleanor—with a driving interest. Eleanor reached over, touched Harriet's shoulder, and left the room.

She stood in the doorway, watching the shape of the sentry drift by, hearing the murmur of the troopers in the barrack across the way, catching the keen hot smell of dust damped down by the passing sprinkling cart. An orange-silver moonlight vaguely diluted the darkness and the mountains directly east of the post lay high and solidly black—with the feeling of danger and mystery and ancient wildness in them.

168

It was odd to stand here and have her thoughts drift beyond control. She had been thinking of Phil Castleton, wondering about him; the next moment all these vivid impressions of the night lifted her spirit to an eager pitch and then, in the sway of this strange restlessness, she remembered Tucson and Benteen and her feelings were quick and pleased and on the shadowy edge of wistfulness. She could not explain that mixture of sensation in her body though she honestly tried to clear it up; there was, she realized immediately, danger in the mood, danger in the memory, and it was with a distinct relief that she saw Castleton cross from post headquarters.

She took his arm, happy to have him near. They strolled along the north side of the triangle without a word. Near the post bakery a beam of light crossed the walk and she noticed the rather hard angle of his face. But he felt her glance; it drew his smiling attention. Beyond the beam of light he stopped and drew her in for a kiss. For her this was the deepest pleasure of the evening. Even the forgetfully severe pressure of his arms brought her nearer to him.

She said, "It's been a long time, Phil."

"I always miss you. Five days, or three years. One's just as bad as the other."

"That's nice to know."

"See anything new in Tucson?"

"We went to a Mexican play and ate enchiladas and hot chocolate. And—" She had meant to add that they had sat on the steps of the church in the moonlight. But she turned aside from it, saying, "It was really a pleasant diversion." A distant uneasiness stirred in her at her own evasion. She didn't like it, she didn't approve—and wondered why she had so definitely drawn away from mentioning the rest of the episode.

He said, "We?"

"Tom and I." She at once heard the change in his

169

voice, its cooling and its brief jumpiness. So she asked, quietly amused, "Jealous?" and knew before he answered that he was.

"Certainly," he said. Nothing more, but that was enough. Some parts of that night, she thought distantly, she couldn't tell him.

"Did you have a pretty hard scout?"

"You've heard the details, I imagine."

"Yes. I'm sorry, Phil. Better luck next time."

They were at the men's side of the quadrangle and as before he pulled her away from the walk so that the voices inside would not register. "What are you sorry for?" he asked.

His tone made her wonder. She knew the depth of his pride and she had expected to hear some echo of his defeat, some unconscious admission of humiliation. She didn't hear it. His voice was cool and quick and quite self-confident. Whatever his thoughts were, he kept them carefully hidden—and this reserve troubled her, as though it were a lack of faith on his part in her. The moment's closeness was broken. She changed the things she had intended to say, which was about the trap he had fallen into. In his present attitude she knew it wouldn't help.

"You wanted to catch Antone, didn't you? I'm sorry you didn't."

"I have learned," he said, "that Antone is clever. A good sagebrush general. He picks his spots always in reference to a safe retreat. This time he faded into a rocky country we could not follow. But I do not have much respect for his striking power. Both Manuel Dura and Al Hazel put too much stress on his danger. I went through a canyon at dusk. Dura and Mixler were both uneasy about it. Nothing happened. We came up against the rocks, with Dura full of old-maid symptoms. We lost two men and accounted for ten or twelve Indians. I regret the loss of the men, but we paid off for it."

He mentioned this with a cool indifference that both puzzled and displeased her. Somehow his words were not right; they were screens against his real feelings. She found herself saying:

"It was O'Grady's third enlistment. Sweeney was very fond of me. They were good men."

"I took my chances, too, Eleanor," he said in the same touch-and-go voice.

"Phil," she said, a little sharp with him, "I am expressing regret. I'm not arguing."

He said, "You will be the only one not expressing disapproval. The post seems to think I'm a poor officer. Yet I would do it again." Then she heard some of the hidden anger get loose. "And I will do it again, given the opportunity. I have no use at all for the damned penny-ante tactics of this campaign. If I were Antone, watching a file of troopers chase him up one canyon and retreat down another, I'd have nothing but contempt for the American uniform. Next time I see the color of his skin I shall follow, on horse or on foot, or on my belly, as long as I have one man left to draw a full breath. Then we shall see."

"Phil," she said, "don't carry a chip on your shoulder."

He stopped. They were on the thick shadows by the post headquarters and all she saw was the line of his jaw. "Eleanor, are you making the common disapproval of me unanimous?"

She had her own temper. "Hold on young man," she said immediately. "If it is a fight you wish to pick, just tell me. I love to push pins into rash young officers who grow too proud."

"So," he said, again cool.

"So," she mimicked, stung by this irritating aloofness. "If I am to be your wife, Phil, you must not use that 'Run along little girl' tone at all. I was straddling army

171

wagon tongues while you were still playing marbles. I know something about this army, mister. You seem to think nobody at the post likes you. If that were really true Phil, it could only mean that you were wrong. I don't think it is true. But one thing you must do, if you really want to get along. You must go halfway to other people."

He used that dry distant tone again, saying, "Tell me the rest of my faults," and at once she knew she had to break through this man's barrier. She said, shockingly distinct:

"One of us is a fool, Phil. Either you for using that tone, or I for standing it."

"Eleanor," he flashed out, on the very edge of arrogance.

"Well?" she asked.

He took her arms, almost shaking her. But he came all the way down from his high, biting anger; and the sound of his words then, humble and afraid, made her remember that she loved him. "Eleanor," he groaned, "never speak like that. This is a hell of a lonely life and if you leave me, how in God's name—"

She said, "Hush," gently and sweetly. "I know. You can't help it. It drives you so hard. I can understand. But others don't—because you never let them see. We'll be together a lot of years, Phil. If I am good for anything, I'm good for you. And I'll help. I know how. Only, you've got to do a hard thing in the next few weeks. You've got to make your peace with the men in the post."

"How?" he said.

"That," she said, with more insight than she realized, "I can't tell you. You're a man—you must do it the way men do."

A long windy breath rushed out of him, telling her how desperate and balked and stormy his feelings were.

172

Then he murmured, "Eleanor, I wish we could be married shortly. Would a month be too soon for you?"

"No," she said. "A month from now, if you want it."

"Fine," he said, "fine," and kissed her again, and wheeled through the night. She didn't realize until now that she stood in front of her own doorway. This wrapped up had she been. Watching his high shape merge with the blackness of the parade, she had her moment of wonder. She understood him—and yet did not. He had so many contradictory sides, rising from the tremendous up and down swing of his personality, that at times she could not follow, and grew a little weary from trying. She hated his moments of sarcastic indifference— for these were the times when he went entirely away from her and forgot her and underestimated her; but he had that hard burning fire she could not help loving. And so she pondered.

Her father spoke from the house: "Daughter, wish you'd come pull off my boots."

"Yes," she said, and didn't move. Somehow and sometimes she knew she'd have to tell Phil about the rest of her evening with Tom Benteen, so that it would not be a secret standing between them. She hated deceit. But deeper than this was a faint fear of the memory of Benteen's kiss. The recurring thought of it could be a dangerous thing. She thought of it now and had no illusions about her own feelings. She had wanted the kiss, and had not regretted it, and this was the danger, this warmth that came back to her as she recalled how he held her in the swirling blackness of Fort Lowell.

"Dammit," complained Major Warren, "I can't go to bed with these things on, Eleanor."

"Yes," she said, and listened to the trumpet pouring the strong golden notes of tattoo across the parade.

Beyond tattoo Lily Marr stepped from the Mixler dobe and stood a moment to watch the far away glitter of the stars. Dust incense clung to the air, and heat rolled flat and cloying along the parade, and the few stray sounds of the post sank without echo into the overwhelming silence of the desert. Castleton and Eleanor went past, not noticing her. The sentry paced his post, back and forth. Tom Benteen appeared a moment in his lighted doorway, his high body indolently slouched. Lily Marr's eyes clung to him as long as he remained there. She lifted her arms and locked them across her chest, and after he threw his cigar into the dust, its lighted tip showering sudden sparks when it struck, and turned back into his quarters, Lily Marr slowly followed the walk around the quadrangle, her head bent down.

She had reached the corner near the bakery when a shadow moved away from the wall and a hand touched her arm. Jack Bean's voice said:

"Just a minute, Lily."

She was a strong-nerved girl. She turned without surprise or shock, pulled against the bakery wall by Bean's hand. She let his hand stay only a moment, afterwards pulling away with a strong resistance. Jack Bean began to speak, but stopped and turned into a taut shadow against the wall while the sentry paced by. He waited until the sentry was out of earshot; his voice was quick and soft and amused.

"Hell, I came through the guard line, right at the feet of one of those soldiers. If I was an Apache I'd have you out of here on a pony now."

"What you want?"

He said, "When I set out to do something, Lily, nothing can stop me. I told you I'd come back, didn't I? I'm going to kill that captain some day. I take nothing from any man, not me. And I'll do what I please, long as I live." He quit talking, waiting for her answer. She remained passive and unresponsive, until he had to speak again in a more aggressive voice, "Whut

174

were you a-goin' up to Summerton's ranch for?"

"To cook."

"I put a stop to that, didn't I? You never got there. Nor you never will. If you get up there, Lily, I'll burn the damn place down. You ain't goin' to be under any roof with another man. Maybe you don't want me—but if you don't it won't be anybody else, either. I'm tellin' you, Lily."

"Go on back to Tucson."

"Which is where you ought to be," he answered. "I can't be ridin' up this way all the time."

"Then don't come," she said. Both of them were silent again, waiting for the sentry to go by. Presently Jack Bean tried a different voice.

"Whut's a man got to do, Lily?"

"Do what you please. Why ask me?"

He said, sharp and suspecting, "There any men up here you're a-lookin' at?"

"What if I am?"

The indifference of her talk set him in a rage. "By God," he breathed, "I'll find 'em and I'll kill 'em. That captain?"

She said slowly, "No, not him. Though he could whip you any time. You don't like that, do you, Jack? You don't like anything above you. But there's lots of things bigger and lots of men better."

He said, "If you was a man I'd know what to do. It is plumb hard not to bat that damn pride out of your head. I set my mind on what I want, Lily, and I get it. I always have and I guess I always will. I'm goin' to trail you around Arizona. Every time you see a man you like I'm goin' to kill him. You'll change your mind. Or you'll be an old maid. Maybe you think I'm goin' to have the Territory laugh at Jack Bean for losin' his girl. No. I ain't. Because I'm goin' to make it too risky for another man to look at you."

She waited out his talk, clearly knowing how bitterly this wild, arrogant outlaw hated such unresisting indifference. It was the one thing he could not understand and could not fight. He said, more quietly:

"Lily, whut you want? I'll get it. Whut you want a man to do?"

Suddenly she moved against him and put her arms around his waist, locking her big strong fingers together. She called out, "Guard—guard!"

Jack Bean heaved backward, trying to reach her locked fingers and break her grip. He was cursing, he kept sliding along the wall, the challenge of the on-running guard coming to him. He couldn't catch her fingers and then, with other men rushing at the bakery, he put his forearm against her throat and shoved until she strangled for breath, still hanging to him. She knew he had the power to break her spine if she didn't let go. But he didn't use his strength, he didn't try; and then she understood more about him. The guard raced in and jammed the muzzle of his carbine into Jack Bean's flank. Stepping back, Lily was at once surrounded by soldiers. The sergeant of the guard swung a lantern forward and Castleton was here—and Benteen.

It was Benteen who lifted Bean's gun from the holster. He held it in his hand, watching the outlaw and watching Lily Marr who stood so composed through all this. Jack Bean's face was white and wild and the light of his eyes burned bitterly against Lily Marr who returned that glance with an iron calm that Benteen never forgot.

"Lieutenant," she said, "this is the man who held up the Summerton wagons."

Benteen studied her. He said, "You've changed your mind, Lily?"

"Yes."

Jack Bean's hat had fallen. Light made a strong shining on his yellow head, on the straining rage that marbled his half-handsome, reckless face. "Captain," he ground out, "I walked through your damned guard line like it wasn't there. I will walk out of your jail the same way. The army ain't big enough to hold me, and no man's big enough. Captain—"

He stopped his talk and his jealous eyes weighed Lily Marr and Benteen with a shrewd suspicion. Suddenly he laughed, quick and flat and dangerous. "I guess I got to take care of you, Captain. God knows I will."

"Put him in the guardhouse," said Benteen, and watched a pair of troopers catch Bean by the arms and swing him across the parade. Lily Marr remained and Castleton remained. Castleton stared at the girl, no trust on his face.

"Rather odd, Miss Marr. You should have done this last time. I don't understand."

"Never mind," interrupted Benteen.

Castleton jerked his head around, affronted by that blunt tone. His jaw made a stubborn cut against the night, black and bold. Benteen ignored him. Benteen kept studying Lily Marr, more and more moved by the serene calm she showed him. There were thoughts in her head that never got out and memories that darkened her eyes. There was a mystery about her she refused to explain; and yet out of her stillness glowed a character very real, very strong. This was what made Benteen soft with his talk.

"What do you want, Lily?"

"Leave him there," she said. "I will do what has to be done." She walked back toward the commanding officer's quarters.

Benteen turned and paced around the corner of the barrack and into the stable. Castleton's steady steps echoed behind him. A lantern swung down from a rafter, throwing a ghostly glow on Benteen. When he wheeled he found Castleton before him and he knew trouble was on the wing.

Castleton said, "When I am under your command in the field, Mr. Benteen, I will accept your orders. When I am in this post, not on duty, I will not have you giving me orders of any kind. I resent the remark you made in front of the Marr woman."

"Maybe," said Benteen, "it was unfavorable. I withdraw it."

"The meaning remains," retorted Castleton, "and your attitude remains. You have always indicated your dislike of me. A blind man could see it. The people in this post are not blind."

"I think," said Benteen, holding his talk to an even drawl, "you are looking for something that doesn't exist."

Castleton flung up his head and half shouted his challenge. "Don't beat around the bush!"

Light glinted across Benteen's sandy red hair, it painted flat shadows over his eyes. His lids dropped, half closing. The wind in his chest gently stirred the front of his gray shirt. His arms hung straight, heavy-knuckled and idle. "I guess," he said, "this is a good time to say what you want to say. Maybe it should have come out long ago. Go ahead."

"Fine" breathed Castleton, sarcasm in each rapid word. "Very fine, very magnanimous. I compliment you on your manners. They are most effective on rank and file. The Major admires your judgment and your discretion—or is it discretion, Mr. Benteen? The commissioned staff is charmed by the quality of your poker. The enlisted men applaud and imitate your soldierly virtues, which are most naturally unstudied—or are they unstudied, Mr. Benteen?"

"Go on," murmured Benteen. The shadowing in the wells of his eyes grew blacker. He raised one hand and softly rubbed his belt buckle.

Castleton's heavy shoulders rose at the corners. He

178

was solid, he was twenty pounds heavier than Benteen. Light laid its oily shine on his long and flushed face. His feet stirred restlessly on the hard-packed floor of the stable; his words rushed on rising unreasonably and unforgivably to the break.

"Maybe I'm not plain enough, Mr. Benteen. So I will be plainer. I do not see the gallantry in you that others appear to see. I do not like political lieutenants who curry the favor of their men by slack discipline. I do not believe your customary silence indicates profound wisdom, as Warren seems to think. Is that plain, Mr. Benteen? I think your caution in avoiding a fight with Antone is something else than caution. I think your transfer to this regiment is a mystery still in need of explaining, and—" He paused for a huge sweep of breath, measuring Benteen as if for attack, "I think you had better keep your damned leisure hours away from Eleanor."

"Through now?" said Benteen.

"Maybe," cried Castleton, "you still don't understand! This army is too small for both of us! Perhaps you want to do something about that!"

Benteen's lips rolled together and the silence ran on, hot and thick and bad. He dropped his arm from his belt. "Phil," he said, "you're an ass, full of conceit. I think I am going to beat hell out of you. I have wanted to do it for a mighty long while."

"Fine!" breathed Castleton, stepping back. "Fine. I propose to destroy your reputation as a fighter before we leave this stable."

This was the moment Sergeant Hanna intervened. Watching Castleton follow Benteen to the stable he had immediately followed as far as the corner of the barrack wall, there hearing the quarrel. Now he walked into the stable with a certain bland deference. He said, "Beg pardon, but I forgot to trim the wick on this lantern. 'Twill smoke up the place."

Benteen stood directly under the lantern, blocking Hanna's further progress; and so Hanna remained by the door, solemnly waiting. Castleton flung him a black, intolerant glance, and then looked around to Benteen who made no move. Castleton said, "I shall see you later, Lieutenant Benteen," and wheeled from the stable.

Benteen considered the face of this inscrutable, taciturn Hanna, understanding him completely. He said, "Hanna, was there any talk around here tonight? I thought you might have heard some."

"No, sor," drawled Hanna, "I niver heard a worrd."

Benteen nodded and walked out of the stable.

Chapter Thirteen

Captain Harrison brought his detail back from the hills, reporting no luck. The wear and tear of five days' scouting showed on him, on Lankerwell, and on the men. "It is," said Harrison, gratefully smacking his lemon-and-sugar flavored whisky, "a killing climate for a soldier dressed in wool clothes and carrying thirty pounds of equipment. Meanwhile Antone, stripped to moccasins and breechclout and a tailless shirt, travels like a shadow. We cut his trail, two or three days old. We never got any closer. Dura says he's shifted north."

Suddenly this blasting hot summer month the Apaches were alive in the Territory. The Chiricahuas came out of the Dragoons to disrupt the mail stage line. A prospector, with an arrow in his back, ran thirty miles through the Rincons, escaping only to die. All down the Santa Rita valley men were forted up in their small ranches. Half a dozen warriors crawled to the very margin of Tucson, killed a Mexican water carrier and raced back into the Catalinas. One afternoon, on the Santa Rita, a sheepherder lay in the partial shade of a paloverde, listening to the tinkle of the bellwether, thinking there could be no Apaches disturbing the flock as long as the bell continued to sound. He fell asleep, and woke, still hearing the jingle; but turning over he saw an Apache crouched ten feet away from him, holding the bell in his

181

hand, ringing it and grinning. The Mexican screamed and sprang up, racing for the distant ranch house. The men in the ranch house saw the Apache's lance pin the herder to earth.

Travel from Tucson to Prescott was cut off, no man caring to risk it except under heavy escort. Pete Kitchen's ranch was raided and his hogs filled with arrows, but Pete Kitchen held on. High on the Mogollon plateau the Tontos were active, closing the courier service between Camp Apache and Fort Whipple. There was a flurry at Date Creek, on the road to Ehrenburg. A stagecoach and six passengers, venturing out of Prescott, never reached McDowell. A trapper and his Indian wife were massacred in the White Tank Mountains. The mines closed; everybody withdrew from desert and hills, crowding the settlements. Down in the Huachucas, near the border, a Mexican rancher's boy was carried into captivity.

Every garrison in the Territory was active. Detachments scouted out of Lowell, north toward Camp Grant. Troops moved into Fort Bowie to guard the eastern gateway of the Territory. Detachments from Camp Apache, high in the hills, scouted southward toward Grant; Camp Verde and McDowell, out on the Salt, were little islands in a barren land.

As soon as Harrison came in, Major Warren put Benteen back in the field. Benteen found a fresh trail beyond the Gila and followed it until his rations gave out and his horses would stand no more; but he returned to Grant with definite knowledge Antone had shifted into the Sierra Anchas. Warren gave the next detail to George Mixler, who surprised an isolated rancheria and brought back a squaw and an elderly brave who said he would not have been caught if he were not tired of fighting. Howell Ford took the next detail; and after that, Harrison went out again.

Meanwhile, Major Warren had relieved Ray Lankerwell

as post adjutant to put him in the field, and named Phil Castleton adjutant. It was, Eleanor knew, her father's way of keeping Castleton in the post. He did not mean to trust Phil with another detail. She was too smart a girl to interfere with army routine and so kept her own counsel as the days wore on. Yet, walking around the quadrangle with Phil in the hot night shadows, she felt bitterness grow greater in him. He had a manner of concealing it, which was to smile more and to speak with a lightness close to insolence. But it was no concealment. By day he walked the post, stiff-shouldered and exact in his duties, keeping to the post headquarters office more than usual—even in the broiling midafternoon's heat. Once, passing by headquarters doorway she saw him seated by the desk. He had a book before him and appeared to be reading it, bent over with his hands supporting his head. She paused, expecting to draw his attention; and then she saw the sightless way he stared at the page and the nerve-drawn expression on his lips and the complete tightness of his shoulders. He wasn't reading; he sat there on the edge of some kind of a break. That afternoon she broke her long rule and spoke to her father.

"When will Phil's turn come again, Dad?"

"Ray Lankerwell served three months. I expect Phil will serve that long."

"Still, you sent Ray out even while he was post adjutant."

"Too much paperwork right now to let Phil go."

She said, "Of course that isn't the real reason."

Warren sat in the easiest chair to be had, loosely and uncomfortably. Heat turned his cheeks dye-red. He scowled through the haze of his cigar's smoke. "Daughter, don't be meddlesome. I raised you better."

She said, "I can't help it, Dad. You'll break him—you are setting him down in front of the camp."

Warren carefully judged her expression and found it hard to answer. He stirred around the chair. "One time," he murmured, "when I was a young fellow in the dragoons, I committed a very serious breach of discipline. I'm a fat man now, but at that time I was as high spirited as young Phil. I could have been cashiered for it. The colonel took my sword away from me and confined me to quarters for an entire summer. I used to watch the troops go out. I'd stand on the porch when they passed — and I knew what every man in that command thought of me. They thought I was a young fool. I got so I hated to cross the parade, or look another man in the face. Sometimes I wanted to hide, but I made myself stand in sight when those details left. Many's the time I thought of resigning, only I couldn't run that way. You don't know what kind of a hell that is, daughter. When I got my sword back and rejoined my troop I wasn't the same young man any more. I lost something. But it made a soldier out of me. It will do the same thing to Phil. Or he'll resign."

"No," she said, "he won't resign. That would be a terrible answer."

"Then let him eat part of his pride away," grumbled Warren. "He has too much of it. I'm sorry for any living thing that's got to destroy part of itself to survive. I'm sorry for any man who has to throw half his ambitions out the window. Maybe in civil life he could try to be Caesar. There is no place for a Caesar in the army." He put his cigar away and rose, not liking his thoughts. He paused before his daughter, older at this moment than she had noticed before — older and a little sadder. "I have stood by and watched poor officers rise above me and I have seen great officers march out their lives in one rank when they should have worn stars. I have seen bribery and favoritism and cheating. I have saluted men I knew to be scoundrels, I have seen officers rot away in some little sagebrush post while others wore gold braid in Washington, D. C., without reason. It is unfair, it is hard, it is brutal—but you've got to learn it, and do your duty as you set it and make that your one consolation. I can't talk to Castleton, and you can't. He's got to sit there and go through every damned bit of it alone. He'll be a great man if he does. He won't be anything you'd want if he doesn't. I don't know whether God hates a political general or a grandstand swashbuckler, but I do. And I cannot take the chance of sending him out with twenty men he'll lead to slaughter for the sake of ambition."

She said, "You don't like him, do you?"

He stopped in the doorway, carefully thinking of that. "Let's wait and see. In thirty days I shall either love him for being a man, or I shall hate him like hell for being a weak fool."

"In either event," she said, quite slowly, "he will be your son-in-law."

"You have always been a loyal girl, Eleanor. You are like your mother—you don't change."

After he had gone, Eleanor stood in the doorway, watching the doorway of post headquarters for sight of Castleton. Benteen came from officers' mess and strolled down the shade of the barrack's ramada. Eleanor watched his loose walk; she watched the way his sandy red hair tipped, she watched the way his long arms swung. He was very tall and, like most cavalry officers, slim at the hips. He wasn't a good-looking man, he wasn't spectacular, he had little of that terrific drive of energy possessed by Phil Castleton. And yet—these things kept going through her mind oddly—he was a figure that she watched with an interest that never flagged. His presence had a way of reassuring her, of binding her to him; he had, behind his silence and his easy-going patience, something that always lifted her heart. At the cor-

185

ral near the bakery shop he swung up and sat a moment while troopers led in a fidgeting horse; afterwards he slid inside the corral, waited for the troopers to snub the horse to a post, and then stepped into the saddle. Eleanor moved around in the doorway, watching the sudden furious boil of dust when the horse was released. She held her breath, she pressed her fingers against the dobe wall. When the horse quit bucking, she realized how still and intent she was, and turned back into the house. Cowen was in the kitchen. She said, "We're going to make up some apple pies for a party tonight, Cowen."

Lily Marr crossed the parade to the guardhouse and stood by the iron-grated door, coolly watching Jack Bean's face. He came forward and placed his hands around the bars. His long mouth cut a quick grin across his cheeks and then he laughed in a way that turned her eyes dark.

"Lily," he said, "I could have killed you last night. But now I got it figured out. You were sore last night. When a woman's sore she's got to love a man. That's why you had me put in here."

She said, "The United States marshal will be here next week. You're going to hang, Jack."

But his grin grew wider; he was sure of himself, he was pleased with her anger and he had no fear. "Lily, this place won't hold me long. When I get out I'll be around Tucson. I'll wait for you there."

"The guard stands in front of this door all night with orders to shoot. You're going to hang, Jack."

He said, "How long you figure to stay sore? What do you want from a man? You had your way—I reckon that ought to be enough. If it's money—" He lowered his voice. "Listen," he said, "have that captain take you back to Tucson today. The money from that wagon is in a coffeepot, on the kitchen shelf, in the old Aguirre house where I always stay. You find Bill Hanley and tell him

186

when the marshal figures to take me back to Tucson. Bill knows what to do. He'll wait in the Catalinas, by the trail."

Benteen, at this moment, was returning from the corral. Lily Marr beckoned to him and waited until he came up. She watched the grin fade from Jack Bean's face; dark and unstirred she watched doubt creep into his eyes, she watched the freshening shine of anger. She said, to Benteen, "He told me where the money is. It is in a coffeepot in the kitchen of the Aguirre house in Tucson. Everybody knows that house. The money belongs to the Summerton ranch. Tell them where it is."

Jack Bean's hands struggled against the iron bars. "Lily," he ground out, "you go too far with a man! I'll find out who gets that money! I'll kill Summerton if he touches it! I'll knock this damn dobe down! Captain, you keep your mouth shut if you expect to live. Damn a jealous woman—"

The guard came up with a tin plate of food and a tin cup of coffee. Lily's eyes followed his hand as it reached up to the high outside corner of the low roof and pulled down the jail key. He unlocked the door. Lily reached out and took the cup and the plate. With all these men watching her, she poured the coffee over the food. "Open the door," she said and when the guard obeyed her she stooped and slid the plate across the floor. The door slammed shut and was locked. Benteen's glance clung to Lily Marr's impassive face; he was trying to read the things in her eyes, on her lips. She stared at Jack Bean, cruelly unforgiving.

"Dogs eat off the floor, Jack. There's your meal."

She turned away, crossing back to the Mixler quarters. Mixler and Shiraz came out, with Shiraz saying some soft thing she didn't hear; and then the two men passed her, going toward the headquarters building. Swinging around, she saw them stop before Major Warren who had come to the door. She heard Mixler speak in a fatigued voice:

"Doctor Shiraz says it will be necessary for Harriet and sonny to get out of this heat. I should like your permission. She wants to go to Apache in the morning."

"Take an escort of six men, Mr. Mixler."

George Mixler lowered his head. He was silent a moment, both these other officers waiting. Then he said, "I believe she would prefer another officer, sir."

Warren spoke briefly: "Then Mr. Ford will accompany her. Does she wish to take all her luggage?"

"Yes sir," said Mixler dully. "She is not returning to Grant."

From her position under the ramada of the Mixler quarters, Lily Marr watched this passing scene, her eyes seeing so much that others would not see. She had this frontier vigilance. The baby was crying loud enough to turn George Mixler in his tracks. He stared at the dobe, caught by indecision, but finally went on with Shiraz toward the sutler's store. Major Warren traveled past her, breathing deeply. Benteen came from the corral and now her glance livened and followed him as he went down the barrack line. Nachee crouched in the shade and here Benteen stopped, also crouching; Al Hazel came up, the three of them holding, a tricornered parley, Nachee drawing patterns in the dust. The baby kept on crying, with Harriet Mixler's voice, low and exhausted and desperate, trying to soothe it, but for a moment longer Lily Marr watched Benteen. Her lips sweetened and stirred and a prettiness came to her dark face. At last she turned into the Mixler dobe, lifted the baby from its wet bed and cradled it in her arms. She walked the room, softly murmuring, "So—so—so." Harriet Mixler lay on the bed with her face turned to the ceiling; it was set and gray. She said, "You'd make a better mother than me, Lily."

Lily Marr said, gently: "What else is a woman for?"

188

After retreat and guard mount, the officers of the post, save for Ray Lankerwell who was on scout, sat down to Eleanor Warren's supper. The oysters were out of a can long saved for a particular occasion, the fresh corn straight from Tucson and still on the cob, the coffee strong in the way all soldiers like it—and the pie a last little touch of drama. Captain Harrison, an honest epicure, considered this pie in some surprise, took his first taste and slapped his hand on the table: "Where in God's name did you get the apples, Eleanor?"

"That was my mother's recipe when supplies got down to nothing. Apple pie without apples. You make a crust. You soak soda crackers until they are soft, season them with cinnamon and lemon extract—and there is your filler. If you're really hungry it does taste like apples."

"Ah," applauded the captain, "you're a fine cook. A woman makes an awful difference to a man. It took me a long time to find that out—and now it is too late. You are very lucky, Phil."

Eleanor said, "Lucky to have the woman or to have the cook?"

Phil surprised her. He lifted his wine glass and he was smiling. "For the woman," he said. Coming from him it was so unexpectedly gallant that she blushed. Her father gave Castleton a quick look. Benteen's chin lifted, as though his drifting interest had been arrested; and for a moment there was a silence. She had her moment of genuine fear then that the silence would change Phil back to what he had been, that he could not carry it off before those weighing eyes. For she knew what was in the minds of these men. Their opinions regarding Phil had already been formed and were not easily changed; this was what he faced. But he kept smiling as he looked around at them. He met their eyes and his voice was quite easy:

"For the woman, for Eleanor."

189

Harrison kicked back his chair at once and they all rose, bowed to her and drank. She was not an outwardly emotional girl and yet the rush of feeling in her, so strong and so grateful, made her drop her head; she was that near to crying. "You are all," she murmured, "very proper gentlemen."

They were still standing. Tom Benteen looked down at Lily Marr. He smiled at her, a deep-lying interest in the smile. "To Lily, as well." So they drank again and waited—and it was George Mixler who added, so quietly, "To my wife." Thus they finished and moved back from the table and lighted their cigars. All of them kept to their chairs except Benteen who moved around the room, touched by restlessness. The old, slanting expression was on his face again—a faintly ironic color to his eyes. Eleanor listened to her father's slow talk, her worried attention meanwhile remaining with Phil Castleton. Yet she was aware of Benteen and when he stopped by the doorway her glance went at once to him, wondering if he meant to leave. He slouched against the edge of the door, all loose and lank. His head turned and he met her glance and held it until she felt something in his head, as definite as speech. She brought her glance away.

Her father said, "This outbreak has just about tied up the Territory. I am not too pleased with our tactics. I think the Indians all through the country have been encouraged by Antone's success. I do not know how long we can keep on his trail without needing fresh horses."

Harrison said, "How in hell can the government expect to police a section twice as big as New England with four scattered regiments of cavalry?"

"The thing that defeats us," considered Warren, "is Antone's mobility. It is like catching a shadow. If it were possible to surprise or surround him I should take the whole force out tomorrow—"

Benteen spoke from the doorway. "Nachee says Antone is wearing down."

Castleton spoke up, not quite able to conceal his suspicion. "How does Nachee know?"

"The last warrior Ford brought in talked to Nachee. Antone is apt to stop pretty soon and make a fight, out of necessity. Or else he will lose his authority among the people he leads. They are getting tired of traveling. So he'll have to make medicine. Only medicine he can make is an attack."

The hour call was then running from sentry to sentry, all those voices level and strong in the hot dark. The guard at number one post challenged through the night. They heard Ray Lankerwell answer, "Officer and detail."

"Halt, officer and detail. Corpr'l of the guard, post number one!"

Presently the clatter of the guard detail rose on the parade and there was a soft, perfunctory exchange of words; and the scuff of the inbound detail. The men in the room rose, anxious to have the news; and afterwards Benteen stepped back from the doorway to let Ray Lankerwell come in. Alkali dust whitened Lankerwell's uniform and clung like dry flour paste to his sunscorched cheeks. His eyelids were puffy and his lips cracked; his voice was husky, his shoulders sagged with a genuine fatigue.

He saluted the major. "Reporting back from detail, sir. We cut a fresh trail in the Pinals and followed as long as we could. Antone is shifting rather slowly through the hills, not inclined to give much ground. I sighted his party in an extremely rough location, at the bottom of a canyon, but could not come up to attack. He had his women and children along. There was a large number all told—fifty or sixty, I should think."

Warren said, "Join us, Mr. Lankerwell, when you have freshened up."

191

Lankerwell left the room and Benteen resumed his position by the door, staring at the dark parade. His long fingers drummed on the dobe wall, which was a key to his frame of mind. Eleanor, never quite getting him out of her thoughts, watched these rising signals of restlessness. All the other officers had turned to Warren and were silent, knowing that he would be coming to some kind of a decision. Warren nursed his cigar at considerable length, his round ruddy cheeks gravely established; and then Benteen turned, as if waiting for something he was certain would come. Major Warren removed his cigar: "All right, Mr. Benteen. We will try it."

Benteen left the room at once, his voice singing over the parade. "McSween."

Major Warren rolled the cigar between his fingers, very conscious of the continuing silence. Eleanor noticed the way his words seemed to trouble him when he spoke. "Mr. Benteen suggested a plan to me yesterday. There is a pattern in Antone's travels, a kind of general retracing of his trails. We are wearing him down, but it is also true he is wearing us down. It is noticeable that he does not break away from these last few details as quickly as he did with the first ones. He grows a little more careless, apparently believing we will not close in. Mr. Benteen goes out tonight, with Al Hazel and Nachee. He proposes to sight Antone and to send the detail back. He will remain on scout with Al Hazel and Nachee, and one or two extra troopers. He will follow Antone, dropping his troopers back on the trail as he goes, as couriers. At that time I shall take the command out."

Harrison said, "The young man will find himself exceedingly lonely company in the middle of those hills, the damned savages creeping all about him. Does he hope to keep out of sight?"

"There is some danger," admitted Warren "However, Mr. Benteen has an aptitude for this type of campaign-ng. He has studied it very carefully and knows as much about Indian habits as any officer in Arizona. Al Hazel has much confidence in him, which is considerable recommendation. And he has been able to get more information from Nachee than any other man. Otherwise, I should not permit the risk."

Lanterns swung brightly along the parade and Sergeant McSween's voice was solidly insistent. There was a racket in the stables, a forming blackness in the shadows. A man shouted, "Conway—where's Conway?"

The officers drifted out to watch and to listen. Eleanor put her hand through Castleton's elbow and stood with him beneath the ramada. Suddenly she wanted to hear him speak, to know what was in his mind. For her father had given Benteen a free hand, which was more than he had given any other officer in the post; and in so doing he had shown a greater confidence in Benteen than in the rest of the officers. All of them knew it as they stood here. The knowledge was in Castleton's mind, undoubtedly rubbing against his injured pride, burning away some of his tremendous faith in himself, building up his resentment. And still he remained silent. She pitied him then for all he was going through, sharing his hurt, proud of the way he had so far this evening covered it up, and drawn closer to him by it. Her hand tightened on his elbow.

The troop was forming line, Sergeant McSween's deep voice pushing at it. George Mixler suddenly detached himself from the group and crossed to Benteen who stood by his horse. Mixler said, "Tom, you're a hell of a fine soldier. I wish you all the luck. Go say good-by to Harriet. She thinks a lot of you."

Benteen laid his long arm across Mixler's shoulder. "George," he said, "have you said everything to her you could say? She's had a bad time. Remember that."

"No," murmured George Mixler, "I can't change her

193

mind. She won't listen."

Benteen turned to the Mixler quarters, ducking hi
head at the low doorway. Lily Marr sat in the rear room
rocking the crackerbox cradle; and Harriet lay on th
bed. Her eyes came around to Benteen, the stony memo
ries fading out of them and a pleased expression soften
ing her lips. Lily Marr saw this, and saw the wa
Benteen's face relaxed into a man's frank appreciation o
a woman; Lily Marr at once rose and quietly left th
dobe.

"Harriet," said Benteen, "you won't be here when
come back. Isn't this post dull enough without your leav
ing and making it duller?"

She took his hand and held it, tightly, as though want
ing his support. "Tom," she whispered, "I'm never com
ing back."

He looked at her, light running along the tanned sid
of his face, and he nodded, as though he knew all tha
she felt. "Tough on you and on the boy," he said. "It'
wise for you to go up to Apache and get out of the heat
As for going any farther away than that—it is your prob
lem alone. You'll be running away. What from, Harriet
Better be sure it is something you won't want any more
A man and a woman go through a lot the first year o
two. It is something you'll remember later—and no othe
man will mean just the same to you. It is a hard countr
and the army's a hard life. On all of us, Harriet. An
you are giving George the worst bump a man can get
But Lord bless you. Be a good girl."

She had tears in her eyes. She whispered, "His name i
Tom George Mixler." Her hand pulled him down and he
hands went around his neck, and she kissed him. He re
mained in this awkward shape a moment, touched by th
lost and lonely feeling that was in her. But he drew bacl
smiling, and ran a finger through a ringlet of her hai
"You're thinking of the fun you had as a girl. You'll g

194

ack and try to be that girl again. But you'll find that ime's gone. You're an officer's wife with alkali in your blood. Wait and see."

He turned out at once, disturbed by the forlorn look on her face, and found Lily Marr waiting beneath the black-shadowed ramada. He had put on his hat but he took it off again. "Lily," he said, "what are you going to do with Jack Bean?"

She was a strong shape in the dark, her shoulders squared toward him and the round oval of her face vaguely shining up to him. She didn't answer his question. She let the silence ride a long while and then murmured, "Be careful of yourself," and turned into the adobe.

Benteen walked directly to the cluster of officers, shaking hands with them. Major Warren said, "It is entirely your discretion, Mr. Benteen. My best wishes." Over on the parade the detail counted off, those voices harking sharply into the soft desert stillness. He came before Castleton, for a moment undecided and uncertain—and wishing to make no scene. But it was odd the way Castleton put out his hand. Everybody was listening. Castleton's voice, cordial as it had never been before, said, "Run him down, Tom. I shall cheerfully admit you the better man if you do."

Benteen murmured, "A generous thought," and later felt the light pressure of Eleanor's hand. She didn't speak and he could not see her face; and he had nothing in his mind then that he could safely say, and so turned back to the detail, swung to his horse and took Sergeant McSween's report. Al Hazel drifted out of the shadows with Nachee. Benteen said, "Right by twos, harch!" The column broke into motion, wheeled by the commanding officer's house, and passed into the dark. Thus Benteen left Camp Grant behind him, heading toward the gap of Aravaipa Creek in the east. The black mountain mass

195

hovered before him and the bright stars lay crystal-scat
tered across the endless heavens.

Eleanor held Castleton's arm while the other officer
moved away, her father into the house, Harrison an
Ford toward the sutler's store for their habitual nightcap
Lankerwell came up and entered the house to see he
father. She was alone with Castleton.

"Phil," she said, "I'm very proud of you. And ver
grateful."

"For what?" he said in a guarded voice.

"For being all that I thought you were. You mad
friends tonight — friends you never had before."

The light from the dobe came out and touched then
both. She turned her chin upward, eager to hear his an
swer. He was smiling and he seemed amused, but in th
depths of his eyes she saw something that cut her plea
sure; it was a hot, stung expression that he could not en
tirely hide. He said, "If that is the way the game i
played, Eleanor, I guess I can play it."

"A game? Wait, Phil —"

"Or whatever it is," he said, and walked away.

She put her shoulder against a post supporting the ra
mada, watching his shape sink into the night. For a mo
ment she had the strong impulse to call him back and t
hold him with her arms and reassure him, in the hop
that it would change him back to the way he had been a
the supper table. He was, she realized, going throug
torment; the misery of it swayed him from side to sid
until he was as unstable as sand. It hurt her to think o
him this way; it troubled her and brought on a fain
doubt that disturbed her loyalty.

The last echoes of Benteen's detail died in the night
The moon-shot blackness closed down and the deser
stillness closed down and mystery trembled in windles
air and the post seemed drained of life. This, she realize
in some surprise, was the way it always was to her whe

196

enteen left. Some sureness and some pleasure and some
eeply satisfying part of her life left with him. There
ere, she thought with a growing unease, secret impulses
her that would not answer to reason and would not be
ppressed; for now the memory of Benteen, his voice
d his smile and his arms around her, was uncontrolla-
y near and real. It struck her this suddenly and would
ot go, and left her ashamed of the power it had over
er will. In a way it was like hunger. She turned quickly
to the house, and began to talk to Ray Lankerwell,
eeding this distraction to stop her thoughts.

Cowen walked into the sutler's store and showed the
utler a face gripped by gloom. "If I was ten years youn-
r, now, I'd be in that detail. What is a man to think of,
ashin' pots and pans after a life like I've had? Give me
quart of whisky, Bell."

The sutler said, "A quart, Cowen?"

"For mince pie—I am going to make a mince pie."

"Where," asked Bell, "did you get the mincemeat?"

"Ah," said Cowen mysteriously, paid for the whisky
d walked out. He hugged the bottle under his arm,
ailing completely around the parade and coming at last
the bakeshop. He slipped into the bakeshop's back
oom, uncorked the bottle and put it in the middle of the
ble. He drew a chair to the table, sat down and crossed
is arms and stared at the bottle with his black brows
eetling above his eyes.

"Now," he said, "ye smoke o' Satan, it is high time we
ad this out. The temptation is on me, and we will wres-
e. Drink is a curse. It rots a man's mind and dulls his
ner sensibilities, it brings on cancer and the man in
cotland said it shriveled all the flesh from his stomach.
rink—"

Half an hour later Cowen stepped from the bakeshop,

walked stolidly into the parade. He halted there, clutched the bottle by its neck and threw it far away from him. He said, "Ah," and belched splendidly and opened his mouth, suddenly howling, "Apaches—Apaches! Hey guard—Apaches! I see the devils right here!" There was a rush of feet along the parade and the yell of the sentry on Post Four. Lights sprang up around the quadrangle and Howell Ford, officer of the day, ran from headquarters. Cowen braced his feet apart, swayed like a tall tree in a heavy wind and fell flat on his face. As the sentry on Post Four ran up he heard Cowen say, deep in the dust, "Let go my legs, you red murderers! Let go my legs!"

Chapter Fourteen

Beyond midnight they camped in the rough country
rtheast of Grant. In the first water-clear light of the
llowing morning they saw smoke signals spiral up in
e distance, to be repeated on another peak. Benteen
oke to Al Hazel. "Ask Nachee what that is."

Al Hazel asked it and listened to Nachee's brief reply.
Ie says it is a warning that we are here. They have seen
”
.

"Antone's band must be split again. Which one is An-
ne?"

Al Hazel did the interpreting. Nachee considered the
10ke signals a long while and shrugged his shoulders,
eaking. "He thinks maybe it is the one in the north,"
id Al Hazel.

"In the Mescals. That's the way we'll go. I want them
know where we are aiming."

They ate bacon and hardtack—the hardtack fried in
e bacon grease—and bitter black coffee and went on,
rding the Gila and entering the rough country beyond

They followed the broken slopes of the Mescals, dip-
ng from canyon to ridge, and camped that night with a
ne-shaped peak of the Pinals directly facing them.
1at day they crossed numerous tracks. Nachee said,
rough Al Hazel, "There has been a raid somewhere.
1ese are Antone's men coming back to the Pinals. You
ill find Antone in there, maybe. He will have Chirica-

huas with him." After supper, as dark rolled quick an
moon-luminous across the hills, Nachee pulled up th
folded leggings of his moccasins and faded out of th
camp.

"That," said Al Hazel, "is what an Injun loves. 1
crawl and prowl, soft as a snake. Nachee's been peacef
so damned long he's gettin' restless. So he's just havi
some fun. Note that look in his eyes when he left? Shin
like the eyes of a cat switchin' its tail and thinkin' abou
trouble."

The day had been long and hot and dusty; and no
the murmuring of the troopers fell soon away and th
camp turned silent beneath the stars, with no soun
breaking it save the grind of the sentry's feet against th
rough soil. Benteen scraped out a hollow for his hip
pillowed his head on the saddle and watched the coun
less sweep of stars in the sky. Somebody stirred amon
the sleeping men and, rising on an elbow, Benteen sa
van Rhyn crouch over the round, dull-shining remnant c
the cook fire. Van Rhyn's face, dully illumined, was ol
and slack-fleshed and gripped by memories that woul
not let him sleep. Lying back on his blanket, Benteen fe
his kinship with all these men; and knew what was i
their minds and in their hearts. They would be remem
bering the broken pattern of their lives, and chance
gone, the ambitions still unfulfilled or no longer to b
hoped for, the faces of women shining out of the pa
and the voices of women, crying or angered or in laugh
ter; the color and the heat of certain high moments tha
once experienced, would be warm to them as long as li
held; the mistakes that now woke a silent groaning, th
memory of barroom brawls that made them tighten thei
muscles and feel strong. Awake, they would be remem
bering all these things and they would be feeling a hun
ger for something they could not name; in sleep all thi
would follow them through incomplete dreams.

These were his men. He knew them, because he knew himself. The memories were his, the hunger was his, and his also was the sense of some great adventure passing him by while he grew old in the dust and the common day.

It was in these hours when he couldn't keep physically busy that the recollections of his own life were so vivid and keen. He thought now, as he had in most hours of the past five years, of Lucy Beauregard, recapturing the inflections of her voice and the quickness of her up-slanting glance. Most of his life since had been influenced by the constant picture she made in his mind. Then—and this was a new turn of thinking for him—he recalled what Eleanor Warren had told him he must do. The memory of a woman in the past was a feeble light to a man; either the woman had to be found again, or forgotten completely. He recalled the softness of Eleanor's face as she had said it; and felt now the nearness of her body as it had been at Fort Lowell, and the gentle strike of her laughter in the dark. So thinking he fell asleep.

Deep in the rough Pinals the following morning they came upon a fresher trail. Antone's scattered people had collected and were traveling ahead of him. A canyon struck into the northeast, deepening and darkening and growing narrower as the surrounding terrain lifted toward a prominent peak. At the canyon he stopped and sent out small scout parties; around noon, with these parties returned, he still had no complete story, and so took the detail along the southern edge of the canyon for a matter of seven or eight miles. Occasionally the print of an unshod hoof came out of the south and dipped into the canyon, this happening often enough to indicate some gathering of Apaches on the north side, in the direction of the peak. Deciding this much, he found a trail into the canyon. Nachee scouted its gravelly bottom and shook his head, speaking to Al Hazel, who interpreted.

"Not this way. Up beyond, on the high land."

They spent an hour finding a narrow ledge leading them out of the canyon to the north side, and within the next hour cut a definitely fresh series of tracks. The way still was northeast toward the high peak. All the surrounding country was badly broken, rock shelter upon rock shelter, and parallel ridges separated by difficult ravines. Pines studded the land, and cactus and catclaw and thin-scattered forage grass. In the middle of the afternoon Benteen, searching for just such a location, halted the detail on a ridge top that had a rocky outcrop around it, affording considerable shelter from all directions. In here he was high enough in the hills and deep enough behind the rocks to be concealed from the scouting eyes of the Apaches. The detail threw off for a rest while Benteen studied his pocket map. Nachee began to draw pictures on the ground with a sage stem, speaking to Al Hazel.

Al Hazel said, "He thinks Antone will be on that peak all right. There's a natural park up there and a lot of mesquite beans. Also a spring. But the country leading to it is pretty tough for an attack. Nachee says he lived there as a boy—sometimes hiding out from the Tontos when they came down on their raids."

Benteen showed Hazel the map. "If Antone keeps on traveling it is not apt to be east. That brings him too close to Fort Apache. As soon as this detail pulls back to Grant I'd guess Antone will do one of three things. He'll stay on that peak to rest, or go on north across the Salt and into the Mazatzal Range, or do as he had been doing before—come back this way. I think it is a decent guess. Ask Nachee."

Nachee listened to Hazel, studied on it, and answered. Hazel said, "He thinks Antone will drift back this way, to show his warriors he is not afraid. And also to dig up mescal they've probably got baking in pits around here."

"This is what we do," decided Benteen. "McSween takes the detail back to Grant. Antone's scout will see him go. But you and Nachee and I stay here. When dark comes we'll move on and do a little scouting. The idea is to keep track of Antone's movements until Major Warren comes up with the complete detachment."

He took a sheet of paper from his pocket and a pencil, and wrote this note to Warren:

Sir: By the enclosed map I indicate where we are, and where Antone probably is. If Antone comes back this way, we shall meet you when your column comes up. If Antone shifts ground we shall follow, but I shall detail Nachee as a connecting link to bring you on to our new location. Should Antone retreat farther it will quite probably be toward the Mazatzals. In this case, according to our tentative plan, I think it would be wise to send part of a troop straight north, by night march, cross the Salt and sweep around the northern base of the Mescals to intercept any such shift, the main command meanwhile marching directly to this point. O'b'tly, T.C. Benteen.

He folded the note and handed it to McSween. McSween waggled a finger at the troopers, who rose from the earth and were ready to travel. But McSween nursed his black mustaches with the back of his hand, reluctant to go. "Lieutenant," he said, " 'tis a hell of a country for three men to stray in. Should ye not keep a few more here?"

"Good luck, McSween," said Benteen.

"Ah, that," responded McSween. "I think I'll leave all my luck here—for 'tis you that will be needin' it."

The detail swung up and passed back through the rocky fissures of the ridge, soon dropping downgrade.

From his position, Benteen watched them sink deeper and deeper toward the canyon until the double file was at last lost to his restricted sight. Just before fading in the rough country McSween turned to look back, not waving—for that would have been a betraying gesture—but holding himself around in the saddle until he disappeared.

Nachee squatted in the center of the area, staring at Benteen; and suddenly he spoke to Hazel, asking an obvious question. Hazel answered, whereupon Nachee grunted a thoughtful answer. Hazel grinned at Benteen. "He wanted to know what we were doing. I told him."

Nachee shook his head and spoke through Al Hazel. "Antone is a fox, Nantan."

This was midafternoon with a violent sun blasting the ridge top and its few scattered pines. Benteen pulled the three horses to the center of the bowl, which was its deepest part, in order to keep them well out of sight; and the three men posted themselves about the rocky outcrop, thus commanding a view of the surrounding land. There was no higher ridge within three or four miles of this spot and the rising basaltic rim which surrounded the bowl concealed horses and men from the lower land.

Somewhere near five o'clock Benteen, looking northward through a crack in the rocks, thought he saw a blur of motion on the adjoining ridge, something that slipped from one cactus clump to another. He called Nachee over. Nachee laid his eyes on that far spot for a full five minutes, never turning a muscle; then he said, through Hazel, "A small deer, Nantan."

Al Hazel said, "A deer now, but it will be Injun later. Antone knows the detail is on the way home. He'll be scoutin' this country." He repeated it in the Apache tongue; and Nachee said:

"They are close by now."

Nachee had turned away from the rocks and now

crouched on the earth, staring at the sky with his eyes half closed, as though keening the dead hot air. The tail of his shirt hung between his stringy legs, his arms lay idle across his knees and there was on his face a complete muscular stillness. Nachee was in his fifties and small of stature as most Apaches were; yet his cheeks were as smooth as Benteen's and in his eyes a clear vitality glowed. His hair, held by a single strip of red calico across the forehead, showed as black as a crow's coat.

The sun dipped westward. When it touched the ragged rim of the hills its livid-red ball seemed to break like the yolk of an egg, spilling out against the domes and spires and rough-cut summits of the Pinals. Light flashed in a thousand sharp splinters along the sky, creating a fan-shaped aurora against the upper blue; and then as suddenly as this spectacular burst showed, it faded and the blueness of twilight trickled down the canyon slopes. The far ridge lines, which Benteen watched quite closely, grew vague before his eyes. Hot silence had covered this summit all day but now, in twilight, the stillness seemed greater—so great that the staccato beat of a woodpecker came in rocketing waves out of the distance. Nachee came off his haunches and walked to the far end of the bowl, crouching beside a break in the rocks.

Beyond this break the land fell sharply to the west. Al Hazel, watching Nachee with a particular interest, came from his station to the horses. He stood with his hand on the nose of his own horse. Benteen dropped back to Hazel.

"He sees somethin'," said Hazel.

Benteen ducked over to the rocks, lying against them with his head pushed against a crack. He discovered nothing, though he swept the cactus-scattered slope carefully. He looked across to Nachee, noting how taut Nachee's body was; Nachee was on one knee, the other foot pushed behind him and ready to shove. He had one hand dropped to the handle of his knife. Scanning the slope again, Benteen saw an Indian rise from a mescal clump and come up.

He walked at a low crouch, his head bent toward the earth. Once he whipped straight, staring at the summit. Then he dropped his head again, and advanced, now near enough for Benteen to hear the small abrasion of his moccasins on the gravelly soil. Twenty feet from the edge of the rocks where Nachee lay, the Indian again halted and this time seemed to smell trouble. He went to his knees, his hands propped against the earth like a runner about to rush forward; and this position he held for a long half-minute without stirring. The slope was steep enough to cut the sight of the bowl; nor could he see the horses in its bottom. On all fours he crawled another two yards and flattened completely on the ground. At this moment Nachee moved.

Nachee sprang forward between the rocks with his arm whipping up over his head. The Indian on the earth came straight up and lunged at him; Nachee's knife hit him in the chest—the sound of it dull and distinct in the silence—and drove through the Indian's lungs. The Indian made one wild shout that raced cleanly clear across the hills, dropped his hands and fell at Nachee's feet. His body rolled a little way back down the hill, lodging against a boulder.

Nachee reached down and wiped the blade against a grass clump and trotted back to the bowl. Al Hazel came up, speaking to Benteen. "That's bad. They could hear that Injun four miles away." He talked to Nachee a minute and waited for Nachee's calm reply. Then he translated the answer for Benteen.

"Nachee says that Injun knew we were here. He knew it when he fell on his stomach. We got to pull out of here."

Nachee pointed to the dead Indian. "Chiricahua—not

Aravaipa. Plenty Chiricahuas with Antone, maybe, Nantan."

The three walked to their horses. The last daylight had gone; the half-moon flushed a pale indistinct glow against all the black edges of the surrounding ridges. At this elevation a breath of cooling wind came with the night, immensely relieving after the long ordeal of the sun. Benteen took a short drink from his canteen while Nachee spoke to Hazel.

Hazel said, "He thinks we ought to go on without the horses. They make too much track. If Antone's scouts come across the tracks they'll find us before tomorrow is far along."

"How far is it to that peak where Antone is?"

" 'Bout twelve-fifteen miles."

Benteen thought about it. "Too long a walk. We'd be dragging around the country all night, no telling where Antone goes meanwhile. We've got to get near him. We'll keep the horses and take the chance. Tell Nachee to aim for the peak."

Hazel gave the order to Nachee who grunted, "Enju," and climbed on his horse. They left the bowl, traveled down the slope and fell into a black trough between ridges, pointing due east at the high coned shape of that peak where Antone seemed to be. The footing was gravelly and they made a distinct racket as they traveled; yet Nachee apparently preferred this to the softer earth for somewhere farther on he turned into another creek bed, followed this until it dwindled out, climbed over a low ridge and took to still another gravel course, so advancing eastward by a kind of right-angled in-direction which ate up considerable time. At midnight, from a high point, they sighted the tall peak again. It lay now in the south. Nachee had cut a wide circle.

He had also brought them upon a shallow trickle of water in the rocks. Stopped to drink and rest, Benteen estimated the time to elapse before the troops from Grant could come up.

"McSween will get back tomorrow noon. Major Warren will probably start out that night. By a straight march he ought to reach the meeting place day after tomorrow morning. Thirty hours. Not long."

"Long enough," said Al Hazel, "if those devils get to smellin' us."

"That's why we can't try it afoot. Should Antone start back through the hills we've got to keep to his trail."

"Ain't as bad as tryin' to fill to a pair of deuces," said Hazel, dryly, "but still it is considerable of a try. You got a level head, Lieutenant, or I sure wouldn't be out here now." He was lying on the ground. Suddenly he heaved himself erect with a quick outlet of violent profanity and began slapping his clothes. "Damnation. I been sittin' on an anthill."

He kicked around the darkness, making considerable noise, and came back to Benteen, his tone somewhat shamed. "I'll spit in the eye of a diamondback any time and I have shook a lot of centipedes outa my blankets. But them damned ants give me the creepin' twitters, ever since Long Jack Bell's time."

"Never heard of him."

"My partner, back in '65. This was a pretty empty country then. We used to prospect clear up tords the Mokyones. Wasn't any troops around here and the Injuns had chased all the Mexicans into Tucson. It was a bad time, for fair. We was over in the Basin, Jack and me, knowin' better than to be there but havin' a hell of a good time, just trappin' and prospectin', when up comes a band of Tontos and jumps our camp. That's pretty rough country. I got away and hid in a hole in the rocks. But they caught Long Jack and had some fun of their own. I guess I was half a mile away but I sure heard him holler till he couldn't holler no more. You understand,

208

Lieutenant? Jack was no hollerin' man, but he did then. They beat the country for me and didn't find me—and pulled out. I crawled back to where the camp had been and saw whut was left of Jack. They'd cut off his eyelids and staked him over an anthill, facin' the sun. The ants sure took care of Jack. Never had much use for an ant since then. Never had much use for a Tonto, either. Which they know. I been huntin' them fer seven years and they been huntin' me. So far the best o' the bargain's been mine, but I sure can figure better places for old Al Hazel to be right now than here."

"How'd you get out of that fight?"

"Crawled back to a minin' camp, which was about eighty miles away."

"Crawled?"

"The walkin' wasn't good," said Hazel. "One of those Tonto bullets busted my laig."

They went on in the first hours after midnight, falling into the canyons and arroyos crisscrossing these hills, and climbing back to ridge tops from which they took their bearings on the tall peak. Presently they came to the black crack of a canyon whose walls dropped sheer to an unknown depth, whereupon Nachee followed the rim until he found a thin crevice for a trail and led them to the bottom. A creek boiled against the rocks, apparently shutting off passage. Nachee, who had been aiming for this spot all night, took at once to the water and kept to it for a tedious mile or more, winding with the rocks and leading the horses breast-deep through occasional pools. Later they ascended a risky trail, reached the canyon's other rim and came at last to a pine flat, beyond which the land rose again.

Nachee spoke to Al Hazel, who relayed the talk to Benteen. "Not far now. We leave the horses here."

Benteen followed Al Hazel afoot across the soft under-footing of the pine flat. Now and then Al Hazel stopped, putting back a hand to warn Benteen. In these intervals Nachee slipped away, was gone, and came back without the least sound, to lead them forward again. They crossed the flats and reached the foot of a short slope, once more halting. Al Hazel's tobacco-scented breath fanned Benteen's face. "Up there. Be a little careful whar you step."

They faded against the earth, climbing on all fours and halting to listen and climbing again across the cacti and stony soil. Benteen eased his weight against his arms, placing each boot toe gently; he laid his palm against the scratchy body of a horned toad, and in jerking back almost lost his balance. One pine tree stood on the summit above him, vaguely traced against the star-glittering sky. At intervals he saw Al Hazel's rump rise and go on and fall. This was the way they traveled, foot by foot, along the last piece of that grade, and finally reached the crown of the hill and stopped and lay side by side, flat to the earth with their heads hooked over a roll of land.

The Indian camp lay slightly below them in a natural clearing, a hundred feet on. The remnant of a fire glowed round and red in the clearing's center. About it were the scattered shape of sleeping figures and the outline of Indian camp utensils and horse packs. The horses were in a bunch beyond the fire, identified by the occasional sneeze and stir of their browsing. One figure slipped in from the dark, crouched over the fire a moment, and cupped his hands, as though eating something. And as he did so a voice came from all those rolled-up shapes, a white man's loud, half-desperate and half-defiant voice:

"If I had one arm free, you godblasted red wolf, I'd sure take my chances on runnin' fer it."

Benteen's head jerked upward; he heard Al Hazel's sweep of surprised breathing. The Indian at the fire didn't turn, didn't pay attention. But at the same time another Indian crossed the clearing and came by the fire. He stopped and kicked one of those shapes—the white man's shape—with a full swing of his leg and walked out of the firelight again, coming straight toward this rise of ground where Benteen lay.

Chapter Fifteen

As soon as McSween returned to Grant with the detail, Major Warren sent for Captain Harrison.

"Both troops will prepare to leave tonight with rations for a week and a pack train to carry extra ammunition. After the column pulls out Mr. Lankerwell will split off with twenty men from K and go straight north, circling the Mescals. I want all equipment and horses carefully inspected. Leave behind nothing but a skeleton guard. We will take all the officers. Sergeant Oldbuck will remain here in charge of the post until Mr. Ford returns from Apache. We march at dark."

Captain Harrison left and presently the long sultry quiet of the post gave way to a brisk activity. Men overhauled their boots and belts, replenished their canteens, drew rations for the march and, in many instances, wrote long-deferred letters home. Some of them, according to common custom, made oral wills, disposing of their belongings to this bunkmate or that friend—and arranging for certain other trinkets and valuables to be shipped home in event of death. It was all part of the routine preceding a march into Indian country; for every man knew Major Warren intended to bring on a fight if it were possible and they also knew, through the returned McSween, that Benteen had sighted Antone. The troopers had tremendous faith in Benteen. If he had sighted Antone and planned to keep him under observation until Warren arrived, it was pretty good proof that a fight was at hand.

Coming back from the stables in the middle of the afternoon, Harry Jackson found van Rhyn crosslegged on the adjoining bunk, sorting out his personal effects—a few old letters, a picture cut from a magazine, some clippings from a newspaper, a tintype of a small girl, and a gold wedding ring. These he had folded into a handkerchief, and now twisted the ends of the handkerchief together. He called Harry Jackson's attention to the handkerchief as he pushed it under the head of his straw mattress. "Harry," he said, "if I don't come back, you take that bundle and mail it away for me."

"Where's the address?"

Van Rhyn tapped the pocket of his shirt. "You will find it in here."

"You'll come back," said Harry Jackson.

"There's an end for all of us," van Rhyn answered gently. "By one cause or another, mine is not far away."

Harry Jackson sat on the edge of his bed. He made a gesture with his hands. "Hell, Van, there's nothing to fear."

Van Rhyn smiled quietly. "I had not mentioned fear, Harry. Fear is for the young ones who love life too much. When I was younger I was afraid to die. I used to lie awake, thinking about it. I used to reach forward with my mind trying to overtake the moment death came, trying to discover how I would act and how I would feel—and it was pretty bad. But there is nothing to fear, Harry. Little by little as a man grows older he gets callous, his senses grow dull and his mistakes and his hurts slow him down and the fun of living fades away. Alter a while he ceases to care very much, or to fight very much, or to feel very much. After that it is a matter of waiting. I shall be glad to go."

"That's no way to talk," said Harry Jackson.

"You are young and you have everything to hope for. That makes all the difference. Never be philosophical,

Harry. Never play the game safe when your heart tells you to gamble. Life is mostly a matter of damned, contemptible conventions, and hypocrisies and cheating devices and pleasant fictions hiding a brutal system. One or two, or maybe three, things ever matter to a man. Those you should live by and live for. Everything else is just so much claptrap. This world is governed by the pack. The pack sets up the rules and it punishes the man who will not live by those rules — just as the wolf pack kills or drives off the lone ones who will not bend to the rules. Never let the pack govern your life. Do what your conscience tells you is right, follow your own star, and be your own master."

Harry Jackson stared at the older man, not wholly understanding. Van Rhyn, ordinarily so quiet and so removed from the rough talk and horseplay of the barracks, showed him a pair of bright, bitter eyes. There was in this man, then, the last flare of an old vitality, the final glow of a fire once very strong. Harry Jackson said, "What two or three things matter, Van?"

"You will have to find out those things for yourself, Harry. When you do find out, you'll be an old man, as I am now. If you have played the game right the knowledge will be a comfort to you. If you have not, your last days will be in that purgatory Dante created out of whole cloth."

"How's a man to know?" murmured Harry Jackson.

Van Rhyn's smile was soft and understanding; his resentment died. "Ah, I wish I could tell you. I have read all the philosophers, but they could not tell me. Make your own answers, Harry. Depend on others for nothing. For nothing at all." He tapped his breast pocket again. "There's three hundred dollars in here. When you take out the address, also take the money. It is yours."

"What for?" asked Harry Jackson, completely astonished.

Van Rhyn pressed the sweat across his forehead. His face was tight-pulled and weary; he was old. "For a drink, for a poker hand, for a woman, for the start of a career. For anything, Harry, that will squeeze one more drop of flavor from the rind of the orange, which is tasteless enough at best. Someday you will understand."

Troopers crossed and recrossed the parade. Men walked their horses around the corral, watching for bruised feet and bad tendons; the sound of the blacksmith's hammer rang metally through the heated day; a detail crossed the Aravaipa to bring fresh mounts from the nearby corral and Indians from Nachee's camp began to collect under the shade of the ramadas. Ray Lankerwell came to post headquarters, reporting to Major Warren.

Warren said, "As soon as we leave tonight you will break off and take your detail directly north, past the Mescals. Turn east into the Pinals, about at this point on the map. You are not to bring on a fight but rather to make a show of forces that will push Antone back should he have intentions of traveling north. If you see nothing in front of you, and no fresh sign, close in southward toward this spot." He indicated it with his thumb. "I shall be somewhere near there. Pete George will go as your guide. If you see evidence of a strong force, send a messenger through to me. If you are not held up I expect you to join me at the earliest moment."

The supper call was running all around Fort Grant's parade and the sun lay half down the western horizon when Lily Marr came from the Warren house and crossed to the jail. The guard was just then bringing up a tin of food from the mess hall. Lily Marr stood back while he unlocked the cell door, slid the tin plate into the cell and closed the door again. She waited until the guard had replaced the key on the high corner of the dobe wall and turned away.

Jack Bean stood with his face at the bars. He put his hands around the bars, his fingers slowly closing, tightly closing. Blond hair fell down across his forehead, almost against his eyes. He had been in this cell a week, tramping

215

its narrow space, enduring its breathless heat. The effect of it showed on him, pulling in the centers of his cheeks and painting a dismal color in his eyes. He hadn't shaved and he hadn't slept much and all this wore him thin and nervous, and left him like a caged wolf slowly dying for want of appetite and air. He stared at Lily Marr, too bitter to speak, while she showed him that old, unrelenting calm.

"A messenger," she said, "went up to Summerton's and told them about the money. They have probably gone to Tucson to get it by now. The marshal won't come for another week. But when he does come he'll take you back with a party of soldiers. Bill Hanley won't help you out of this. You're at the end of the rope."

"Lily," he said, "I'll get loose. Before God, I will. And I'll pay you back—and I'll pay the captain back. I'll pay everybody back."

"No," she said, in the same rubbing, insistent calm, "you never will. This time the wheel stopped on your number and you pay off for what's been done."

His question jumped at her. "What've I done?"

"Maybe you better start thinking about that. You never had time to think about it before, but you've got a lot of time now. Better think of those burnt wagons and the Mexican yelling when the bullet hit him. You remember how he yelled, Jack? I do."

"A Mexican," said Jack Bean, "is nothin' but a Mexican."

"Maybe you better think of Bill Goff."

He answered that swiftly. "Bill knew I was after him. I never catch a man without a gun. He saw me comin' and he had his draw."

"Maybe you better think of Charley Brewerton."

"He made his remarks about me, Lily. When a man makes his remarks he's got to stand the consequences. I walked down the middle of the street at him, and I waited till he reached for his gun."

216

"Maybe you better think of Charley Brewerton's wife who takes in washing to live. Or Bill Goff's little girl, who's got no parents left now."

He pulled up his chin. "That's somethin' those fellows should have figured out before they got proud. I'll stand my mistakes; they should stand theirs."

"Then stand yours now," said Lily Marr. "You are going to die for them."

"Lily," said Jack Bean, "when a man calls me into question I'll see him answered, till hell freezes over. I take nothing from nobody."

"Yes," said Lily Marr. "You'll take anything they've got, cattle or money or horses. Charley Brewerton said you were a thief. That's why you shot him. But you're still a thief, Jack."

"Listen, girl," begged Jack Bean in a furious voice, "there's ways of lookin' at that—"

"Just two ways. The honest way and the thief's way."

Bean cursed Lily Marr and swung away from the door. She heard his heels kick into the floor. She heard his fists slap against the dobe wall; she heard the in and out sawing of his breath. The sun dropped down and twilight suddenly came and men were moving out of the mess shack. The trumpeters came across the parade to take stand by the number one post, from which point all calls were sounded. Lily Marr's voice, as even and colorless as fate, followed Jack Bean into the jail.

"You always talked about your rights. Maybe you better think of other people's rights. You never liked the idea of any man being as quick as you were with a gun. You had to shoot him to find out if he was. You couldn't stand the thought of anybody being better. If they were better you wanted to kill them. But there are better men in Arizona than you'll ever be. You never thought there was anything strong enough to hold you in one place. Well, here you are, Jack."

217

He said, from the depths of the jail, "I'll get loose, by God!"

"Nobody will remember you when you're dead. Nobody will remember where you're buried because in all this country you haven't got one friend who cares enough to put a board up to mark your grave. Someday, a few years from now, somebody will say, 'Who was Jack Bean?' And somebody else will say, 'He was a small-time tinhorn who went around waving a gun making believe he was big.' I guess that's about it. Just a tinhorn who never had sense enough to stop and think. What've you got to be proud about?"

She waited for him to answer, but he didn't answer and he didn't come back to the door. Twilight rolled around the post and suddenly the trumpeters were blowing the quick, peremptory call To Horse and troopers began to form on the parade. Lily Marr went back to the Warren quarters and stood there.

A few minutes earlier Phil Castleton had come over to say good-by to Eleanor. Now they stood in the shadows of the post bakery, turned silent by the trumpets. Eleanor watched Castleton's face come alive with its old, rash eagerness; even in the shadows she observed his old temper flare up and she knew that if the chance came to him he would throw his whole future, career and friendships and life itself, into a last gamble. The thought worried her, it depressed her and made this moment unpleasant. She said "Phil" very softly, but he had turned and was looking across the parade at the forming troops and his thoughts had gone away from her; and then she had one more cold shocking suspicion: There was so great a desire in him that nothing else could find a place, perhaps not even love, as she understood love to be.

She said, "Phil, I wish you luck."

That turned him. He was smiling and his whole face changed under excitement. He said in a rapid voice, "This time I think we'll catch up with Antone."

218

"Whether you do or don't, Phil, I'll still be here when you return."

"I'll bring you back his scalp. I'll do better. I'll count a coup on him. I'll touch him and say as Indians say, 'Now your spirit is mine and I am a great warrior.'"

"I'll still be here, Phil," she prompted him patiently.

He laughed outright and brought her against him and kissed her; there was at the moment no gentleness to him, no thoughtfulness, none of that small and faintly sad uncertainty of a man going away from something desirable, possibly forever. He kissed her and let her go, and still smiling, he walked at a fast long stride over to his troop. There was an echoing roll call in the dusk and the slap and strike of gear and stepping horses and moving feet; all this rose to a certain key that stirred the camp. George Mixler ran forward and shook her hand and looked at her quite closely.

"Sometime in the future I wish you'd write Harriet a note. Say that you think she did the right thing. It will please her and make everything else a little easier for her mind."

"George, why say that?"

"I've got a feeling about this trip. It doesn't matter at all, of course. I'm glad we're going. My love to you, Eleanor, and good-by."

He ran into the shadows. The men were counting numbers and afterwards the sergeants of K and I swung exactly around on their heels, reporting troops. Eleanor saw her father shift in the saddle and listened to his steady voice sing out the commands. There was a blur of all these men, rising to saddle and the slap of legs and the grunt of the mounts; and this, to her, was part of a memory that went away back into her childhood, the same routine, the same sound and the same quick rush of excitement and eagerness — and the shock of pride running through her from seeing her father turn his horse, from hearing his voice sing out the marching order. The long line broke and wheeled into column of twos, swung eastward through the guard gate, passed it and rattled on the stones of Aravaipa Creek; and then, long after, sank into the deep silence of the hills.

Presently the post was a lifeless row of buildings under the glittering Arizona sky. Eleanor stood with her shoulders to the bakery shop wall, hearing the shuffling of the sentries, the slowly closing fear out of her mind. Waiting was always the hardest part, but this was the army and this was the whole meaning of army life—this moment when the troops swung away, outward bound on campaign. Somewhere deep in her mind was a recurring image of Castleton; it lay back below other thoughts just now, vaguely stirring, vaguely troublesome. She let it be so, afraid to bring it forward and see it for what it was.

There had been, at that last moment, one more scene. Standing by his horse, waiting the command to mount, Harry Jackson saw Rose Smith come out from the barrack wall and stop by Canreen. She had something in her hand. She pushed it into Canreen's pocket and then said, "Be good, Ben."

Ben laughed out his assurance. "Never you mind, Rose, I'll bring back a pair o' moccasins—"

The order to mount stilled him. Up in the saddle, Harry Jackson turned to watch Rose Smith's face. It pointed toward him, white and still in the shadows. Major Warren's order swung the troops into line and they moved out to the guard gate. Rose Smith walked quickly forward, abreast Harry Jackson's horse. She said, small-voiced, "Be good, Harry." After that Harry Jackson passed through the gate and he saw no more of her.

At Camp Apache, that same night, Harriet Mixler stood by the open window of her room, staring into the southwest where Grant lay. She had arrived at the post this same morning and Major McClure's wife, looking at her pallid face and alarmed by the completely exhausted sound of her voice, had immediately taken the baby from

220

her. So she stood now alone in this room, dressed for bed and deeply breathing the cool air of the high hills — the first refreshing breath she could remember in many months. This was heaven compared to Grant, the dreary trip was behind her, and the baby was in good care. It was beyond taps, with the post asleep. Adjoining her room was the room of young Lieutenant Kessler and his wife. She heard them talking, she heard Kessler's laugh and the suppressed reply of the woman; and then the closing silence left her thoroughly alone and friendless and letdown. She put her hand to the window sill, watching the black crooked outline of the southwestern skyline, and went down into her own empty thought.

Chapter Sixteen

Benteen watched the restless Apache cross the camp site and slowly climb the grade. Al Hazel was beside Benteen, so near that Benteen could hear the ticking of the guide's huge stem-wind watch. In this silence the sound seemed loud enough to warn the Indian, now about forty feet away and closing up the distance with a catlike pacing. As he advanced his stringy shape was silhouetted by the ruby glow of the fire embers behind him. He had his head down and he swung it from side to side as though scooping information out of the air, for his ears and his nose. At twenty feet the slope lifted him until his shoulders were on a line with Benteen's eyes and his course was dead against Benteen.

Al Hazel was still motionless; Nachee had lost himself somewhere in the dark. Benteen, knowing this next moment was nothing but a gamble, laid a strong muscular strain on his arms, holding them still. There was a chance yet; and the chance presently came.

The white man in the Apache camp suddenly began to howl. He didn't say anything, he didn't speak any intelligible words; he only yelled, the pure sound pouring out of his lungs and carrying all over the hills.

The Indian crouched by the fire didn't bother to move, but the one now within three paces of Benteen stopped and turned and called back to the man by the fire. That one said something, still not moving, whereupon the Indian near Benteen went rapidly down the slope. Figures began to stir on the ground, wakened by the white man's continuous screeching. Two shapes trotted in from the far edge of the flat. The white man, Benteen realized, had gone crazy from thinking of what lay before him. The Indian who had walked down the slope now reached the white man and stood a moment over him, grunting in Apache, but the white man, apparently tied hand and foot, rolled along the ground, his cry growing thinner and higher and wilder. Abruptly the Indian turned aside, seized a gun from the ground and brought its butt twice down on the white man's head, killing him instantly. The crushing sound of that gun butt against bone skull traveled up the slope and made Benteen dig his fingers into the dirt; it went slowly through him as a wave of sick, soft feeling. The Indian stood over the white man and smashed his head once more.

He walked near the fire-glow, slowly turning as if to retrace his path up the slope again, and at this moment Al Hazel's elbow dug into Benteen, and they gently backed down from the top of the ridge. They waited under the pines, missing Nachee. Al Hazel murmured, "That was Ben Stevens, Lieutenant. And he was smart."

"Crazy," suggested Benteen.

"Not him," countered Hazel. "He knew whut was in front of him, so he made 'em mad and got it over with quick."

When Nachee arrived it was so softly that they didn't see him until he whispered at Hazel. Al Hazel murmured, "He says this is Antone's main camp. Antone is in that bunch. Nachee thinks there is another camp farther along the ridge. Whut's your idea now?"

Benteen whispered, "How many up there?"

"Maybe twenty-five or thirty. Which is why Nachee figures there's another camp. Antone's got a strong party in these hills."

Benteen crouched against the base of a pine tree, calculating his time. It was near three o'clock, with a faint paleness to the star-shine and a faint change in the sky, from metal black to lesser black. In another hour or more daylight would be along. Silence hung to the hills, deeper than any silence in the world, the silence of motionlessness, the silence of that hour when even the night-prowling animals had fallen asleep and the sibilant, furtive voices of earth insects had ceased. This was the cool hour, with the scent of pine and the scent of aromatic vegetation clinging to the air; and this was the ebb hour when a man's mind grew dull and his hope sank down and his vitality ran out. After a day and a night of steady going, Benteen felt it. There was no push in him at all.

He said, in a toneless murmur, "We'll back out of here. Tell Nachee to pick a high spot across the canyon, where we can watch the country and keep an eye on Antone if he moves."

Al Hazel's arm hit Benteen in quick warning; and Hazel faded against the pine trunk, blending with its black up-and-down shadow. Nachee was out of sight. In the nearing distance was the faint scrape of a moccasined foot. One of Antone's warriors had come to the rim surrounding the camp, and now kept advancing.

The trees made a thin scatter along the land, and rock hummocks here and there built up deeper spots of shadow; and so it was difficult to catch the outline of a moving shape. Benteen saw him first as a faint streak of motion, forty feet away. He came on, disappeared behind a rock mound, and reappeared within four paces of where Benteen stood. This was as near as he got, for he made a quarter turn and slid by the trees at a quick, almost soundless shuffle and headed westward toward the canyon. And, Benteen suddenly realized, toward the horses.

He was still a gray shape against the night when Nachee's shape rose from the rocks and closed in. Those two shapes at once violently blended and there was a sharp scuffle, the 'tunk' of a knife driving home, and the little disconnected rustle of a body loosely falling on the flinty soil. One shadow trotted back, which was Nachee. He murmured something to Hazel and thereafter all three of them walked to the horses and retraced the way into the canyon.

Complete blackness smothered them as they reached the canyon's bottom and threaded the creek southward a mile or more; when they rose from it, now on the west rim, a gray break showed low in the eastern sky. Nachee led them steadily into higher and rougher country. They passed through rocky defiles that covered them completely from the freshening morning twilight, across piny flats, between masses of catclaw and mesquite; and at last, in the first full sunlit hour of day, they reached a broken-topped elevation above a narrow pass which cut irregularly east and west through the hills.

There was some shelter here and a view from all angles. Looking over the rocks surrounding them on three sides, Benteen saw how hard a country it was and realized then how easily Antone had escaped every detail sent after him. There was no clear trail in any direction; nothing but these rough ridges broken by deep draws and sudden canyons, and hillslopes whereon broken rock lay blackly in the growing light. Benteen scouted the surrounding terrain with his glance, seeing nothing that moved. Westward at the end of the pass stood the butte to which he had brought the detail the day before. This was about six miles distant.

Al Hazel had already gouged himself a place on the ground and had pillowed his head on an arm, taking a quick rest. Nachee squatted in the middle of the small space; he had his arms over his knees. His head was tipped up and he was watching the sky with an expressionless, unmoving attention, as though he waited for the sky to tell him something.

Al Hazel drawled, "Makin' medicine. It is his religion, Lieutenant. The sky and the earth—and water. I ain't an educated man but it is my observation that a man's religion usually narrows down to whut he needs most. An Injun lives right against the earth. When he prays, somethin' like you and me, it is fer the water to last and the mesquite beans to be plentiful, and fer the sun to be kind. Ain't a bad religion. What more could any man want? Nachee right now is seein' things in that sky you and me wouldn't."

Nachee spoke to Al Hazel, who said, "We got a couple-three hours to sleep. Nachee will take first watch."

Benteen spread out on the ground, gouged a hole for his hips and shoulders and pulled his hat over his face. A stray thought ran through his mind and was never completed, for he sank into the luxury of pure, depthless sleep at once.

The burning of sun against his skin woke him in the middle of another sweltering morning. Al Hazel slept on, snoring steadily through his open mouth. Nachee lay between a rock cleft, watching the pass and the land east of the pass, which was where Antone's camp lay. Benteen took a swallow of flat water from his canteen and stood up to kick life into his legs. Nachee's head turned at the sound, whereupon Benteen pointed to the ground. "Better sleep." Nachee grunted and turned back to his observations. But he said something over his shoulder which drew Benteen forward. Edging himself into the rocks so that his head wouldn't show over the rim, Benteen set his eyes on the eastern end of the pass. The sun struck the land at a long angle, turning it gray and brown, and against this light he made out nothing until the flash of a metal object telegraphed across the distance. Entering his glance on that spot he at last saw a file of Indians crossing over; they were leaving the camp of the night before and going over to the high ground on the south side of the pass.

Al Hazel strangled on his snoring and sat up. When he

226

aw Benteen shouldered into the rocks he came over to ave his look, at once locating the Indians. He spoke to Nachee and listened to the reply.

"Nachee says that's all men. No women or young ones. o Antone's just looking around, not breakin' camp."

"Circling back in the direction of Grant," said Benteen. That's the way he did it before."

"Al Hazel sat on the ground and rubbed his shoulders. Rheumatism again. Always get it in the hills. I butchered n arrow out of this arm ten years ago and I still feel the amned thing." He looked pretty tough, his long lips ulled together as though he tasted something acid. A hort beard covered most of his face; beneath his eyes the kin pouched up, giving him an expression that was both hrewd and dissipated. When he removed his hat a round ald spot began to shine. He was, Benteen knew, not more han forty, but a hard and active and sometimes extremely ough life had prematurely aged him. He washed out his nouth with a drink of water and refreshed himself with a hew from his plug. The taste of the tobacco at once rightened him.

Meanwhile Benteen moved to the north side of the ocks and began to watch the land they had crossed by lark. That way the country lay in a complete tangle of ntersecting arroyos through which Antone's warriors night crawl in complete cover until they arrived at the vall of rock surrounding this small peak. He mentioned his to Al Hazel.

"I guess they'll be down there some place," agreed Hazel. "Just a question of how long it takes 'em to find ur trail out of the canyon. Soon as they spot two horses hod and one barefoot they'll know who's here."

The long morning rolled on. Near noon Benteen distributed hardtack from his saddlebags. He broke his own piece into a tin cup and soaked it with water. Nachee lipped his ration into his shirt pocket. Al Hazel made no retense of eating. "I reckon I'd just as soon go hungry,

227

Lieutenant, till I can get me some meat."

At two o'clock Al Hazel spotted a file of Indians crossing the pass a few miles westward. "That's Antone, cuttin a circle," he said. "He's lookin' at the tracks of the detail you sent home. And he'll be followin' our trail now, from the other end."

In the long burning middle-afternoon hours Benteen saw a warrior rise from an arroyo at the eastern base of this summit and look steadily upward. Presently he dropped from sight. A little later two of them showed again, mounted, and struck up the slope, cutting a wide detour. They were in and out of sight, beyond a carbine's range. Benteen and Al Hazel — who had come over to watch — saw the pair reach a high point and disappear westward; somewhere in that direction the larger party of Indians now rode.

Al Hazel considered the sun. He hauled his watch out of his vest pocket and said "four-thirty," and snapped the hunting case shut. "Four hours till dark, Lieutenant."

The sun beat down into this shadeless spot and the rocks began to burn, trapping and building up the heat. Benteen knotted a handkerchief around his neck. The backs of his hands began to blister, the skin around his ears pulsed whenever the handkerchief rubbed it; blood collected in his eyeballs, enlarging them and changing his vision.

In the adjoining heights northward a dust ball rose from an arroyo, betraying travel. It would be, Benteen guessed, Antone's larger band closing in. The two Apaches had probably caught up with Antone and were leading him back. Nachee said, "Nantan," bringing both Benteen and Hazel over to the side of the peak which lay against the low pass. Another party slowly crossed the pass now, taking the same trail the band of warriors had followed in the morning. The line was long and strung out and lifted high clouds of dust. Nachee spoke to Al Hazel, who interpreted.

228

"Squaws and kids, he says. The women are movin' camp. He says they'll pitch new camp in those heights."

"How's he know?"

"They're movin' late in the day. And there's water up here. Nachee knows that country."

"Swinging back in the direction of Grant again."

Al Hazel said, "Movin' away from the white man they butchered."

Benteen returned to the north side, now seeing dust boil out of the nearer arroyos. An Indian showed himself on the skyline, horse and all, and poised this way long enough to display his interest and his lack of fear. Hazel said, "Look down slope—the way we came last night."

Heads showed along the low eastern rocks, within five hundred yards of Benteen's position. There were four or five of them, all steadily moving in and out of the rough breaks. Nachee came back from his position facing both Benteen and Hazel and raised his arm and swept it around him; it was a slow and graphic gesture that covered everything. Al Hazel grunted, "You bet—we're surrounded."

He had shown almost no concern to this point, governed by the self-confident taciturnity of all frontiersmen; nor did he display any particular alarm now, but he went over to his horse and pulled out his carbine, filled his pocket full of shells from the saddlebag and returned to Benteen.

The country was alive with Antone's men. Posted behind the rocks as the bitter-burning day dragged on, Benteen saw the shift of black heads in the rocks and the gradual nearing of those heads. North, in the adjoining rough country, dust continued to banner up from point to point, hanging to the air long after it had risen; and from these telltale streaks, Benteen could see the route of the main party as it came up from the west and wound through the arroyos.

On the south side was the natural protection of the swift-falling wall of the pass. East and west the broken rocks marched directly to this summit, and up the east

side the smaller group of Apaches now patiently crawled
To the north, where the mounted Indians maneuvered, a
casual depression made a cleared spot of perhaps two
hundred feet between the summit and the next rim of broken ground. That yonder elevation was as high as the
summit, and Antone's riders were masked by it until they
arrived at the cleared spot. Thence onward, they would be
in the open if they chose to rush in with their horses.

Suddenly Nachee stooped in the dust, patted his palm
against the ground and began to sing a tuneless chant that
came out of his throat as an "Ahhhhh — eeeeeah —
Ahhhh." This was beyond six o'clock, with the sun almost
touching the eastern rim of hills. Al Hazel fed shells into
his carbine and hung it over his arm, like a hunter. Benteen lifted his revolver, looked at the loads, and laid it on
the rock in front of him. And it was then that the long
spaced line of Antone's larger party broke from shelter,
riding to the top of the nearby rim.

They were mostly stripped down to breechclouts, leggings and a few daubs of paint, though some wore shirts
whose tails dangled against their thighs. Part of them had
lances and bows; part of them carried guns as good as
anything the American cavalry used. Their legs curved
against the bare flanks of the horses, their toes dangled
down; and at this distance, which was not more than sev-
enty yards, Benteen saw the shoulder straps of an American captain pinned to one brave's shirtsleeves — the relic of
some old battle. Coolness ran along Benteen's muscles; he
felt the quick slugging of his heart and the dryness of his
throat. Poised against the skyline, they made a startling,
barbaric show; they were the hardest, craftiest, most mer-
ciless fighters in the world. This, he thought, in the moment before he closed his mind against that kind of
thinking, was what lay in the back of every trooper's mind
on the frontier — this final picture. And here it was.

Al Hazel drawled, "See that little feller in the middle
with the face like an old dried potato. The one with the

shoulder straps on his shirt. That's your friend Antone, Lieutenant. That's the Injun you been chasin' all summer. There he is."

Antone moved his horse forward from the straggling skirmish line and turned a circle in a kind of insolent invitation, in a kind of feinting suggestion. But Benteen, all the while remembering the Indians creeping up through the rocks on the east, saw the shape of something cross the edge of his vision, and hauled around in time to discover an Apache make a long jump from rock to rock, not thirty feet removed. Benteen threw up his gun, took a snap shot and caught the Apache in the middle of his leap. Antone yelled across the clear space and the horses began to bunch up, on the edge of a run. Al Hazel's carbine roared against Benteen's ear. The warrior adjoining Antone sagged and caught at his pony's mane, and dropped. Hazel's second bullet killed a horse. Antone wheeled back and carried his party over the edge and out of sight.

The party of Apaches who had spent all this hot afternoon creeping up the eastern slope suddenly raised from the rocks and rushed on, ducking from cover to cover, low-bent and evasive and howling. Benteen steadied his arm, carefully firing. Al Hazel jumped beside him, the carbine laying hard echoes into the last bright glare of the day. A bullet struck a rock surface and screamed all through the hills as it ricocheted on. One Apache raced forward sinuously, straight away from his sheltering hollow, straight against the parapet. Benteen's sights fell dead on his chest but as his finger squeezed out the shot the Indian dropped from view. He was against the same rock that Benteen touched, only its thickness and its height between them. Al Hazel's carbine knocked one more Apache into the boulders; the rest had faded.

Benteen suddenly heaved himself belly flat across the rock. His head hung down the opposite side, his eyes glared straight into the Apache's eyes, no more than a foot

231

from him. The Indian reached up, seized Benteen by th
back of the neck and attempted to haul him forward. Ber
teen, on the edge of falling, got his gun around, thrust
straight against the Apache's face—and saw the face ha
vanish from the shot. Hazel grabbed his feet; he fell bac
against Hazel, blood dripping from the rock-scraped sid
of his jaw.

The sun was suddenly gone and purple shadows bega
to flow along the ridge slopes, through the pass into a
the pockets and barricades and arroyos of this broke
country. Antone's main party had faded behind the hillto
on the north, but dust still moved there and now and the
a warrior came to the summit and cut little dog-trottin
maneuvers before the watching three, as though temptin
them to come out. Al Hazel watched these antics care
fully.

"A little show fer our benefit. Hopin' to keep us chee
ful whilst the rest of that bunch circle this point and com
up the sides. Which they will now be doing. This spc
ain't exactly good fer an invalid, Lieutenant."

Benteen crossed the small depression of the summit an
pushed himself through a break in the rocks, lookin
down upon the pass. This rock wall fell in stiff grades fc
a matter of three or four hundred feet before leveling int
the floor of the pass. The pass itself was hardly a hundre
yards wide; and its far wall rose into the hills at a less di
ficult angle. The original problem, Benteen thought, wa
to take a horse down this first wall.

He traced a zigzag course with his eyes, trying to men
orize the lay of the slope before the swift-falling shadov
blotted it out. The moon had already begun to throw o
its pale glow and would, at full dark, partly light th
way—an advantage in keeping to the trail, but a disadvar
tage insofar as getting clear of Antone was concernec
There were, as yet, no Indians down in the pass; c
seemed to be none. That way was open, if they could gc
to it quickly enough.

"Lieutenant," murmured Al Hazel in his unhurried way, "we had better watch sharp. Hard to tell an Injun from a rock in another ten minutes."

"As soon as it is dark enough," said Benteen, "we'll risk the slope." He took Al Hazel's place by the barricade while the guide went over to have his look. Presently Hazel called to Nachee, who remained all this time by the east edge of the rocks, as patient as fate; he trotted to Hazel and the two of them talked a moment, Hazel pointing into the pass. Hazel called, "Better be pretty soon, Lieutenant. When we pull out of here they'll be right on us."

Benteen stared at the rocks beyond this little area. There was no sound in the deepening twilight and no visible motion. All the shadows began to blend until he found it impossible to distinguish between boulder and moving shape. He called over his shoulder, "We may get separated when we leave here. Tell Nachee to pull out by himself and go find Major Warren. Have him tell Warren to wait for our arrival at the butte. We'll keep a lookout on Antone. We will also keep a lookout on the butte—and close in as soon as we see the troops."

He crossed to the west angle, hearing Al Hazel translate the instructions in a voice that quickened and grew blunt and was at last touched by something very close to excitement. The situation, Benteen thought, was bad when it could swing the guide out of his consistent calm. The shape of the rocks directly beyond this small clearing at last blurred entirely and he found himself straining forward, the revolver pushed ahead and half-lifted; he found his legs hardened and all his muscles drawn tight. These shadows were tricky. They moved, they pulsed, they had an odd bulk that drifted toward him; and out of them suddenly emerged the sibilance of sound. Al Hazel yelled, "Watch!" His carbine cracked the creeping quiet. The shadows before Benteen ceased to be shadows and became rising shapes half-vague before him. On these he placed

233

his shots, seeing one shadow and another drop—until they had all dropped. Indians hated to face this kind of fire, they hated running against anything solid. So they had dropped and were elusively crawling forward, deep-buried in the rocks. Al Hazel's gun blasted the night again.

Benteen turned from the rock parapet. He said, "Al, come on," and stepped beside his horse. He waited a moment until Hazel and Nachee had reached him, until they were ready to rise to the saddle and run. Blackness dropped, with the reddish stain of moonlight diluting it. Al Hazel murmured, "Better make this fast, Lieutenant. They'll be crawlin' between us and the pass."

Benteen said, "Nachee goes first," and listened to Al Hazel repeat it to the Indian. Then he said, "I'll be the tail end. Let's go."

He was in the saddle. He laid a shot back of him, as a diversion that would keep Antone's men low in the rocks for a moment. Nachee faded through the narrow break on the pass side and Al Hazel faded through it, both dropping at once from Benteen's view. When he followed and got beyond the rocks he saw the two ahead of him, whirling zigzag with the descending slope, making a great racket on the stony ground. Behind him was the rising yell of Antone's men and an interval in which he waited, as he pushed the horse recklessly downward, for the first crack of a shot. That interval grew longer and harder, it grew more and more painful. He heard his horse grunt at each descending plunge; he saw Nachee and Al Hazel's shape wheel right and left, run and stop and turn, and run again. Low in the saddle, he felt the first shot breathe by him. After that Antone's men searched for him with their guns. Slugs hit the rocks. A fragment of splintered stone stung his face and he rode in the smell of heavy dust.

He was half down the slope when his horse, misjudging the grade, stumbled and threw him forward from the saddle; he landed flat on the gelding's neck and balanced this way, seizing the animal's mane to keep from falling, and in such a manner he fought for his seat all across the last hundred feet of the decline and came at last to the bottom; the sudden pitch of the horse on level ground threw him completely off. He lighted on his knees, holding to a stirrup with his hand. Al Hazel galloped back from the darkness, calling, "All right—Tom!"

The horse stopped the moment weight went from its back. Bullets slashed the ground and as Benteen rose, still clinging to the stirrup, he had one backward and upward glance, seeing the firefly dance of muzzle light from the rocks above him. He jumped into the saddle and raced southward across the pass with Al Hazel beside him. The firing had quit.

"Where's Nachee?"

"Faded. He's all right—he'll meet Warren in the mornin'."

Behind them now was the rattle and clatter of Antone's horses on the hillside; Antone was following down the slope. At the far side of the pass Benteen turned again and made out the weave of shadows behind him, but Al Hazel was laughing in the dark, pleased with his luck. "I reckon that's close enough to brag about, Lieutenant."

He took the lead, finding some kind of an open way up the side of the ridge, talking to his horse as he pushed it: "Git on, Star! By God, you better pull for yore breakfast. Them's Injuns you smell."

They were half up the stiff slope, with Antone's men somewhere at the bottom of the pass, all scattered in the dark. Turned, Benteen made out those tangled shapes and was tempted to chance a shot but did not. At the top of the ridge, Al Hazel swung to the left, raced forward at a dangerous tilt, and shot into an arroyo. They followed to its blind end, clawed out of it and swung right. In this fashion, see-sawing from one direction to another, they rode for a mile or more before pulling down. They heard nothing behind.

"Shook 'em for a little while," decided Al Hazel.

"Ridin' like this at night we got all the best of it, though they will track us by the smell of dust. So we walk slow."

Benteen's horse showed the effect of the run. It limped increasingly as they went along; traveling head down, all steam gone, unsteadied by its need for wind, its heart mauling the big chest and sending hard reverberations up its frame. They drifted up the side of a ridge, through an open pine stand whose needle-carpeted flooring left no dust smell, bearing westward and gently higher with the contour of the hills until, two hours or more from the time of their brush with Antone, Al Hazel halted and got down.

This was some kind of a clearing in a gulch. Al Hazel said, "Castle and Butler's old mine," and walked forward, leading his horse. Benteen followed, seeing the square shape of a log house lift from the shadows. Hazel hauled back a door whose rusty hinges squalled in the silence, and stopped on the threshold, listening and smelling. He threw some rocks inside. "Guess there ain't no snakes or skunks," he decided and led his horse into the place. Benteen, loosening the cinches of his saddle, also put his horse through the door. Al Hazel came back, closing the door, and led Benteen across the remains of an old dump, past the dismembered skeleton of a mill and on to the faintly cool breath of a mine's mouth. Here again Al Hazel gingerly poked around the ground with his feet and threw a stone or two into the tunnel.

"Never sleep with a snake unless there's worse things to choose from," he said, and went into the tunnel, dropping at once. "By God, Lieutenant, I'm tired enough to be an old man." Benteen heard him suck greedily on his canteen, grunting his relief at each gulp.

The floor of the tunnel was solid rock, overlaid with a scatter of loose stones. Benteen brushed them halfheartedly out of the way before settling, took a pull on his canteen and felt no relief from the stale water. He lay back, sore in every joint, and so tired that when he thought of saying something to Al Hazel about taking turn at guard the words were too heavy for his throat. They were in a hard spot, but weariness outweighed everything else, even the need of safety; and so he fell at once asleep, indifferent to anything.

Chapter Seventeen

Benteen woke in the first grayness of morning to find Al Hazel coming back from a scout. Hazel had a can of water and a few pine branches; he started a small blaze in the tunnel and boiled up some coffee. By the firelight Benteen saw the guide's taciturn face marked by fatigue. Al Hazel said, in a cranky voice, "A little risky, but by God, I got to have my coffee."

They drank the coffee, hot and strong and black, from the can; and broiled bacon over the firepoints and killed the fire. This was the first approach to a meal Benteen had had since the noon of two days ago, and the effect of it was like a jolt of whisky. The floor of this mine was printed on every muscle of his body and his joints dryly ached, but he felt cheerful again and faced the pearl-gray daylight at the tunnel mouth cheerfully.

Al Hazel said, "There's a spring up the hill. I watered the horses and put 'em back in the shed. Your horse is considerable lame, Lieutenant. Both front legs, which is from comin' down that slope hell bent fer election last night. Whut you want to do now?"

"Climb the nearest ridge and have a look."

"Antone's camp won't be more'n three-four miles east. But we got to keep smart. These hills are alive with those damned Apaches—and the closest ones will be the Tontos."

238

Benteen said, "How's that?"

"They saw me in the rocks yesterday, Lieutenant, and fer a Tonto that was like advertisin' Fourth of July. That tribe's been wantin' my hair fer close to fifteen years. They'd crawl belly-flat across forty miles of cactus to ketch me. I sure have had some narrer squeaks."

Benteen said, "Think this is another narrow one, Al?"

The guide nursed the coffee tin between his hands and took a long pull. Coffee dripped along his mustache. He swiped it away with the back of his hand and looked across to Benteen; his eyes were blackly bedded in pouched skin. "Kind of narrer, Lieutenant. Was a time when a situation like this would have made me smile. Never was loath to match my legs or my eyesight or my wits with an Injun—not as long as I was young. But when a fellow passes forty, the game gets considerable hard. It is hell on a man like me to wake up feelin' like he's been drug at the end of a horse. That's when a fellow knows he ain't young any more. Well, I guess we better get this over with."

"Major Warren ought to be pretty near the butte by now," considered Benteen. "As soon as we have a look at the country, we'll go that way."

He went to the mouth of the cave, followed by Al Hazel's cautioning voice: "Wait a minute, Tom." The black shadows were breaking away from the hillslope, from the pine thickets, from the rough pockets. The pearl-luminous twilight of morning drifted in. All this was a kind of motion along the earth. A dump ran out from the tunnel fifty feet or more and broke off on the descending slope; there was the one cabin standing in the clearing and the faint trace on the ground where other buildings had been. Across the gulch the hill ran up into pines; behind him a similar hill rose to a broken summit. In all directions beyond the gulch trees made a scattered screen.

Al Hazel was beside him, studying the trees with a troubled attention. Afterwards he shrugged his shoulders.

239

"Never can tell," he grumbled. "They're not fur away now."

They turned about, climbing the slope. A magpie rose before them, a long-tailed streak in the growing light. Al Hazel grunted, his feet slipping on the ground. Halfway up the slope Benteen heard the guide's breath deepen and he knew then that the last forty hours had drained Hazel's strength considerably. At the top of the slope a flat crest extended fifty or sixty yards eastward and dropped away again. From that margin Benteen saw the land roll north and east and south, potted by arroyos and pine clusters and slashed by crisscross ridges. Sunless morning swelled out of the east, so clear and transparent that it telescoped distance. He saw the deep course of the pass and the rocky barrier across the pass, which was the country they had come from the night before, and this verified his sense of direction. The butte at which he was to meet Warren lay about four miles behind him. The light kept growing brighter in the east; and on a peak close by a wisp of smoke raveled up to the sky.

Al Hazel nodded at it. "There's your Injun camp, Tom."

"All right," decided Benteen, "that's what I wanted to see. Now we'll go find Major Warren." He was pleased with the way all this had turned out, and said so. "The trip's been a little bit tough, Al, but we've got Antone spotted."

"Maybe," murmured Al Hazel. "An Injun is a shadow, Tom. The women and kids are yonder, and part of the warriors. But all of 'em ain't. The rest are closer to us, I'd bet my shirt on it. Antone is a sly devil, and them Tontos are lookin' for me right now."

He was dissatisfied, he kept sweeping the foreground with his glance; he stood by the trunk of a tree, hat pushed back from his round forehead. In the mat of his beard his eyes blackly sparkled and his lips were thinned from the pressure of his thoughts. His vest draped slackly

240

around his solid chest and the chain of his watch swung gently as he turned. His shoulders dropped at the points and Benteen caught weariness in them again, and in the way his legs were planted apart. Hazel said, "Damned pretty country, Lieutenant. I've had a lot of fun in it. You fellers will maybe civilize it and then it will fill up." He shook his head at the thought, not liking it. "I'd ruther have it like it is, for a fact. Ought to be one place left in the world where a man can do jest as he damn pleases."

"A long time yet," said Benteen.

Al Hazel pointed to the smoke signal. "Someday those things won't show against the sky. Then it will be a different country. I don't take much to your kind of civilization, Tom. Put a man in a town, in a house, give him a steady job and let him worry about his paycheck—and he ain't a natural man any more. The Lord never meant us to live that way."

They recrossed the flat and walked down the slope. First sunlight rushed through the sky, stepping up the brightness of the old clearing below. The dirt of the dump made a yellowish scar against the surrounding soil and the foundation marks of the mine buildings still cut a pattern against the encroaching grass and cactus growth. Dust rose around Benteen's boot tops as he slid with the grade; a few loose stones bounced downward. At the dump Al Hazel held back while Benteen pulled the horses from the small cabin. He led them to Hazel, noting how still-placed Hazel was; the guide's eyes, narrower and brighter, searched the tree thickets. He took his horse, swinging up with Benteen. Double lines cut quickly across his forehead and he moved his shoulders in a gesture of discontent. "Let's get out of here."

They crossed the dump and fell into the bottom of the gulch, riding up its shallowing trough. This was northward, generally back toward the pass. The land rose beneath them, reaching into the hill slope. They quartered the slope, the pines lying in front. Benteen's horse kept favoring its right front foot; it moved at a stiff, jaded pace.

"Take the left side of that hump," Al Hazel said, "which—"

Benteen, turning to look at Al Hazel, caught the tag end of motion in the trees above. He threw weight into his heels even before he was sure of his sight. Al Hazel had also seen it

"By God," he grunted, "git out of here, Tom! Up—go on up!"

Benteen hit his horse with his heels hard enough to break the gelding into a grunting, climbing run. He had his head turned and now saw four Apaches come out of the timber at a dead gallop, angling down the slope to intercept them. The stillness of the morning echoed their sudden shouting, and echoed as well Al Hazel's quick gunshot. Hazel yelled, "Keep goin', Tom!" and fired again.

Benteen swung away from the slope, shooting off toward nearer trees. The grade kept lifting him; he felt the strain of it on the gelding. The beast's pace faltered until he used his spurs again, so rushing up to the lip of the ravine and arriving at level ground. In front of him lay the scattered pines and the wrinkled contours of broken earth. Looking behind, he noticed that Al Hazel had dropped back and at once he slowed his pace and drew his revolver.

Hazel had tried another shot from the saddle. It knocked a horse down, throwing one of the four Apaches. The other three came on at a circling sweep, low bent on their ponies, and still howling. Benteen fired and called, "Come on, Al—" and threw his glance to the front and suddenly hauled the gelding half around. For at this moment half a dozen warriors rose out of the little pitted hollows of the pine forest and rushed straight at him, all dismounted.

He yelled, "Al!"

Al Hazel's voice came robustly back to him. Thereafter

he had no time to look around. The Apaches before him were dropping on the ground; they were taking aim while one tall warrior rushed straight for the head of the gelding. Benteen wheeled again, took a snap aim and knocked the Apache down. He was broadside to the others, a plain target; and suddenly he knew this was fatal, and wheeled to charge them. They were thirty feet away, brown-shaped on the earth. He saw their rifles rise at him, and in rushing forward, he watched the gun muzzles shift as they rolled aside to get clear of the gelding's hoofs. The horse rawed away to keep from stepping on the nearest. A gun, lifted straight up, roared in his face, and then he was past the line, rushing away from it. Swinging to cover his rear he saw them wheel around at him; but behind them was a sight that made him rein in.

Al Hazel's horse was down. Al Hazel stood with his back to a pine, holding his gun against the three mounted Apaches who came at him in full halloo. Al Hazel fired and killed the nearest, and then, raising both arms, he threw the gun at the other two. There was a louder and louder yelling and a pair of the dismounted Apaches swung around and ran for Hazel. Benteen wheeled his horse, firing at the Apaches blocking his way. He yelled, "Al—get behind the tree!"

It was then too late. A bullet caught Hazel and turned him until he faced the tree. He caught at its bark, painfully trying to swing back and he was like that, slowly pushing himself around when one of the foot-racing Apaches reached him, swung the barrel of his carbine crushingly against Hazel's head.

Benteen howled "Al!" firing pointblank at the warriors coming toward him. Al Hazel was dead at the foot of the tree and the sound of gunfire rocketed into the morning and dust began to shimmer in the piny shadows—and the head of another column of Antone's men reared up from the mining camp ravine and charged forward. There was nothing left Benteen but to run and so he slashed on through the pines with the hark of guns behind him and the faint whispering of lead at his ears. There was another pocket in front of him. He raced into it, escaping their fire, and climbed out of its far side, galloping deeper and deeper into the timber.

He was beyond the effective reach of their shooting, with sweat pouring across his face. The big horse was slogging along, fighting for wind, and slowly losing speed; one backward glance showed him a flickering pattern of Apaches cutting through the trees, spreading as they followed.

This flight had carried him northward and now, through the trees, he caught an occasional sight of the pass and its open ground. The butte was out there at no great distance, with a pretty effective rimrock shelter if the horse could carry him to it; otherwise he had only the protection of the trees and the possibility of jumping into some shallow pit and making his fight.

This was what he debated in a hundred yards of dead run, and came to his conclusion and at once swung toward the pass. Another hundred yards brought him to its rim, the pine trees behind him. The slope pitched steeply into the pass and after he took it he looked up the clean sweep of the pass and saw the butte jutting against its end like the battlement of a castle. He saw something more as well—and this was a sight he never forgot afterwards to the end of his life.

Out around the pass, riding in double file, came Major Warren's command. Dust boiled around the horses; the figures of the troopers was a solidness against the dun earth and metal flashed against the sunlight and the troop guidons fluttered to the small breeze created by the forward riding of the column.

This was a mile or less away. He saw them and raised an arm—and was seen at once as he came rocketing down the slope. The column stirred and the dust rose in whirling clouds and the guidons whipped straight to the immediate

244

un of the command. Benteen rushed off the last of the rade and halted to look above him; one Indian stood igh on the lip of the wall, staring at the advancing trooprs; a moment later he faded from view.

Warren's big body rolled backward in the saddle, bringng the detail to a halt before Benteen. Benteen saw the ough-red surface of the Major's face break expressively. Warren's voice bawled out:

"Where, Mr. Benteen?"

Benteen slipped off his horse. Warren said, "That beast s about dead. Hannevy, give Mr. Benteen your horse and rop back with the pack mules."

Hannevy spurred forward and dropped out of the sadle, running back with Benteen's horse. The column sat ark and eager under the bright-hot sunlight. Benteen nounted Hannevy's horse as he spoke:

"There's part of Antone's band on the rim, behind me. hey will be falling back to the main camp. That's three r four miles down this pass—up on the rough ground to he right."

"How many in front of us?"

"Twenty or so. More coming up, though."

Warren called, "Harrison, take a platoon up this slope. Push right on! We will parallel you and cut in."

Harrison bawled a few words. A platoon of I troop wung from the line, trailing Captain Harrison up the stiff itches of the slope. Warren swung his arm overhead and he rest of the column fell into a steady gallop down the pen floor of the pass. Benteen said, "They will retreat long the edge of this pass. There's an old mine about a nile on, and a clearing they might cross in their retreat."

Warren said, "Anything over on the north of the pass low, Mr. Benteen?"

"Antone had his camp there last night. This morning he hifted to the south."

Warren said, "Mr. Lankerwell should be coming up oon. Where is Antone's main camp from here?"

Benteen pointed to a round black butte-top in th southeast; this lay perhaps four miles distant by crov flight. Warren, heavily rolling to the long forward pitch o his horse, studied the butte-top at a considerable interval Afterwards he called back, "Mr. Castleton," and waite for Castleton to ride up. He said then:

"You will take fifteen men from your troop, with Ser geant Hanna, and continue down this pass when we swin out of it. Keep on until you are approximately abreast tha butte, then move into the hills, approaching it. You are to block any retreat from that direction until we come up Do you understand—you are not to make an attack Should you see Mr. Lankerwell coming out of the north dispatch a messenger to bring him up."

Castleton dropped back to the column. There was, ove the rattle and run of the column, the muffled scatter o firing on top of the ridge. A trooper came to view on it rim and plunged down the slope at a long angling descent He rushed at Major Warren: "Captain Harrison's respects sir, and the Indians are givin' ground in front of him, bu not fast. They are collecting in the timber, About thirty More are drifting in from the southwest."

Benteen said, "Then the rest of the warriors from th camp have come along. There will be fifty of them Maybe more."

Sweat rolled freely along the Major's empurpling face sweat began to stain his shirt. He rolled around in the sad dle, shouting back, "Mr. Castleton—never mind!" Hi blue eyes were brilliant bright. "By God, it looks like a fight. If he does not give ground rapidly he is waiting fo his chance to attack." The headlong run of the colum had carried it well down the pass. Major Warren's eye considered the slope they paralleled and he pointed hi arm at an irregular break in its rim. "A convenient spot We have pretty well gotten behind them. We turn up!"

The column swung over the pass floor, straight at th grade. Major Warren grunted as his horse hit the slope

…d started upward; they were at a climbing walk, zig-zag-
…ng with the contours. Benteen forced his horse forward,
…aking an advance point, and so arrived at the rim first.
…. front of him the land showed its potted surface and its
…atter of pine trees; through a long, erratic defile he saw
…e scar of the mine dump. A show of dust hung around
…at spot, raised by recent passage of horses. Now and
…en, from the west, where Harrison was, an occasional
…ot signaled a running action between troops and the
…paches. Warren heaved up the slope and the column
…me on and halted at his arm signal; he was breathing
…it of the very bottom of his lungs; the points of his
…hite mustache drooped down, sodden with sweat. But he
…ocked an ear to the west, listening to the shots and mak-
…g up his mind.

"They're giving way before Harrison. Coming this way.
…hat dust over there in the clearing?"

"Antone's warriors coming up from the east to join this
…ght. They have been thick around here since daylight."

Warren led the column forward again, following the de-
…le as it slanted irregularly toward the mining dump. "I
…ant to get on that hill above the mine."

They came out of the defile, swinging away from the
…ine gulch and striking the ridge in a more heavily tim-
…red part, climbing by hard stages. "I wish to God," said
…ajor Warren bitterly, "I wasn't such a hearty eater. It is
…ell to carry the weight of two men on one pair of but-
…ocks. Where's Hazel?"

"Dead," said Benteen.

"Ah," sighed Warren.

The column scrambled over the last rocky folds of the
…llside, horses sliding and scrambling through the loose
…yers of crumbling stone. Sweat smell grew rank. Mixler,
… the rear of the column, was calling at his men to close
…. Hanna's thick Irish voice cursed Trumpeter Patch. "Ye
…amned little whelp—move on—move on!"

They reached the piny flat on the ridge top and trotted

along it until they came at last to a spot directly above th
mine dump. Here Warren halted the column to study th
canyon bottom and the ridge beyond. Firing thickene
over there and grew considerably nearer. Major Warren l
the moments run on while he weighed it all in his min
He said presently:

"Mr. Castleton, take six men and go left along this ridg
top. It seems to curve around into those trees. Scout th
trees. If you see anything in that direction, send word
but do not bring on a fight and do not charge into an
timber. Hanna, go along."

Castleton whirled away with his detail. Mixler came u
and reached out to shake Benteen's hand. "Looks like yo
had an active time." These two officers stood by whil
Warren quietly talked out his mind.

"That firing is not pronounced, so I think Harrison
in no trouble yet. We could ride into it, but that woul
scatter the Apaches. If they are withdrawing in front c
Harrison it is likely they will come into this clearing. I
such case we shall fight on foot. But if they avoid th
clearing and try to slide around us then we must stick t
the horses. It is like seining fish—you've got to find whic
way the fish propose to swim or else you scoop up nothin
but water. We shall wait a moment or two longer."

Carbines scattered long echoes through the timbe
across the ravine. The sun threw its hard yellow glar
against this waiting column, burning wherever it struck
The troopers held double-ranked formation, loose in thei
seats, but black-jawed and showing the flash of excite
ment in the rounds of their eyes. Benteen studied thes
men carefully, noting how calmly the old-timers, lik
McSween and Conrad Reicherts, held themselves. Trum
peter Patch had never been in a fight before; he kept roll
ing his eyes around him, watching his companions, as i
seeking some sort of comfort from them, as if trying t
discover some of his own uncertainty in them. Bentee
understood what was in the boy's mind. He could remem

248

ber back to his own first engagements, catching again the rush of blood, the quick squirming fear and the still greater fear of showing fear. This was what Trumpeter Patch would be going through now, and Harry Jackson who sat with his head down, staring at the knuckles of his hands. This was the silence of the column, but behind that silence were the crowding hopes and fears and the back-reaching memories. Mixler pulled his horse over to be beside Benteen. Benteen grinned at him and Mixler nodded gently, and turned his glance to the pines on the far ridge.

Suddenly the yonder firing strengthened and dust began to show. Benteen murmured, "They're coming out of the trees."

Chapter Eighteen

Major Warren spoke conversationally, "We will fight on foot," and gestured with his arm. The column stirred into front line without further command; men sprang off, ducking under the heads of their horses, three men handing their reins to the fourth, who was the horse-holder. The horse-holders, Corporal Oldbuck in charge, trotted out of the line of skirmishers.

Warren said, "You will take the right, Mr. Benteen. Mr. Mixler, the left."

The troopers scattered thinly along the brow of the rim, crouching among the rocks, resting behind the base of the pines. McSween walked along the line, grumbling, "Ye've got nawthin' to hurry about, either. And mind the orders. I will beat the ears off the man who fires before he's told."

Benteen walked to the right side of the line, taking position behind a tree. From this position he looked across the ravine to the opposite rim and saw Antone's band break out of the timber and trot into the clearing; they came in a straggling, reluctant wave, and as he watched them break into sight he realized that the full force of Antone's warriors was represented here. There were more Indians here than troopers.

Warren said, still even-voiced, "Take aim on the horses."

Meanwhile Phil Castleton, sweeping down the spine of the ridge, reached a point where that ridge curved westward and joined the other ridge girting the mining camp gulch. Trees thickened here and the junction of the ridges made a chopped-up area that cut off any very definite view ahead. All he clearly saw was the margin of the gulch on his right hand. There was a freshening fire somewhere ahead of him, which was Harrison pushing in against the Apaches. Hanna rode beside him and the other six troopers came behind. Van Rhyn was here and Canreen, and Lefferts and Hollander, and the two inseparable partners of I troop, Gordon and Maris.

They turned with the rough ground, keeping out of the hollows as much as possible. His first tangible sight of the flight was a smoky curling of dust through the trees, marking the quick passage of horsemen and this, he judged, was a fresh party of Antone's men coming out of the south to join the main band. He knew then that it was a serious fight, for it was not customary for Apaches to bunch up and throw themselves against cavalry unless they were extremely certain of their ground. He was remembering now the talk of old-timers around the post. They had said that Antone would fade like a shadow until his own prestige forced him to a fight or until support came out of these hills to join him. This was the way it stood.

He debated sending back a messenger to tell Warren of the new Indians drifting in; and dismissed the impulse, not wanting to cut the strength of his detail down. He had his hard moment then in realizing he was out of the main fight. Warren had put him here to act only as a flank guard. Knowing it, knowing that he stood aside as the engagement swept around him and left him high and dry, he had his bitter wish for twenty men behind his back. With that many he had no doubt of his ability to drive into the timber and roll the Apaches back against Harrison, or throw them pellmell into the ravine for Warren to handle.

Dust thickened as he went along and the firing was quite close, so close that a stray shot clipped a pine's high branch directly ahead of him. Then, staring along the ragged up-and-down earth, he saw Apaches drifting in the timber. At once he threw his arms outward as a deploying signal. It brought his men into line abreast him and here he stopped for a moment, standing in his stirrups with his body thrown forward and all his wild eagerness coming up.

Hanna murmured, "Driftin' this way."

The Apaches eddied toward Castleton; they were loosely scattered through the trees and they were in no hurry. Now and then some of them wheeled back and disappeared, as though testing the strength of Harrison's men, as though guilefully drawing Harrison's men deeper in the trees. The dust boiled up more and more and the shot echoes beat out harder. There was, he thought, increased activity farther to the north, near the pass; the main fighting seemed to be over there. These Indians in front of him formed the elusive flank of Antone's band. He saw only seven or eight of them in the dust.

He looked down at his closed fists, he drew his deep-reaching breath, and settled in the saddle. He glanced to either side, his cheeks tight and his long chin hardened. Hanna's black old-soldier's eyes were taciturn, but he knew what Hanna was thinking, even as he spoke: "Come on!"

He rushed ahead, lifting his revolver. Hanna spurred near, carbine coming up, and all the others rose and fell with the shifting terrain. They drove out of the potholes, straight into the trees and into the whirling dust, straight into this shadowy confusion. Apaches shifted before him and he began firing at the slipping shapes and he began calling, "Come on—come on!" Around him suddenly was the blast of the troopers' guns.

The trees surrounded him on all sides. He saw an Apache capsize from the saddle, and saw another rush across his path, low and fast, firing as he raced. They dissolved before him. As he pushed through the pines, it was as if he reached out his hand for a sure grip and closed his fingers on nothing but air. But they were around him. He felt the whip of their lead, close and strong; and at once, snarled in the timber, he found himself caught in a swift attack. They were closing around him thicker than he had ever thought they could be. In these shadows they were lesser shadows, their fire cross-ripping him.

He plunged on, firing at these shadows, and calling, "Come on—keep together—come on!" A pine branch cut him across the face, carrying away his hat and blinding him momentarily. He heard Hanna's horse grunt and go down; he heard Canreen cry, "Ah—!" He was ahead of his men, too far ahead, and in the cloudy dust there was nothing he could lay a shot on. Wheeling around he saw Hanna standing over his dead horse, tall and spraddle-legged, firing and cursing and firing again. Canreen was crawling forward on his hands, his head lobbing down. Lefferts sprang out of his saddle and plunged against a tree for shelter. Hanna bawled, "Get down—get down—'tis another trap!" Gordon lumbered forward on foot, scrambling over a deadfall and dropping behind it. Maris followed. Van Rhyn charged his horse straight at this shelter and then reeled back, vainly grabbing for the swell of his saddle; he was down, at once lost to sight.

Castleton remained on his horse. He continued to turn the horse, he slashed his shots at the blur of Apaches ringing him. They were like the insubstantial visions of a dream, unreachable, yet thickening constantly. Antone's men were all rushing up to this spot for the kill. Hanna looked up at him, his black, wise eyes full of things that he couldn't mention. All he said was, "Ye had better get off that hawrss—we'll be here awhile." Firing swelled and crashed into this spot; there was a steady fall of pine needles on Castleton's head.

From the east ridge Benteen watched the Apaches come down the far slope into the mine ravine, still unaware of the soldiers before them. Benteen murmured, "Aim at the horses, and wait for the command to fire." Harrison's men were putting a steady pressure on Antone's band,

253

forcing them out of the timber. But there was a growing rattle of carbines off to the southwest. The center of the fight swung that way, quickly and in surprising volume. Benteen turned to Warren, seeing the major's face veer in the same direction. An Apache spurred out of the timber and shouted something to the Apaches now in the gulch, whereupon part of the band swung back up the side of the gulch. Suddenly Warren bawled out, "That's Castleton in a fight! God-dammit! Benteen, take your men around there!"

Benteen rushed for his horse, followed by the whole right half of the line. The horse-holders rushed up. Warren yelled at his own section, "All right—fire!" They let go on the mounted warriors in the ravine. From his saddle, galloping along the spine of the ridge, Benteen watched the Apache horses fall, watched Indians race back for shelter, he saw them lie low on their ponies and break in all directions.

He came down to the junction of the ridges with his men hard on his heels, struck the potholes and heard the full force of the fight in front of him. Smoke and dust rolled up from the trees; the Apaches were howling full-throated in there. He could see them weave through the timber and he thought he saw one trooper still in the saddle.

"On foot!"

He was on the ground, with McSween trotting beside him. Troopers fanned out, lumbering in and out of the potholes, dismounted. They hit the trees, they went on through, taking shelter and firing and slipping forward again. Smoke smell and dust smell were rank underneath the pine boughs and the Apache horses made a confused flitter through all this. Benteen saw Castleton wheel his horse and rush deeper into the pines, headlong and crazed and thoughtless. He yelled at Castleton. The troopers drove away at the Apaches. Horses smashed into the pine trunks. One little warrior, flat on the bare back of his

254

pony, skimmed in front of Benteen, trying for a shot. Benteen knocked him down. Gordon and Maris raised their heads over a deadfall, saw Benteen come up, and rose to join the line. Gordon yelled out, "Now you red sons of suches!"

Benteen jumped over the deadfall and stumbled against the small shape of van Rhyn dead on the ground. Canreen sat with his back to a tree; he held a hand across his belly and stared at Benteen, shaking his head. Sergeant Hanna lay curled up on the pine needles with one big fist still gripping his revolver. He had his eyes open but he was dead.

Harrison's men were coming near, pinching in the Apaches from the other side. Benteen heard Harrison's crusty voice calling; and he saw the Apache horses wheeling back toward the mine ravine. This was a quick turn in the fight, and immediately he called to his men, bringing them around toward the ravine. "Come on—follow me!"

McSween stuck with him, the thin skirmish line doubled around. McSween grumbled, "Keep back with me, Lieutenant! Don't get so damned far in front!" Apaches flashed in front of them, rushing for the clearing. But gunfire boiled up from the clearing, which was Major Warren's piece of K troop checking Antone's retreat; and Harrison kept pressing in from the northwest. Pinched this way, Apaches rolled back up the gulch and through the trees, coming hard by Benteen. Benteen balanced his revolver on the driving shape of a wire-thin Tonto who came on afoot from the gulch. He dropped the Tonto and turned to signal his men forward. They were in the middle of it, the very heart of this whirling fight. McSween ran back, seeing Conrad Reichert lose his horse. He bawled, "Watch out, you damned Dutchman!" Harry Jackson ran through the pitted hummocks, the rest of the detail on his heels. Standing against the pines, or kneeling in the soft turf, they met Antone's recoiling warriors and beat them back into the ravine. Harrison appeared from the timber, his cheeks chalked by sweat and dust and his lips pulled apart as he sucked in the dry, hot air. A piece of K slashed through the pines behind him, reached the mine gulch and fell into it, yelling.

Benteen yelled, "Horses!"

The horse-holders rushed in, the detail hit the saddles. Benteen followed Harrison to the edge of the gulch and stopped a moment to look down. Indian ponies lay slaughtered below and Apaches, both afoot and mounted, shrank back from the firing. Warren came down the steep opposite slope with his men, and Harrison drove the last scattered remnant of Antone's band off the ridge, into the bottom of the gulch. A few warriors, dodging this enclosing maneuver, raced to the head of the ravine, bent on reaching the potholes where Castleton had been trapped. Benteen pointed at them and carbines battered the dead-burning air, dropping some of the ponies. The rest of the fugitive Apaches rushed on, vanishing.

The firing dropped off. Antone's band was shattered, his men were dead in the hills and in the ravine, or they had fled across the ravine, or they stood now at the bottom of the ravine, sullen and no longer fighting. Benteen saw the troopers collecting below him, and led his men down. Warren stood on the end of the mine dump, considering the scene, completely soaked in his own juice. A few last shots echoed at the end of the ravine. Troopers straggled back and horse-holders came off the hill. Castleton rode down from the timber, hatless and with a streak of blood across his face. Three troopers were carrying George Mixler across the rocks. Mixler turned a little in their arms and raised his hand across his eyes. Benteen went over to meet him.

"What's the matter, George?"

Mixler was gray-white, and feeling pain. He shook his head. "I don't know. Hit somewhere."

Shiraz came up the gulch. The troopers put Mixler on the ground, arranging themselves to block the gun away.

Shiraz unbuttoned Mixler's shirt, and bent over, his fingers pushing across Mixler's chest. Suddenly Benteen turned aside. Manuel Dura called from the opposite slope, "Hey—thees is Antone," and he pointed at the ground.

Troopers trotted toward Dura and Benteen walked over, looking down at the small, wizened face of the Apache who had, for so long a time, laid his terror across the Territory. He was past middle age, stringy and shrunken; with an astringent, unforgiving expression on his face, even now. He wore a striped shirt, with the captain's bars pinned to a sleeve; and around his neck was a cord holding a brass medal with a picture of Washington on it, a peace-treaty medal handed down to him by some older warrior. Benteen reached out and ripped the captain's bars from the shirt.

Details were climbing the slope to bring back the dead troopers. Somebody said, "Hey Jackson, Canreen wants to see you." Benteen started back to Warren, but turned aside, for Castleton stood in front of Warren, and the major's red face was full of anger. The three troopers carried George Mixler into the dobe, Shiraz following. Benteen took a drink from his canteen and suddenly crouched on the ground, turned dizzy by heat and hunger and the drain of the last four days. Manuel Dura walked up to him, and McSween came up. McSween said, "Give me your hand. You'll get out of this sun."

"Manuel," said Benteen, "Al Hazel is up there. Over on the right, just after you get to the top of the slope." Dura went away at once, murmuring under his breath.

McSween pulled Benteen to his feet and slipped an arm under Benteen's elbow. "Hell, Lieutenant, it would be a bad thing now to see you on the ground. Any other man, but nawt you." Harrison walked over from the Apache prisoners. He stared hard at Benteen. He took Benteen's other arm. "I don't wonder, Tom."

Warren called both of them and they walked on to the mine dump. There were these four on the dump—Warren,

Castleton, Harrison and Benteen. Castleton's cheeks were rigid. He kept his eyes on Warren, almost sightless in the way he stared. Warren said, "We will camp here. It is unnecessary to go on. Antone's dead, which is the end of this particular expedition, and the end of trouble around our district. Mr. Lankerwell should be here before long—I have dispatched a messenger to reach him. When he comes I shall send him on to Antone's camp. We will take the women and children to Grant." He paused, shifting weight on his feet, irritably pressing sweat away from his eyes. Then he said, "Mr. Castleton is under arrest, and will exercise no command during the balance of this trip. That is all."

Benteen walked down the slope toward the cabin, the back muscles of his legs barely bracing him. He went into the cabin and crouched beside Mixler. Shiraz had finished working on Mixler and shook his head at Benteen. "Not a pleasant prospect. It will be a bad trip back, for him. Better stay in here, Tom. You look pretty well washed out. I'll get you a drink of whisky a little later."

Mixler said in a husky voice, "One for both of us." He groaned a little and moved his head from side to side. But he managed a small smile when he looked at Benteen. "You turned out to be a pretty good soldier, old boy. I shouldn't like to have been in your shoes."

Benteen murmured, "Part of the game, George. For both of us."

"Sure," groaned Mixler. "For both of us. I guess I'll get mine on the ride home. Still, it is a comfort, in a way, to know what you'll do under fire. I'd never been in a scrap before. There's always a little doubt. I used to envy you, because you already knew what you could do. Now I know what I'll do. Pretty good feeling."

Harry Jackson crawled over a deadfall, up in the timber, and found Gordon and Maris kneeling by Canreen. Canreen was on his way out; it was in the slackness of his big lips, it was a nearing shadow in his eyes. But when

258

Harry Jackson came up he moved his arm a little and had his say: "Take my watch, kid, and give it to Rose. And listen. I been through the mill and I look at a woman different than you. You're pretty young and you got some strict ideas. But that girl Rose is all right. I wouldn't hold nothin' against her for the way she's made her livin'. Never hold that against any woman, kid. When you get a little older you'll see what I mean. You been sore at me, but you're all right, too."

Maris said, "We got to pack you back to camp."

"Sure," said Canreen. "But just wait a minute, then I won't feel it. That Camp Grant graveyard is a hell of a dry spot for a man that's been as thirsty as me." He closed his eyes, his big lips softly turning.

Harry Jackson said, "About Rose. You think—"

"Never mind, Harry," said Maris, "he don't hear you anymore."

Chapter Nineteen

There was no reason for rising at reveille, yet when th
call came Harriet Mixler at once dressed and watched th
sun break across the high rock ramparts behind Cam
Apache. Strolling in the morning's bright winy coolness
she saw the details of post life with understanding eyes
and was a little surprised that she should. It flowe
around her in aimless regularity—troop drill and fatigu
detail, commanding officer's orderly stiffly wheelin
down the walk, horses milling in the breaking pen, th
water cart's to-and-fro traveling, the sick call line in fron
of Doctor Panzer's door, the Indians crouched in th
quartermaster building shadows.

It was a pattern marking off the hours of her life. Rev
eille, roll call, stables, mess, drill, and recall; the lon
browse of afternoon, the sharp summons of the musi
again, and the stiff line of troopers massed against th
low sunlight as the bugles blew retreat and the flag cam
down; and at night, in the smothered stillness, the sentr
call running from post to post while tattoo broke acros
the dark and rode in continuing waves out and out int
the hills, at last dying. And taps—the end of the patter
for one more day.

She had never thought this life could leave any impres
sion on her. Once away from it, she felt she would soo
forget it, as she might forget an unpleasant dream. An
yet this listening for things that were familiar, this fain

pectancy which came when the buglers walked to their ation at the guardhouse and breathed tentatively into eir instruments just before sending their calls across the mp, this conformity to routine, this faint stir of some- ing deep inside when the troops, stiffly marching pla- on front, passed in review before Major McClure—this ld her something about herself.

Camp Grant was far away in the lowlands, sweltering the desert heat. Sitting quietly in the background of a eerful group in Major McClure's house, she thought out that heat with a shrinking sensation. The heat and erything that had gone with the heat. It was, she told rself, the tragic period of her life. Nothing before had er been like it; nothing ever would be like it again. om this detached place, she looked back rather clearly, realize one poignant truth. Her girlhood had died at rant; there were things she could never believe again, ere were things she could never feel again.

It was rather late in the evening. Major McClure told s bear story and Mrs. McClure brought out coffee and very elaborate pudding. Four other officers of the post d gathered here with their wives, carrying on a robust d cheerful conversation. This was the way army people laxed. They had health and they had hunger and they d the wonderful ability to throw off the day, when the y was done, and to grow loose and lazy. She sat some- hat apart from the group, watching them; watching ung Lieutenant Kessler in particular. He had a pretty d somewhat provocative wife, and now and then his es would lift to her and something passed between em, warm and urgent and possessive.

McClure said, "How's that baby?"

Harriet smiled. "Sleeping and quite contented."

"Apache's the place," said McClure. "That damned rant is a hellhole. I feel sorry for any woman living ere. We ought to get Eleanor to come up for a stay."

261

"Eleanor," said Mrs. McClure, "wouldn't leave troop. At any rate she has other and equally interestin reasons for liking Grant."

"So? Who?"

"Men are so blind. Young Castleton."

McClure looked at her. "Ah," he murmured. "Castle ton, eh?"

It was the brief way he spoke the name, the way h quickly left the subject, that told Harriet of his attitud Suddenly, in her heart, she was afraid for Eleanor. man's judgment of a man was an illuminating thing; an none of the officers around Castleton liked him. Mea while McClure, helping himself again to the puddin; shot an affable glance at Harriet. "Be very nice now old George were here. Round out the evening for you."

Mrs. McClure threw her husband a wife's astonishe and fretful glance; the small silence was quite heavy. M Clure suddenly realized his lapse. He raised a hand an coughed behind it. "Dammit, Madge," he grumblec "you didn't make enough sauce to cover this pudding."

Harriet sat small and quiet in the chair, listening t their talk cover up the mistake. All of them knew, c course. The regiment was a close-bound family, wit nothing long remaining a secret; and suddenly she fe outside the family, apart from it and no longer sharin its closeness. They had been kind to her, but there was difference. In the kindness itself was the difference, a though their minds held reservation and judgment.

McClure said, "Messenger came up from Grant thi afternoon. Benteen went on an extended scout, picked u Antone's location. Warren has taken his whole comman out. I expect they may have a brush with Antone. Be fo tunate if Warren can break up that Apache. Relieve th pressure of this campaign considerably. I am sending detail down to Grant in the morning to get the paymas ter."

Harriet rose, saying, "I think I'll go see sonny," and
ned from the room. Taps was just then sounding
oss the parade. It swung her around and turned her
athing deeper and made her stand straight, with her
all hands tightly closed. She listened to the call with a
emn attention, hearing something so timeless and
thful in the long-drawn notes. There was a sadness in
 call that turned her a little humble, there was a
ength in it that took possession of her and bound her
 this parade ground and to the lights shining from the
rracks, to the tramp of the sentries' feet on the hard
th, to the smell of dust, to the feel of the faint wind
ling off the hills. She had straightened and her eyes
tched the stars so bright and high in the southwest
, where Camp Grant lay.

Major Warren brought his command into Camp Grant
noon. From the commanding officer's ramada Eleanor
tched the column file through the gate. She stood very
ll, gripped by the fear that always came when troops
urned. The men were deadbeat, sweaty and beard-
ackened, blistered and parched by the sun, and round-
oulded from the fatigue in their bones. The dead
re blanket-wrapped across their saddles, and on these
apes her glance clung. George Mixler lay cradled in an
provised carrier between two mules. Her father sat on
 horse uncomfortably, looking tough and old and
oked by the sun. Her eyes rummaged the column, man
er man. Hanna wasn't riding as guide of K, and then
 knew the name of one of the blanketed shapes, and
sed her eyes, blinking away quick tears. When she
ened them again she saw Castleton. A long breath es-
ped her, but her attention remained on the gate as they
d in and her fear was as real and as suffocating as
fore until she saw Benteen. Then all the fear went out

263

of her and she put her head down, afraid at the mome
to look at his high, loose shape. Al Hazel's wife stood
the quartermaster's building, crying out a question
Spanish. The captive Indians, men and women and ch
dren, crowded to a corner of the parade. I and K troo
swung front into line, waited for dismissal, and filed
toward the stables. Eleanor went immediately to Geor
Mixler. Shiraz and two troopers were lifting him from t
carrier and when she saw Mixler's face she knew he ha
been badly hurt. They carried him to Shiraz' quarters.

Captain Harrison walked on, smiling a little throug
his cracked lips, "We got Antone, Eleanor," and conti
ued toward his dobe with a definite limp. Castlet
threw the reins of his horse to an orderly, cut across t
parade and disappeared in his dobe at once. He had n
looked at her. Eleanor thought, "Something has ha
pened," and watched Benteen come up.

She noticed at once the ragged mark on his chee
which was the result of his fight with the Apache on t
rocks above the pass. His face was thinner, he wa
sweated dry, he was ridden down to muscle and bone.
had an effect on her, an actual physical effect. Sh
touched his arm, looking at his eyes. He was smilin
and she knew, from the way his face changed, that h
was pleased with the pressure of her fingers. It was
feeling that at once lay in both of them. But his face ha
some of the old reserve on it; it held away something.

She said, softly, "I said my prayers for you, Tom."

"Sometime," he said, carefully picking his words, "
want to talk to you, Eleanor."

She looked down and was disturbed. "Is it somethin
you ought to talk about, Tom?"

"We'll be living in the same camp for a long time."

"Will that be bad, for you?"

"I don't think—" he began. But he shook his head "
need a little sleep first."

Al Hazel's wife sat in the dust, against the wall of the quartermaster's building. She was crying, rocking her shoulders slowly from side to side. Eleanor breathed, "Where's Al?"

"He's dead," said Benteen. "We had quite a scrap with Antone, Eleanor." He went on, turning into Shiraz' quarters to see Mixler.

The crying of Al Hazel's wife was a steady moaning in the hot, windless air. Eleanor went over and crouched in the thick dust. Al Hazel's wife stared at her out of dully red eyes. She put her head on Eleanor's shoulder, crying and speaking in Spanish. Eleanor held the woman, saying nothing. A detail of soldiers circled the Indians in the yard, her father crossed the parade to his quarters and Benteen left the Shiraz dobe, entering his own. He ducked at the doorway and put his hand against the wall, as though bracing himself. Castleton's quarters were directly opposite her; he sat on the edge of his cot, his shoulders crouched forward, his arms across his knees. He was smoking a cigarette and his head was dropped forward. Presently Al Hazel's wife rose. She said "Ah," and moved her arms apart, and walked back along the line of the quartermaster's building. Eleanor went at once to Castleton's dobe and for the first time in her life stepped unbidden into an officer's room.

"Phil."

He didn't look at her. His long jaw was hard-set; his voice came at her roughly. "Go away, Eleanor. Not now—not now."

"Phil—what happened?"

The question pulled him back and he turned and showed her the rank anger of his eyes. It hurt her to see so much heartless, unthinking feeling there. He stared at her as though he had no trust. "Didn't your father tell you?"

"I haven't seen him, Phil."

265

"Then," he said, "how do you know anything's wrong? Maybe Mr. Benteen gave you the details."

"No," she said, "do you think he would?"

"Ah," breathed Castleton, "Mr. Benteen is an officer and a gentleman and wouldn't stoop to common gossip—is that the way you feel about him?"

She hated that domineering sarcasm and yet realized how deeply stung he was, how completely his fury changed him. So she spoke quite gently. "Do you have to hurt me, Phil?"

He said in a stony, flat voice, "I am under arrest for going beyond the letter-of-the-law of your father's orders." He drew a breath and she knew he meant to add something to that phrase. She waited, dreading what that addition might be. She wanted him to be honest. Above all other things she wanted him to show neither self-pity nor evasion. These qualities she despised. They were, to her, cardinal sins in an officer. Suddenly, not quite sure of what he meant to say, she broke in:

"We can live down any honest mistake, Phil. We can go on, we can keep trying—we can whip any kind of bad fortune—if we face everything straight."

"We?" he said in that high, intolerant voice.

She gave him a long look. "Am I not part of your life, Phil?"

She hoped it would break his temper. She stood there, desperately waiting for him to rise and come to her and include her in his misfortune, to show her some relieving gentleness and understanding. And yet he did not. He said in a dry monotone:

"There seems to be no place in this command for an officer who exercises any judgment of his own. Apparently we are to be little sticks jerked by strings."

She had, when deeply affronted, her own quick temper; and now he had outraged her sense of fairness, her hope, and her long-placed faith.

266

"Stop being a fool, Phil! Stop excusing yourself and pitying yourself. You should know better—your training should have taught you better. There is no sense in trying to dramatize yourself as a young hero on a horse, leading desperate charges. I'm ashamed of you!"

He said, red from throat to forehead, and shaken visibly by his resentment, "Are you? Are you indeed? Perhaps, Eleanor, it would be better if you tried not to guide my life for me. I do not wish to hide behind a petticoat."

She opened her mouth, and shut it tight on her feelings; and she studied him a long, long interval, at last saying, "I think it would be better to wait until we are both less quarrelsome." Going out, she returned to her own quarters. Her father sat half collapsed in the easy chair.

"Daughter," he groaned, "see if you can get these damned boots off."

She knelt down, and had her head lowered when she spoke. "Why is Phil under arrest, Dad?"

He said, "Don't interfere, daughter."

"I know," she answered him, quite humble. "But that's the man I'm marrying. Shouldn't you tell me?"

"I gave Mr. Castleton orders to conduct a scout and keep out of a fight. His gallant notions led him straight into trouble."

She pulled off one of his boots and, still kneeling, asked softly, "Was Hanna with him, Dad?"

"Hanna and van Rhyn and Canreen. Now don't ask me anything more."

"No," she said. "Nothing more." She stood up. Major Warren, watching her now with a shrewd eye, saw no expression on her face and heard none in her voice: "I'll make up some lemonade for you, Dad."

She went to the kitchen and was there when she heard him say, in pleased reflection, "It was something of a

267

sight to see Benteen come off the ridge to meet us. The Apaches had him cornered. They were on the top of the ridge. It was as close to hallelujah as that young man will get for some time. I am mentioning him in my report to Crook."

Coming back from the stables, young Harry Jackson found Rose Smith at the corner of the barracks, turned his way as though waiting for him. He came up to her, embarrassed and oppressed by the message he had to give. Reaching into his pocket he pulled out Canreen's gold watch and held it to her.

"He told me to give this to you."

"He's dead, isn't he?"

Young Harry Jackson nodded, still holding the watch. She didn't take it. She watched him, the shine of the sun in her quiet-black eyes, and he felt something rise in him then he had thought entirely dead. It took the heaviness out of him, it made her as she had been before—a desirable woman. It surprised him a little to hear his own voice.

"Rose, I'm not such a hell of a greenhorn. Like I said before, my enlistment runs out next year and I propose to settle in Prescott. It would be a good place to start. For the both of us."

Her lips, softly pliable, changed and pressed together. A shadow rushed across her face, or seemed to. "There's something you'd have to forget, Harry."

He said, very gravely, "I'd forget."

Her eyes had a glowing deepness, and sudden sweetness made her face younger and prettier. Her lips moved, kind and red and strong. He had not noticed before how dark her hair was against her temples, or how smooth her skin was; all this came to him now, quite quickly, and left him excited and pleased with this moment and the things that were ahead of him. But she was shaking her head.

"You keep the watch, Harry. Canreen was a good man, in his way. You keep the watch, to think of him and maybe once in a while to think of me. You wouldn't forget, Harry. It would come back. It would always come back."

She stepped nearer and brushed her lips across his cheek and went quickly toward the sentry line, toward the ranch on the flat. Harry Jackson didn't turn to see her go. He stood fast with the watch unnoticed in his hand—and wanted to cry.

Midafternoon's heat pressed in on the post, one thin layer on another, and the soil of the parade ground glittered against the sullen light and the powder-dust mushroomed up as a man's foot touched it. A detail took the dead troopers out to the little cemetery behind the post and K and I troop stood in single rank around the fresh graves, listening to Warren recite the services: "Man that is born of woman—" This was all, this and the crash of the carbines and the buglers blowing Last Post, and the march back. Lily Marr walked with Eleanor, as far as the guardhouse, and stopped here while Eleanor went on. Lily faced the grated door and Jack Bean who stared out from the rank jail cell.

He looked at her, neither in hate nor in liking, but she knew something now. Each day of this past week, coming before him, she had watched his eyes; and now she saw what she wanted. This man had always been wilder than the wind, enduring no restraint. He had never known quietness, he had never felt anything as strong as his own will. She watched him, calm and certain, showing him no feeling.

"I guess you saw Lieutenant Benteen come back," she said. "You'd like to see him dead. But he's alive. He'll still be alive when you're hung. Sergeant Hanna was killed. He was a better man than you are, Jack. Why wasn't it you in his place? What have you done that's

269

worth keeping you here when somebody better has to go?"

He put his fingers around the bars. "Lily, I reckon I know what hell is. It is a place where a woman kills a man by keepin' him alive. An Apache couldn't do what you're doin' to me. Go on away."

"The marshal will be here this week."

Jack Bean shrugged his shoulders, not answering, and Lily Marr knew he didn't care. She came nearer the bars, speaking with a low, smooth softness. "When it gets dark tonight I am coming by this door, and reach the key and throw it in. The guard will kill you if he catches you coming out. There won't be any horse to cross the desert on and there won't be any water. Maybe you'll get to Tucson."

He grated his answer back to her. "I wouldn't take nothin' from you, not even to keep from dyin'."

But she was almost smiling. "Yes you will. You'll do anything to live. And maybe you'll get to Tucson. But you won't forget you owe your life to me, and you won't forget you laid in jail a week with the Territory laughing at a tough man who wasn't tough. You are not the same man that went into this place, Jack."

He shook his head. "Not from you, Lily. I don't want nothin' from you."

She was still near to smiling when she turned away and crossed to the dobe where George Mixler lay; at the doorway she turned, observing the last low sunlight with a smooth, half-pleased expression on her face.

Supper and retreat and the bugles strongly sounding while the flag went down; and again the sudden twilight fading into dark. Eleanor stood under the headquarters ramada watching Tom Benteen cross from officers' mess to the stables. She kept her eyes on him until he turned

270

the corner of the barrack. Afterwards she put her arm against a post of the ramada, waiting. Horsemen came over the San Pedro gravel, to be immediately challenged by the sentry. "Halt — who's there?"

"Officer and party from Fort Apache."

"Halt, officer and detail. Cawprul of the guard, post number one!"

Doctor Shiraz came from his dobe, paused long enough to gather a breath of air, and turned back. He had been inside all afternoon with George Mixler. Her father left headquarters office, paused at Shiraz' door and walked forward. He called into the dark, "Orderly," and stopped by Eleanor, his round cheeks gloomy. "I do not think George will live." The orderly walked way, boots scuffling the boards. The detail from Apache swung into the parade, six horses and an ambulance wagon. Turning about, Eleanor saw Harriet Mixler come swiftly down from the seat. Warren went around on his heel, into the house.

Harriet came near Eleanor, her white drawn face vague in the moonlight. "I left the baby at Apache. Is George here? Do you think he will see me? Do you think — ?"

Eleanor breathed, "Harriet — Harriet —" She held Harriet's arm. She was almost whispering. "You will find him with Doctor Shiraz. You'll —"

Harriet said, "Oh," and caught up her skirts, rushing down the walk. She called "George!" Her voice, thin and high as a child's voice, made a forlorn and diminishing echo on the night air. Castleton, coming out of his dobe, suddenly stepped aside to avoid her on-running shape. He wheeled and watched Harriet run into Shiraz' house. Afterwards he paced forward, stepping heavily on the boards. He had his head lifted and his face, illumined by the moonlight, was distinctly sullen. Eleanor said, "Phil —" He saw her, made a quick avoiding wheel, and entered Warren's house.

Eleanor put her hands across her breasts again, tightly locking them. She walked swiftly away from the row, out into the parade and beyond earshot; and kept on traveling with her head down, past men's quarters, past the bakery, past the shining of the sutler's store lights. At the guardhouse she noticed Lily Marr suddenly turn into the shadows, sinking away from sight, but her thoughts were so confused and troubled that she paid this no attention. In this manner, still walking, she came against the still figure of Sergeant McSween.

This was at the corner of the rectangle, near Doctor Shiraz' dobe. McSween had his shoulder tipped against the dobe's wall and seemed to be listening. He straightened up—"My apologies, Miss Eleanor"—and gave her room on the walk.

"It's all right, McSween."

"Ah," he murmured, "there's many a thing that can't be right. 'Twould be too much to expect from a damned funny life. I miss Hanna. I do miss that Irishman a hell of a lot. Now 'tis the Lieutenant Mixler. Which is sad when there are others not near worth the keepin' that do not seem to die."

They heard Harriet Mixler cry out a word. McSween said, "Now I should not be standin' here at all," and strode away. Eleanor walked on.

Harriet came into the room, finding George on the bed. Shiraz got out of his chair and stood back, turning completely around so as not to observe this. Harriet knelt at the bed and George Mixler's drowsy eyes opened up and were a cloudy, puzzled blue. He said, through his mouth's thickness. "How did you know this?"

"I didn't—I didn't. I left sonny at Apache. I came."

"Wanted to come back, Harriet?" he murmured.

"Yes, George. But how—what happened?"

He seemed not to hear her. He rolled his head from side to side on the pillow, he ran his tongue across his

272

lips, and faintly framed the words on them. "It is good to know—that you changed your mind. My young wife, my lovely wife. I should like to have seen the boy again. Do not let him entirely forget me." He breathed suddenly and painfully and she heard the fading, breathless tone: "My love, all of it—as it's ever been—to you."

She saw him loosen; she heard him sigh again. He was smiling and sleepy and there was no motion in him. Harriet turned her head to Shiraz. Her big round eyes, so dark and so frightened, begged at him; and her face held the fear that the face of a child holds when its deepest faith is broken. This was the way she looked at him. Shiraz put his hand across his mouth so that she might not see its changing; and shook his head.

Chapter Twenty

As soon as Castleton came from her father's house, Eleanor crossed the parade to him, placing her hand on his arm. Light gushed through the doorway, shining on both, and she knew that he could see the concern and the loyalty on her face if he looked, if he broke out of his tremendous self-absorption. His old attitude governed him again—a distrust of others, a domineering faith in himself, a rankling, bitter anger at the way his luck ran. She had a pretty clear view of him at the moment and saw so little that she could love.

This was a swift and sudden thought that shocked her: She saw so little that she could love. All these minutes, pacing the parade with her troubled thoughts, an odd discontent had been stirring in her, a tremendous dissatisfaction. She had not been able to name it, but it was as though something lay near her that she could not reach, as though she struggled through a cloudy confusion with the promise of some complete relief and happiness quite close by and could not reach it. All she saw at this moment was the stubbornly resenting cast of Phil's features. The interview with her father had hit him badly.

"Phil," she said, "walk with me."

But he held his place, intractably wilful. "Eleanor," he said, "there is no hope for me in this regiment."

She murmured, "Are you sure?"

"It has been made pretty clear," he said in dry sarcasm.

"Are you thinking of a transfer?"

His chin, she noticed, was very heavy. It lengthened and unbalanced his face. He had removed his hat and his black hair sparkled in the light; and in an unruly, sulky way he was handsome. She had made many an excuse for him, she thought; now it was cruel to see her excuses fade. It was cruel the way her mind worked, picking him apart.

"No," he said, "there is no place in the army for an ambitious man. It is nothing but a dull mill. I am resigning."

"Phil!"

He looked at her. "We can have a little fun out of this, Eleanor. If we go to Tucson we can be married there, catch the stage to San Diego and the boat to San Francisco, going back East by the Pacific Railroad."

She didn't answer. Light made a cool, sparkling glow in his eyes. His own talk began to change him and make him a little eager to be out of this country. He was looking forward, impetuous and wilful again; he was near smiling. "It will be a good deal like paradise, after Grant."

"No," she murmured, "no, Phil," and felt the heaviness of her heart.

It brought him up. There was a gesture he always made when irritated. He lifted his chin a little, watching her with a hardening reserve. "I don't understand."

"I couldn't."

"I thought a woman followed a man," he said, sarcasm in his voice once more, "if she loved him."

She drew a long breath. "If a woman loved a man, I suppose she would."

"Then what has this been?" he demanded.

"Whatever it was—and I did love you once, Phil—it isn't love now."

He hated resistance and showed it in the tightening of his lips. The expression on his face then was almost brutal. This sudden insight shocked her and left her clear-headed, so that his speech made no impression.

"Is the army a religion to you, Eleanor?"

She knew then. She knew what had been in her mind and in her heart so long. It was like relief, like cool air after insufferable heat; she had a feeling of freeness that had not been hers for a long, long while. Standing in front of him she could look at him and feel no regret. For this first time in the years she had known him she had no hunger for his nearness, no quick heart-lift at his presence. She spoke quite evenly.

"Only one person in the world will ever matter to you, Phil. That person is Phil Castleton. You are leaving the army because you cannot stand the truth. You're running away. And you will always be running away. There never will come a time when you learn to be tolerant, or to know what love is, or what fairness is. Well, I wish you luck. I really do."

She waited for temper to pour out of him, or hurt feeling, or pleading—or anything. But nothing came and she realized that he was seeing himself at the moment, not her; he was wrapped around by that wilful pride and self-centered egotism. He murmured "Ah" in a dry, quick breath, wheeled on his boots, almost rushing across the parade.

She watched him go. There were heavy shadows on the parade and into these he faded physically and was gone. And afterwards, in a manner that forever afterwards puzzled her, he was gone as well from her heart

276

nd her conscience, leaving no trace, no emptiness vhere he had been. This was the way it happened if oyalty was pulled too tight and worn too thin. The ime came when, as with her now, it broke completely. These were her thoughts. She was free of him, she was ooking back, seeing him as she had loved him and hen, in this new lucid light, she was seeing him as he ad come to be. She was free of him—and realized ow great the strain and self-deception and anxious ope had been.

The sudden bawl of a sentry rose from the post akery. "Corp'ral of the Guard—prisoner's loose!"

Eleanor ran over. Boots scuffed up from the corner f the quadrangle and Benteen trotted out of the sta-les, a lantern swinging in his hand. Her father came n, cursing at the loose stones under his bare feet. The door of the guardhouse stood wide open and Ben-een, throwing his lantern high up, said, "How'd he et out?"

The sentry said, "It was closed when I walked past t last time, sir. When I turned the beat and came ack, it was open. Just one minute between times."

Major Warren said, "Who carries the key?"

Benteen said, "It usually hangs on top of that pro-ecting timber, sir. Somebody threw it in to Bean."

"Now who would do a thing like that?" grumbled Warren. "Well, he's gone now but he'll have one hell f a time getting to Tucson, or anywhere. We won't ttempt to overtake him. Not worth it. Hereafter I vant that key kept in the personal possession of the ergeant of the guard. Very slipshod. Very."

He limped back to his house, grumbling audibly, 'Guardhouse key hanging outside! Like the key to a emale seminary. Good God."

The guard detail faded in the dark, leaving Eleanor nd Benteen together by the open door. Benteen swung toward her. He was smiling a little. He had slept and shaved and the dead exhaustion was gone from his eyes. He had, she thought in slow, deep admiration the kind of vitality that could shake off any punishment. She stood before him, pleased by his smile and not wanting him to go, and trying to let him see this

"Lily — of course," he murmured.

"I think so."

"The way of a serpent, an eagle or a woman," he murmured.

So near him, alive to the shadows of his face, to the way his mouth turned and the way his sandy-red hair lay against his bronzed forehead, she discovered thorough understanding in his gray eyes. He had this insight and this tolerance; he had the gift of looking into others. It bound people to him, the unruliest trooper in the command, the officers, the women of the post — and it bound her to him. She realized it in one swift, wondering flash and waited for him to speak.

"She broke him, Eleanor. She put him in this hot hole and took the sap out of him. Then she turned him loose." He shook his head, the slow smile continuing. "A little odd."

"Any woman in love," she murmured, "is odd, Tom. They see so much — and so little."

"She deserves better. There is something in that girl —"

Steps rustled in the darkness. Lily Marr said in her calm voice, "Mr. Benteen —" She came into the glow of the lantern and confronted Benteen with her small shoulders resolutely set. Softness controlled her expression, making her pretty and gently excited. Her lips were pleased. But it was the way she watched Benteen that turned Eleanor around and took her away from these two; it was something Lily Marr's eyes held,

278

something sweet and sad and beyond hope. The girl was in love with Benteen.

Benteen said, "What for, Lily?"

She brushed the question away. "I want to go to Tucson with the next detail, Mr. Benteen. And I thank you for all you've done for me."

He said, "You think he'll be there, Lily?"

"If he gets through the Catalinas he'll be there."

"Suppose he doesn't?"

She had a way of lifting her shoulders, a way of holding her face composed. It expressed everything, it was the reaction of a strong, hardy spirit that knew the meaning of trouble and could look at any disaster without crying. "If he doesn't, Mr. Benteen, then I guess I'll grieve—and go on living."

"What'll he say when you see him?"

She was quite serene. "He was a man who never thought twice of what he did, and never once of other people. But he will now. And he'll be glad enough to see me. It is something he can't help."

He was troubled about her. He showed it. "You deserve better, Lily."

She said, very quietly, "No, there's a place for all of us, Mr. Benteen. And I guess my place is with Jack Bean. I think," she said, coolly planning ahead, "we will go to New Mexico. They won't know much about him there. He won't be very wild. He's a better man than you think." Then she paused and added a slow-voiced after-thought, "I guess I know him pretty well, the bad and the good."

"I wish you luck."

"I guess you wish most people luck," she murmured. I guess you know people better than most do. I'll be one, but I'll remember you very well. Very well."

The light showed her strong shape against the night and the round darkness of her eyes as she lifted them

279

to him and held his attention. Brief feeling moved across her long lips; it was a shadow that stirred her features and left them composed again. There was this moment, then she turned and walked into the darkness.

From the ramada of her father's house Eleanor saw the scene. She noticed how Benteen turned about, facing her as if he meant to come on. He remained this way quite a long while and at last wheeled and, with the lantern swinging its quick arc across the black, headed for the stable. Eleanor drew a deep, disappointed breath—and continued to wait.

Turning the corner of the barrack's wall Benteen discovered a shape posed in the dark and threw his lantern around until its pale glitter identified Sergeant McSween. McSween's leathered old soldier's cheeks showed him nothing but a settled melancholy; and so Benteen went into the stable, killed his lantern and hooked it to a peg. Another lantern swung above the doorway of the stable, diluting the blackness with its fan-shaped beams. Horses stirred on the hard-packed dirt, their teeth crunching against oat rations, their halter ropes softly sliding on the feed boxes. The smell of the stable was a rank compound of sweat and leather and manure and hay; strong and pleasant to a cavalryman's nostrils. A man's steps scuffed the area beyond the stable. Benteen, expecting McSween's approach, turned toward the door and found Phil Castleton paused there.

There was a hazel brightness in the man's eyes and a paling of his skin from temple to neck; and Benteen knew what fury was then, from seeing it. Shock went through him; it was an instantaneous flash striking every nerve and leaving him cold in the compressed heat of this summer's night. Alive in his head, this swiftly, was an ancient, brutal eagerness. He knew what Castleton meant to do. It was like a smell, like a sound. The walls of his stomach closed in. He felt the steady, sloshing beat of his heart along the base of his ears, along the side of his jaw. It kept quickening; and for a reason he never knew, the odor of the stable got ranker and ranker.

Castleton said in a rising, shallow tone, "Come at it, Benteen—come at it," and without waiting, drove his big body straight for Benteen. He grunted when he jumped, and grunted again in throwing his right hand at Benteen's jaw.

Benteen's head dropped, Castleton's knuckles ripping along his hair. Benteen pulled up his forearms, rolling Castleton's right hand away as it beat in; but Castleton's weight carried him backward and the next blow, ripping up through his elbow and his guard, cracked him on the corner of his chin. Benteen's shoulders slammed against the stable wall and his head hit the dobe, the echo of it roaring in his ears; and for a moment he saw the crystal sparkle of the lantern and Castleton's long-jawed face and the whip of his arms only as a blur. He turned his shoulder to take the edge from the beating, but these were blows that stunned him, as punishing as the down-sweep of an ax-handle. He kept rolling his shoulders; he pushed a leg against the stable wall and shoved himself low and fast against Castleton again, taking the shock of Castleton's ready fists as he went in. He smothered the man for a moment, wrestling him back toward the stalls, he kept against him, coming around with his fist and battering Castleton's temple. Castleton, quite near the stalls, wheeled aside and away, and Benteen's long reaching arms smashed him twice across the mouth.

Castleton danced back, his breath sawing the dull quiet of the stables. They were under the lantern. They slowly circled, arms up and doubled; throwing quick punches and blocking. Benteen kept his head low, his mouth against the knuckles of his defensive fist. Blood dropped against those knuckles from his nose; he tasted it in his mouth and he had the smell of it. Castleton feinted, went backward and afterwards rushed in. They were close then, fists swinging hard and fast, meaty echoes ringing in the stable. It was a hard and wicked little flurry, savagely effective; and then they were circling again. Benteen panted through his teeth, "Come on, plebe, come on and fight."

From his position at the corner of the barrack wall, Sergeant McSween saw this and lived it and felt it. He stood away from the wall, his muscles working and his breath groaning in and out. He sighed, "Ah," when the on-rushing Castleton hit Benteen on the face. McSween heard the crack of it and saw Benteen's head bounce; and then those two, head down, were circling and waiting, and rushing in and slugging and stepping back. Somebody ran across the parade, coming toward McSween. McSween put out his arm—"Stop here"—and turned to see Eleanor Warren beside him. He was shocked. He said, "Ah, for the love o' Gawd, Miss Eleanor, don't watch it—don't! If the Lieutenant Castleton licks him I'll kill him, I will! Go on back!"

Benteen's head sagged, heavy-weighted. The surface of his fist was oily with blood and slid smoothly along Castleton's cheek when it missed its mark. Castleton hit him twice; he felt the jolt, but not the pain; the ability to feel sharp pain was gone. There was a grayness before his eyes. Beyond this grayness Castleton moved in and out, and Castleton's mouth was a longer and thicker stain against his skin. Castleton stepped at him and moved away, and stepped in again. Benteen rushed him, taking his beating as before, but he knocked Castleton's arms aside and felt Castleton's teeth break against his fist. He carried Castleton back.

282

There was a sharp bridle peg at the edge of the near-est stall partition; he heaved Castleton into it, and saw something half-wild twist across Castleton's face. Cas-tleton's arms went down and he was suddenly uncon-trollably sick. Benteen hit him across the bridge of the nose; and hit him again, fair and full against that long bloody jaw. Castleton's mouth was wide open, his eyes turned aimlessly from side to side. Benteen seized him by the neck and flung him around, and smashed him hard enough to drive him against the wall. There was a bale of hay lying here and Castleton's legs tripped on it and he sat down, holding himself mo-tionless a moment; afterwards he bent over with his arms almost touching the floor, breath bubbling and sobbing in his lungs.

From her position outside the stable, Eleanor saw Benteen move against a stall partition and hook his arms over it. He supported himself this way, his legs wide apart and shaking. He dropped his head against the partition, motionless for a long, long moment. She sighed, "McSween—go help him!" But McSween whis-pered, "We saw nawthin'. We saw nawthin' at all." She stood still, watching Benteen swing from the partition. He pushed the flat of a hand across his face, squeez-ing sweat and blood away from his eyes. He shook his head. There was an empty burlap sack on the floor; he lifted it, dirty as it was, and scrubbed his face with it. His shirt hung wide on him, all its buttons ripped off.

"Phil," he breathed, "you through?"

Eleanor, straining her ears, heard no instant answer. Benteen wiped his face with the sack again. He re-peated his question. "You through?"

She heard Castleton groan, "Oh, my God, what a mess!"

That was all. She slipped across the parade and

stopped beneath the ramada to look into the house. Her father sat in the easy chair, smoking silently and furiously on his cigar. Turned back, she saw Castleton go slowly over the parade. A little later Benteen followed, entering Doctor Shiraz' quarters.

Her father said, "Eleanor, are you out there?"

"Yes," she said. "Yes." And was still beneath the ramada, a long half-hour later when Benteen came down the walk. He stepped into the beam of lamplight and she noticed that he had scrubbed himself clean and treated the cuts on his face with some kind of caustic; there was a long red burn on his cheek, and his lips were a little smashed at the corners. He looked at her, the fight still a smoky flare in his eyes.

"You gave me some bad advice, Eleanor," he said in a very slow voice. "Maybe a man shouldn't carry the memory of a girl around in his head—when the girl's beyond his having. But it is better than something else."

"What else, Tom?"

"I believe," he said, "you must know."

"Yes," she murmured, "I knew it at Tucson. It has been nice to know."

"It will be impossible for me to live in the same regiment with you. That is what I meant to tell you this afternoon."

"Phil," she said in one swift breath, "is leaving the army and I am not marrying him."

He was tired, or he was confused, or he was deeply moved by the thought of it. For he put his head down and held it this way so long that she almost put out her hand. When he lifted it again she saw the oddest expression she had ever found on a man's face—so close to smiling, so near to sadness. All he said was, "Eleanor," and brought her toward him with his long arms.

284

This, she thought as she lifted her lips, was like Tucson—as deeply satisfying, as rich. Only it was different, it was for her an answer that stilled her mind and made her humble at the thought of the years ahead. One small, dissenting thought did come to her, making her pull away:

"She had something of you, Tom. I won't ever have that part, will I? Is there enough for me—will you ever regret?"

"No," he said. "No regrets. Maybe a memory, for me—as you will have yours. There is nothing simple about living, and no sure answer for any of us, I guess. But no regrets."

Over at the corner of the parade the trumpeters were spitting faint sounds into their instruments, ready for taps. She put her arm through his elbow, knowing what he meant. Harriet Mixler crouched before her husband and watched him slowly go out beyond her tears and her hopes. Fresh scars in the cemetery marked the end of good and gallant men. This was the army, this was the frontier, with Lily Marr waiting for the next detail to take her to Tucson and Jack Bean and whatever life with him might mean. Al Hazel's wife sat somewhere with her tragedy and the men of the troop, half-asleep on their cots, would be softly speaking of yesterday, and pleasantly dreaming of tomorrow. The dead were dead and the living looked forward.

The smell of dust was keen in the hot air and the stars hung brilliantly remote and taps, long and deep and sustained, ran the night, promising the end of one day, promising sleep. Tomorrow the sun would rise and reveille blow, with dust again boiling out of the corrals and Sergeant McSween's iron voice harking along the parade. The thin blue file of troopers would cut a silhouette along the flats of the San Pedro; and

285

Tom Benteen would come down the walk toward her, tall and cheerful, with the half smile behind his eyes. This would be the way of it, until whatever end there was in store for them. She tightened her grip on his arm, dreaming and sad and gay.

"The best of it," said Benteen, "to them, wherever they may be. And to us. It is a fine life, Eleanor. We shall have trouble and we shall have fun—but no fear." The long falling melody of taps faded into the deep silence of the desert; along the quadrangle lights winked out.

"No regrets and never any fear," he said, and kissed her.

WALK ALONG THE BRINK OF FURY:

THE EDGE SERIES

Westerns By GEORGE G. GILMAN

SCALE TO THE HEIGHTS OF ADVENTURE WITH

MOUNTAIN JACK PIKE

By JOSEPH MEEK